THE
WEEPING
TIDE

Also by Amanda Foody

The Accidental Apprentice

WILDERLORE

THE WEEPING TIDE

AMANDA FOODY

Margaret K. McElderry Books

New York   London   Toronto   Sydney   New Delhi

MARGARET K. McELDERRY BOOKS
An imprint of Simon & Schuster Children's Publishing Division
1230 Avenue of the Americas, New York, New York 10020
This book is a work of fiction. Any references to historical events, real people, or real places are used fictitiously. Other names, characters, places, and events are products of the author's imagination, and any resemblance to actual events or places or persons, living or dead, is entirely coincidental.
Text © 2022 by Amanda Foody
Cover illustration © 2022 by Petur Antonsson
Logo illustration © 2021 by David Coulson
Cover design by Karyn Lee © 2022 by Simon & Schuster, Inc.
Map illustration by Kathleen Jennings
All rights reserved, including the right of reproduction in whole or in part in any form.
MARGARET K. McELDERRY BOOKS is a trademark of Simon & Schuster, Inc.
For information about special discounts for bulk purchases, please contact Simon & Schuster Special Sales at 1-866-506-1949 or business@simonandschuster.com.
The Simon & Schuster Speakers Bureau can bring authors to your live event. For more information or to book an event, contact the Simon & Schuster Speakers Bureau at 1-866-248-3049 or visit our website at www.simonspeakers.com.
Also available in a Margaret K. McElderry Books hardcover edition
Interior design by Karyn Lee
The text for this book was set in Georgia.
Manufactured in the United States of America
1222 OFF
First Margaret K. McElderry Books paperback edition January 2023
10 9 8 7 6 5 4 3 2 1
The Library of Congress has cataloged the hardcover edition as follows:
Library of Congress Cataloging-in-Publication Data
Names: Foody, Amanda, author. Title: The weeping tide / Amanda Foody.
Description: First edition. | New York : Margaret K. McElderry Books, [2022] | Series: Wilderlore ; 2 | Audience: Ages 8–12. | Audience: Grades 4–6. | Summary: Lore Keeper apprentice Barclay helps his teacher investigate a carnivorous algae bloom and its possible connection to recurring attacks by the Legendary Beast of the Sea.
Identifiers: LCCN 2021024142 (print) | LCCN 2021024143 (ebook)
ISBN 9781534477599 (hardcover) | ISBN 9781534477605 (pbk) |
ISBN 9781534477612 (ebook)
Subjects: CYAC: Animals, Mythical—Fiction. | Apprentices—Fiction. | Adventure and adventurers—Fiction. | LCGFT: Novels.Classification: LCC PZ7.1.F657 We 2022 (print) | LCC PZ7.1.F657 (ebook) | DDC [Fic]—dc23.
LC record available at https://lccn.loc.gov/2021024142.
LC ebook record available at https://lccn.loc.gov/2021024143.

TO GOLDIE AND PEACH,
MY FIRST PET AND A CARNIVAL PRIZE—
YOU WERE BOTH EXCELLENT GOLDFISH

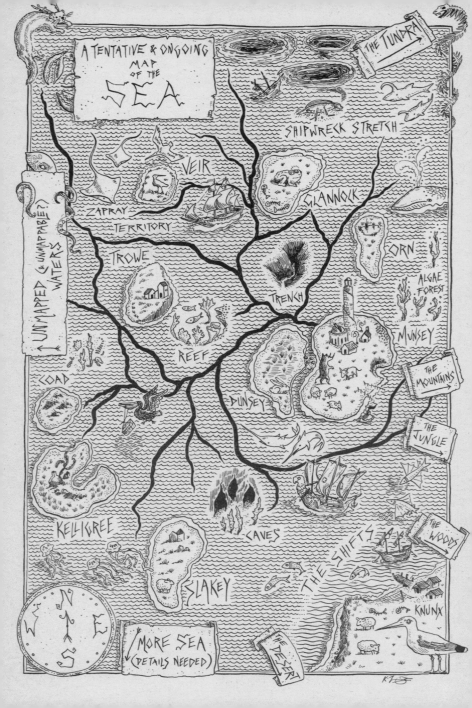

ONE

Barclay Thorne was running so fast he nearly ran straight off the edge of the world.

"Whoa!" he shouted, swerving just before the ground dropped into cliffside. His arms flailed out as he lost his balance, and he tumbled backward onto the tall grass and soppy mud. Then he crawled to the cliff's edge and stared out at the most incredible sight he'd ever seen.

It was gray—gray water stretching out on and on until it met gray horizon. For thirteen weeks, Barclay had been traveling, and though he'd passed many places on his journey—quaint villages, grand cities, and untouched wilds—this was the first moment he felt truly on an adventure.

They had finally reached the Sea.

"This isn't the Sea," said a voice flatly, and Tadg Murdock stepped beside him. Tadg was a Lore Keeper apprentice, just like Barclay. And he'd faced the Legendary Beast of the Woods, just like Barclay. But they were far from friends. "This is a gulf. It doesn't look anything like the Sea."

Barclay bristled. *He* had no way of knowing that. He was from the Elsewheres, which was Lore Keeper talk for any land without magical Beasts. More precisely, Barclay was from Dullshire, a small and silly town nestled beyond the edge of the Woods, another of the six Wilderlands. And one very, very far from here.

"What does the Sea look like, then?" asked Barclay. He couldn't imagine a body of water bigger than this. With a nervous gulp, he inched forward and peeked down the drop. Waves lapped at the rocks hundreds of feet below.

Tadg rolled his eyes. "Believe me—when we get to the Sea, you'll know."

Whether or not that was true, Barclay refused to let Tadg spoil his adventure. Barclay glanced behind them to make sure they were alone, and then he whispered, "Root, you need to see this."

At the summons, a huge wolflike creature appeared at Barclay's other side, his fur so dark and shaggy that it looked like coils of wildfire smoke. He had black eyes and black claws to match, and stark white bones jutted out at the base of his spine.

Barclay had once found Root terrifying, because everyone from the Elsewheres was raised to fear all Beasts and their dangerous magic. But now he slung his arm around Root's back and leaned into the Beast's side.

"Have you ever seen anything like this?" he asked.

Root shook his head, wagging his tail eagerly.

Beside them, Tadg could only grimace.

"What is it?" Barclay asked, though Tadg never needed an excuse to be a grouch.

"It's home," Tadg grumbled.

"What did I tell you?" snapped their teacher, Runa Rasgar, behind them. She'd stopped at the edge of the cliff-side road. "Put Root back in his Mark."

Runa was *not* the sort of person anyone might like snapping at them. She wore the leather coat and chainmail of a warrior, and a gruesome scar was etched across the right side of her face, leaving a rippled trail of white and pink across her fair skin. She was a famous Guardian Keeper, a six-time Dooling champion, and fearsome enough to have earned the nickname the Fang of Dusk.

Per usual, Viola Dumont, Barclay and Tadg's fellow apprentice, hovered in Runa's shadow. She tsked with mirrored disapproval.

Root whined. Because most of their journey had cut through the Elsewheres, they'd each kept their Beasts confined to their golden tattoolike Marks, where they rested in stasis and out of sight. Barclay had learned the hard way how even the whiff of Lore Keepers could send Elsies scrambling for their torches and pitchforks.

"But we haven't seen anyone on this road all morning," Barclay protested. "Root just wants to run. Can't he—"

"I'm afraid not." Runa pointed farther ahead. "Get up and you'll see why."

Barclay stood and peered down the hill. A village of cobbly gray stone huddled along the shore below, smoke billowing from its crooked chimneys.

Excitement swelled in Barclay's chest. Their travels were over at last.

"Sorry, boy," Barclay told Root, then returned him to his Mark on Barclay's shoulder. The Mark prowled across his pale skin, as though annoyed. But then Root padded a few times in a circle and curled up to take a nap.

The group started down the winding dirt road to the village.

Beside Barclay, Viola clicked and clacked as she walked. Her coat was so covered in gold pins, buttons, and baubles that Barclay could scarcely see the wool beneath. She claimed they distracted her pesky dragon, Mitzi, from nipping at her ears or poofy hair buns of tight curls. Even so, she had a tiny welt on her cheek where her light brown was skin swollen from when Mitzi had last nicked her.

"How do you always get yourself so dirty?" Viola asked him.

Dried mud was crusted all over Barclay's clothes and hands. When he lived in Dullshire, he would've panicked at breaking one of their many ridiculous rules, which forbade everything from uncleanliness to hiccups.

But now Barclay only shrugged. "How come you always agree with everything Runa says?"

Viola fiddled with her pins, looking embarrassed. "I do not."

"Yes you do," Tadg muttered.

"Don't you have some flowers to stomp on?" Viola shot at Tadg. "Or sunshine to complain about?"

Tadg gave them a very Tadg-like frown and stormed ahead.

Soon they reached the village, which was a dreary, unhappy place. All of the doors and window shutters looked to be made from rotted driftwood. Sheep milled about the main street beside the beach, munching on the brittle grass that sprouted amid the sand and cobblestones. It smelled of salt and Springtime and a *lot* of manure.

"This is the town of Knunx," Runa declared. "It's the closest Elsewheres town to the Sea."

Just like Dullshire, Barclay thought.

In fact, a lot about Knunx reminded Barclay of Dullshire. The villagers he passed ogled their group suspiciously, and even without their Beasts roaming free, Barclay knew their group must look peculiar. Barclay's shoulder-length black hair hung wild and tangled from the winds up on the cliffs. Viola clattered with each step. And Runa's menacing presence made every shopkeeper avert their eyes.

Seeming to sense the unease around them, Runa halted at the edge of the docks along the beach, which bustled with sailors and fishermen. Her gaze swept over Barclay's untamed hair and Viola's bizarre coat, then rested on Tadg's simple blue sweater.

She pointed at Tadg. "You're going to ask these sailors for passage to the Isle of Munsey."

Tadg's usual scowl deepened. "Couldn't Orla send a ship? No one here will agree to take us."

"Orla has been preoccupied. We'll need to find a way there ourselves."

As they spoke, one of the sailors—a burly man with a coil of rope slung over his shoulder—bumped hard into Tadg's side. Tadg looked daggers at him as the man strolled away.

"I better come with you," Runa said hastily. "I'm not sure we'll be welcome here for long."

While the two strode off down the docks, Barclay asked Viola, "What's the Isle of Munsey? Who's Orla?"

Viola, being the daughter of the Grand Keeper, the leader of the Lore Keeper world, always knew these sorts of things.

"The Isle of Munsey is where the Sea's Guild head-quarters is," Viola replied matter-of-factly, "and Orla Scudder is the High Keeper." High Keepers were each in charge of one of the six chapters of the Guild, and they answered to the Grand Keeper. "You would know this if you did the reading Runa assigned you."

Barclay loved reading and rarely failed a challenge when it came to homework. But because Barclay was an Elsie, he had a *lot* more to learn about the Wilderlands than Viola and Tadg. And so during their journey, Runa had assigned him the grueling task of catching up.

"I *am* doing the reading," Barclay said. "But if I have to memorize one more fact about the Great Capamoo War or the Ickypox Plague, my head might explode."

Beside them, a fisherman heaved a net of today's catch onto the pier. A foul stench filled the air—every fish in the pile was dead. They spilled out over Barclay's and Viola's boots, leaving streaks of gunk across the wooden boards.

Viola yelped and jumped back. *"Gross,"* she groaned.

Barclay pinched his nose. However these fish had died, it must've happened a while ago. They'd already gone too rancid to eat.

At the mess, the fisherman mumbled something to them that Barclay didn't understand but that he guessed meant "sorry." Then the fisherman looked the two of them over, and his eyes widened in alarm.

"Lore Coimadaí." This time, whatever he said, his voice was harsh. He reached into his pocket and pulled out a spiky conch shell. Then he clutched it to his chest and darted away from them.

Because Barclay spent most of his time with Runa and his fellow apprentices, he often forgot that they all heard one another in Lore-speak, which all Lore Keepers could use once they bonded with a Beast. So even though they each came from far-flung parts of the world, they could understand one another. But the fisherman was an Elsie.

"Do you know what he said?" Barclay asked. Viola had a knack for languages.

"I've never learned Sea-speak, but if I had to take a guess . . . I'd say it's their word for 'Lore Keeper.' And his shell reminded me of that twiggy charm you used to carry. Remember? The one that made you smell like a skunk."

Barclay's cheeks grew hot. After he'd accidentally bonded with Root and been run out of Dullshire, Barclay had taken his charm with him. After all, it supposedly warded away Beasts, and Barclay had been about to venture into the vast and frightening Woods, which was *crawling* with Beasts. He'd later learned that the charm was useless. All it had done was make him look very, very foolish.

"Dullshire has no idea that Lore Keepers help protect them from Beasts. They just know that Beasts are dangerous," Barclay said hotly. "I bet Knunx is the same way."

Viola crossed her arms. "It's not like we keep what we do a secret. Elsies are just ungrateful. You saw the way that sailor knocked into Tadg. He definitely did it on purpose."

"Knunx knows that Lore Keepers bond with Beasts. They think we could be bringing danger." Dullshire did far worse things to suspicious travelers, the kindest of which was sending a herd of goats chasing after them or pelting them with moldy fruit.

Viola elbowed Barclay in the side. "You just think that because you're an Elsie."

The words shouldn't have stung like they did. Not just

because Viola was only teasing, but because Dullshire had treated Barclay terribly—even before they'd banished him. But Barclay would always care about some of his companions there. Like Master Pilzmann, the local mushroom farmer. Or Mrs. Havener, the librarian who'd lent him books about adventure. And most importantly, Dullshire was where Barclay's parents had lived.

And where they were buried.

The Legendary Beast of the Woods, Gravaldor, had killed Barclay's parents when he'd destroyed the town almost eight years ago. Dullshire was wrong about a lot of things, especially Beasts. But Barclay also understood why they were afraid, and so it was hard to blame them for it.

Not wanting to explain his messy feelings to Viola, Barclay trudged across the shore. On the docks, Tadg and Runa were in a fierce debate with another sailor. Though Barclay could understand Tadg ("I'm not being rude, old man!" he shouted, then rudely gestured with his hands), the fisherman's words were foreign to him. His voice lilted up and down, as though the words swelled like the sea. But judging from his angry tone, the conversation wasn't going well.

A chilly breeze tore across the beach. Resting nearby on the sand was a ship with snapped masts and shredded sails, and Barclay ducked behind it as shelter from the wind. Then, miserably, he took in his bleak surroundings. Everywhere was wet sand and muddy sheep wool and scratchy burlap. Seagulls circled overhead, their shadows looping across the dunes. Sinister storm clouds gathered behind them.

This time last year, Dullshire had just finished their week-long Midspring celebration. The townsfolk had dyed eggs bright colors and hung them from the tree branches, which all bloomed with pink and orange flowers. Barclay had even convinced Master Pilzmann to get festive, and so they'd strung mushroom garlands across all their windows.

This year, Dullshire celebrated without him.

You're a Lore Keeper now, Barclay reminded himself, and the thought comforted him—a little. Because Barclay wanted to be a Lore Keeper more than anything. He wanted to protect towns like Dullshire and Knunx, even if they never thanked him for it.

Besides, Dullshire didn't want him anyway. They'd barely ever wanted him—before he was a Lore Keeper, he was just a scrappy orphan who accidentally broke too many rules. Barclay might've had a few fond memories of his home, but that didn't mean he'd ever belonged there.

Tadg stalked across the beach, his fists clenched. Barclay watched from afar as he yelled at some unsuspecting sheep, who paid him no mind.

Runa joined Barclay by the damaged ship. The wind was so strong that her braid had come undone, and she spit strands of blond hair from her mouth. "Unfortunately, no one is willing to sail us across the gulf to the Sea, no matter what we pay them. They claim it's because there's a storm coming. But I'm not sure that's the only reason."

"They're just scared, is all," Barclay mumbled. There he went, defending Elsies again. He didn't even know these people.

Runa looked out onto the water grimly. "They should be scared, given the news I've heard."

Unnerved, Barclay was about to ask Runa what she meant when his Mark gave a painful twitch, as it always did when danger neared.

Not a moment later, a scream ripped across the pier. A woman crouched at the helm of one of the docked ships, swatting away a seagull.

Only the seagull didn't resemble the ones Barclay had seen while traveling along the cliffs. It was at least three times as big, with four wings and a beak as long and sharp as a spear.

It wasn't a seagull at all. It was a Beast.

"Well, that can't be good," Runa said. Except she wasn't looking at the docks. She was looking at the sky.

Hundreds of the Beasts swirled overhead, a flock so dense it was darker than the storm clouds.

Then, all at once, they dove.

TWO

The seagull Beasts swarmed the village, attacking anything that moved. They swooped and squawked, the powerful beats of their four wings blowing up gales of sand that seemed to swallow Knunx in a dust cloud. Shopkeepers screamed and fled indoors while sailors dove for safety into the cold waters. The sheep stampeded down the road, knocking over crates, tables, wheelbarrows, and anyone in their path.

Barclay and Runa lunged for cover beside the beached ship.

Thump! Thump! Thump! Thump!

The Beasts' spearlike beaks pierced the boat behind them. Barclay jumped out of the way a moment before he would've been impaled.

"What are these Beasts?" Barclay shouted, lifting his

arms to shield his eyes from the flying sand. "And why are they attacking an Elsewheres town?"

Though Beasts had occasionally stolen into Dullshire chicken coops, the town had never seen an all-out invasion like this.

"They're Sleábeaks," Runa answered. "And I'm not sure why they're here. One or two Beasts, maybe . . . but hundreds? Go find Tadg and Viola. The four of us need to protect the villagers."

At that, Runa sprinted toward the water. She whipped her arms to the side, and a massive wave of ice rose from the ocean toward the sky, freezing a dozen Sleábeaks inside. Barclay's mouth dropped open in awe. Even after weeks traveling with Runa, Barclay had never seen her use Lore and never once met her Beasts.

She moved in a blur. Frosty air glimmered around her fingertips as she dodged and ducked her way to the water's edge. Then, her chainmail coat glinting like a knight's armor, she created a tunnel of ice to shelter sailors as they ran across the beach—

A Sleábeak's wing struck Barclay hard in the chest. With a surprised "oof," he fell back onto the sand. *Stab!* The Sleábeak tried to spear its beak into him, but Barclay rolled over just in time. *Stab!* That one punctured his scarf, pinning him down by his neck.

"G't'ff—! Hey—! Don't—" Barclay tried to shove it away, but the Sleábeak thrashed wildly. Its solid white eyes whirled from side to side, as if in a frenzy. Barclay choked as his scarf was yanked tight.

Finally, Barclay raised his hand toward the Sleábeak and thought, *Wind!* A spiral of air blasted from Barclay's palm toward the Beast, sending it whirling away.

Gasping for breath, Barclay clambered to his feet and searched the havoc for his friends. He spotted Viola braced on a ship's stern, Mitzi flying above her head. Being only a baby dragon—a whelp, technically speaking—Mitzi was smaller than the Sleábeaks. But she was far more agile. She darted swiftly out of the way before the other Beasts could peck at her silver wings or sparsely feathered tail.

Viola, meanwhile, was using her Lore to shine great bursts of light from her hands, so bright that the blinking made Barclay dizzy. The Sleábeaks didn't seem fazed, though. They flapped around her like moths beckoned to a lantern flame. She shrieked and tumbled onto the docks.

"Viola!" Barclay called, running toward her. He summoned a second gale of wind and blew the Sleábeaks around her away.

Viola staggered to his side, Mitzi clinging to her shoulder.

"I don't understand!" she panted. "It's like the Sleábeaks are all in a fit! Why would they—"

"I don't know," Barclay said. "But we need to find Tadg."

He looked to the sheep pen, where he'd last seen the other apprentice. But Tadg was gone.

"Come on." Barclay squeezed Viola's hand, and the two

dashed from the beach into town, Mitzi soaring after them. The streets were strewn with sand and feathers and shattered window glass. Villagers whacked at the Beasts with brooms or fishing rods. The Sleábeaks drilled their beaks into walls, covering every surface with holes as though Knunx was a giant dartboard.

"There!" Viola pointed around the corner, where Tadg stood braced against a wall, batting at two Sleábeaks with a rake.

Barclay blasted the Sleábeaks away. Several roof tiles from the nearby buildings flew off with them.

"A rake?" Viola snapped at Tadg. "That's the best you can do?"

Another Sleábeak swooped toward them, and a sizzle of gold static shot up the rake. Tadg walloped the bird with a loud *zap!* The Sleábeak cawed and soared away.

"It's metal, so it conducts electricity," Tadg said. Tadg's Beast was a Nathermara, a huge electric lamprey. His Lore let Tadg control water and create lightning.

Though Beasts were hard to hurt and quick to heal, Tadg must've made the Sleábeak angry—*very* angry. It shrieked and swerved back toward them, and another dozen Sleábeaks nearby flew to join it.

"We're about to be skewered!" Barclay croaked.

"We should get inside." Viola shoved Tadg's and Barclay's backs. "Go! Move!"

They scampered out of the birds' path down a wide street.

Tadg bolted to the closest door and pounded on it. "Let us in!" he called. But no one did.

Barclay's Lore granted him speed—it would be easy to outrun these birds. But that would mean leaving Viola and Tadg behind. So he dug his heels into the cobbled street and turned around. He raised both arms and focused hard.

Wind!

This time he summoned a vortex. It spun like a tornado, slinking up from the ground and widening into a gigantic funnel. Any nearby Sleábeaks were sucked in and launched back out into the sky. But even after the three apprentices were safe and the street was clear, the vortex didn't stop.

Barclay couldn't *make* it stop. He might've been able to summon wind, but wind was also wild. The more powerful the Lore, the less he could control it. Soon roof tiles, broken shells, and sand were swept into the air, pelting Barclay's skin and forcing him to squeeze his eyes shut. The strength of it all nearly threw him sideways, so he sank to his knees. Even the ground itself seemed to shake, and something loud crashed behind him.

After almost a full minute, the wind finally stilled, and Barclay peeled open his eyes. The cottages around him, already riddled with holes, were now missing whole planks of wood and most of their roofs. The debris littered the street in a circle around Barclay, as though he had been the eye of the storm. Any caws of the Sleábeaks sounded far off in the distance.

But Knunx wasn't saved just yet.

"Look out!" Tadg shouted, and Barclay spun around to spot one last Sleábeak flying straight toward him.

Something hot and bright burst in front of Barclay—*fire*.

"What the—" He lurched back as a flaming wall erupted between him and the Sleábeak. The Beast gave a frightened cry and flew off, and the fire extinguished.

"Are you all right?" someone called, and two figures emerged from a nearby alley. The first was a very haggard-looking man. His pale face dripped with sweat. His shirt hung in tatters. And a bit of dried blood was crusted to the stubble on his cheek.

Beside him was a boy who looked no older than Barclay. He had curly blond hair and the lightest skin Barclay had ever seen, like pickled cabbage. His expression was equally sour, though much of it was hidden beneath the collar of his massive fur coat. A small flame danced above each of his fingertips. Then he closed his fist, and the fires snuffed out.

They'd just saved him, but Barclay was so startled that all he could manage was a shaky, "Wh-who are you?"

"Fellow Lore Keepers. Which makes us friends, so I hope," the haggard man answered, smiling at them cheerily. "Fiery Skellets, what did this street ever do to you? I've never seen such a mess—not to mention droppings. . . . Oh, I'm only joking. It's a good thing none of you look too worse for wear."

Barclay begged to differ. Tadg's sweater now sported several holes. Feathers and twigs stuck out of Viola's hair buns. And Barclay's cheek throbbed where a piece of debris had sliced him as it blew past.

Beside Barclay, Viola's eyes widened. "But . . . *you're* hurt." Barclay followed her gaze to the man's side. His torn shirt was soaked in blood.

"What, this?" The man chuckled and smeared away all the red. Though Barclay couldn't spot a wound, he did see two scars along the man's abdomen, like a pair of puncture marks. But they looked very old, far too old to be from today. "I have healing Lore. But it's not much help in *winning* a battle, I'm afraid."

"So you're the one who saved Barclay," Tadg said to the boy, whose hand was now stained with soot. "And caused the earthquake."

"Earthquake? I didn't feel anything of the sort." The man cocked his head to the side, then patted the boy's shoulder. "Yasha uses fire Lore. Outshining his teacher again . . . makes a habit of it."

The boy—Yasha—waved his hand dismissively, as though such powerful Lore had been nothing to him. "It was lucky I spotted you, is all."

"But what are you doing in the Elsewheres?" Barclay asked.

"We only just arrived," the man answered. "We're trying to find passage back to the Sea. Orla mentioned that her problems have only been getting worse since we left. Now I see she's right! Imagine, a whole flock of Sleábeaks terrorizing an Elsie town!"

It seemed that whatever problems the Sea faced, the High Keeper had summoned more help than Runa alone.

Before Barclay could ask what those problems *were*, Viola looked up at the dark sky. "The Sleábeaks are gone. We should find Runa."

"Runa?" The man frowned slightly. "You can't mean Runa Rasgar, the Fang of Dusk?"

"Yes. She's our Lore Master," Viola explained. "Come on. You can meet her."

The group shuffled back to the beach, where the remnants of Runa's ice Lore thawed in the chilly Spring afternoon. Runa argued with another villager on the pier, but the villager seemed to be the one doing most of the shouting. Runa spotted them and mouthed Tadg's name.

Tadg rolled his eyes. "She can't speak the language well. I'll be back."

He left the four of them lingering at the edge of town. The wreckage the Sleábeaks had left behind was dramatic— Knunx had more holes than a cheese grater. Half of the boats were sinking, and the stampeding sheep had destroyed almost all the fencing.

"You're bleeding," the man said to Barclay. Then he rummaged through his baggy pockets and various knapsacks, all of which looked full to bursting. "No, not the Scaromilk . . .

Oh, there's my good knife! I've been looking for that. . . . Hm, kritters, poison antidotes, a snorkel and . . . Aha! I knew I had some more left."

Triumphantly, he whipped out a silver, slimy piece of seaweed and slapped it onto Barclay's cheek. It smelled like sauerkraut.

Viola giggled.

"Mind if I patch it up? It'll only take a minute," the man said, though Barclay would've preferred to have been asked *before* having the kelp stuck to his face. The Lore Keeper held his hand over Barclay's cheek, and a soothing, tingling feeling spread across his skin.

"Oh, um, thank you," Barclay told him.

"No need! Us Lore Keepers need to look out for one another."

While he waited for the man to finish healing him, Barclay watched Tadg join the argument with the villager. Unlike Runa, he had no problem yelling right back at the woman.

"How do you think it's going?" Barclay asked.

The man chuckled. "Do *you* normally shout when a conversation is going smoothly?"

"But we saved Knunx from the Sleábeaks!" Viola said gruffly. "They should be thanking us."

"Ah, I'm afraid it doesn't work like that. But . . . good news! Your cheek stitched up nicely. Lucky I had some leftover pickled Gunkwort. Between that and my Lore you couldn't get better healing anywhere."

"Thank you," Barclay said again. "But can I . . . take this . . . off?" He tried and failed to wrench the slimy Gunkwort off his skin.

"Eh, it'll stick there for hours. Maybe days . . ."

"*Days?*" Barclay repeated. Viola's giggles dissolved into laughter, and even Yasha cracked a smile.

"It'll fall off when it's ready. Oh, better gird yourselves . . ."

The villager Runa and Tadg had been arguing with stomped over. She jabbed her finger three times into Barclay's chest, and even though she wasn't hurting him, the woman was very large and frightening. And Barclay was tiny even for an eleven-year-old.

"I don't know what you're saying!" he said, his voice drowned out by the woman's yells.

Then, ignoring Viola's and the man's protests, the villager grasped Barclay by the wrist and dragged him with her down an alley.

"Wh-whatever it is," Barclay blubbered, "I was only trying to drive the Sleábeaks away! I was *protecting* the town from . . ."

He trailed off when he saw where the woman had led him—a completely ruined home, collapsed into a heap of rubble. Though the woman kept yelling, Barclay no longer seemed to hear. He was reminded all too well of a festival in Dullshire, when his Lore had gone out of control and destroyed the town's famous clocktower. It was one of his worst memories, when everyone he knew had turned on him.

Had *he* done this?

Even if he had, this time wasn't like what had happened in Dullshire. He'd saved Knunx, not destroyed it.

But the angry crowd who swarmed around him disagreed. They shouted at him, and even though Barclay didn't understand the words, their voices were so loud and mean that he trembled all over.

"*His* fault?" Tadg snapped at a villager, caught up in yet another argument across the street. "It's thanks to him that your whole sorry town doesn't look like that!"

Barclay had never heard Tadg defend him before, but he was too frustrated to feel grateful. Because Tadg was right. Knunx should be thanking them. But instead, they would probably distrust Lore Keepers more than ever now.

Something struck Barclay's back, and an extremely rotten crab apple tumbled to the ground. Someone had thrown it at him, no different from Dullshire.

The crowd parted as Runa marched through to Barclay's side. "Come on. We've clearly overstayed our welcome. And we need to find someone to sail us to the Sea before this storm hits."

If the villagers had more rotten fruit, they didn't dare pelt it at Barclay with Runa beside him. And so, his stomach in knots, Barclay let Runa lead him, Viola, and Tadg back to the beach. The haggard man and Yasha waited for them on the pier.

"Cheer up, kid," the man told Barclay. "You took on a whole flock of them, which was far more than I managed."

"And you are?" Runa asked, staring at the man carefully,

as though she couldn't tell whether they'd met before.

"Edwyn Lusk." The man gave a small flourish of his hand. With his other, he held the strips of his shirt together. "And this is my apprentice, Yasha Robinovich. We're also looking for passage to the Sea." He glanced overhead, where dark clouds rolled across the sky. "Though this might not be the weather for it."

"Do you know Sea-speak? This one"—Runa frowned at Tadg—"isn't much of a charmer."

Tadg scowled.

"Only enough to order a drink, I'm afraid," Edwyn responded.

"That'll do," Runa grumbled, dragging Tadg by the sleeve of his sweater and motioning for Edwyn to follow.

After they left to walk down the pier, Barclay stared miserably out at the water. Maybe if he had controlled his Lore better, he could've changed Knunx's mind about Lore Keepers. But Dullshire had banished Barclay despite knowing him all his life. His dreams were probably a lost cause.

"Oh, don't be so sullen," Viola told him. "The Elsies here would never have thanked you, no matter what you did."

"I thought your Lore was very impressive," Yasha told him seriously. "Have you been an apprentice for a while?"

"Only since Midwinter," Viola answered for him, which was fine with Barclay, who was in no mood for chitchat. "What about you?"

"For about a year. Started when I was eleven."

"Oh! I've been an apprentice for that long . . ." Viola

stopped herself and cleared her throat awkwardly. Before she'd been Runa's apprentice, she'd had a different teacher—Cyril Harlow, Runa's famous archnemesis. But Cyril had fired Viola as a student, and Viola never liked to talk about that. "I mean, you're probably way ahead of us, then. I'm Viola, by the way. Viola Dumont. And this is Barclay Thorne—"

"Dumont, like Leopold Dumont? The Grand Keeper?"

Viola looked sheepish. "He's my dad, yeah."

"I've heard that he has *three* Mythic class Beasts," said Yasha, sounding skeptical. "Is that true?"

Barclay wondered if Yasha had even caught his name, and he tried not to feel snubbed. He couldn't help that Viola was far more interesting. Her father was head of the Lore Keeper world, and Barclay was just a boy from the Elsewheres who could barely use his powers without destroying everything in sight.

Leaving them to their happy conversation, Barclay slumped across the beach. More than anything, he wished he could go running with Root—to run so fast that they became the wind and his problems were left far behind them. But Knunx had had enough of a fright for one day.

Then a woman tapped his shoulder. She was very old, her wrinkles like ripples left on the sand. Her floppy knitted hat reminded him of Mrs. Havener from Dullshire.

Barclay stiffened, expecting her to yell at him like everyone else had.

Instead, she held out a shell. It was a conch, like what the fisherman had clutched earlier.

"I'm sorry. I—I only wanted to help," Barclay told her, uncertain if she could understand him.

She smiled and placed the conch shell in his hand. Barclay realized it was a gift.

"Thank you," he told her, even though he knew the charm was worthless, just like his skunk charm had been. But it was a gift of thanks from someone in a town so much like Dullshire. And that made it precious.

The old woman looked like she wanted to say something, but then Runa, Edwyn, and Tadg walked toward him, and she ducked away.

"The good news," said Runa, "is that we've found someone willing to take us to Munsey."

"The bad news," Tadg grunted, "is that his brain's leakier than these boats."

The man in question appeared behind them. He was hugely tall, with a parrotlike Beast on his shoulder whose glittering scarlet feathers matched the man's red beard.

"Why, hello there," he greeted them, bending low to be more level with Barclay, who only reached the man's chest. "I hear we have some stranded Lore Keepers in need of a ship." He grinned, his wooden pipe bobbing from his mouth. "It so happens that I'm a Lore Keeper too. And I love sailing during a storm."

THREE

An hour later, Barclay offered Yasha a wooden bucket while Yasha puked off the starboard rail of the *Bewlah*. The vessel was medium-sized and flew tattered, graying sails made of a bunch of different fabrics patched together. Bewlah, the parrotlike Beast who was the ship's namesake, sang a limerick at Yasha while perched atop his head.

> *There once was a boy with blond curls*
> *Who couldn't sail without needing to hurl.*
> *Without a latrine,*
> *His face had gone green,*
> *But a bucket he might give a whirl.*

Barclay tried to swat the Beast away, but she paid him no mind.

"Sorry about Bewlah," the captain apologized from where he stood at the helm on the upper deck. Though the ship seemed large for a single sailor, the captain was so large himself that he must've counted as at least two extra crewmen all on his own. "She's mighty rude to children. Doesn't like them."

At that, Bewlah began pecking at Yasha's ears.

"Get off me," Yasha grumbled, swatting at her. Bewlah flew to the sailor's shoulder. Then Yasha seized the bucket Barclay had offered and threw up in it. He uttered a quiet, grave thank-you, and Barclay gave him space and slinked off to join Root at the bow. Root lapped his tongue as the sea breeze ruffled his black fur.

"Hey, buddy," Barclay told him. He slumped against the ship's rail and scratched Root behind the ear. This was supposed to be his first grand adventure, yet he couldn't shake the image of the angry villagers from his mind. Over a whole season had passed since he'd been thrown out of Dullshire, but for some reason, the wound felt painful and raw all over again.

Sensing his misery, Root nudged his head into Barclay's side, bumping into the conch shell stowed in his pocket. Barclay took it out. Even if it had been a gift, it was just a useless, superstitious charm. He should probably pitch it into the water.

"You're still carrying that shell?" sneered Tadg, who sat cross-legged with Viola on the deck.

Barclay hastily tucked the shell into his satchel. "I'm not—I mean, I just haven't thrown it away yet." But he would, once they reached the Sea.

Tadg was in a mood, apparently. He glared at Viola and barked, "Why do you always have to read that? Haven't you finished it by now?"

Viola peeked over her copy of *A Traveler's Log of Dangerous Beasts* by Conley Murdock, a Lore Keeper famous for his dazzling and daring studies of powerful Beasts—like the time he'd ridden a Pterodragyn or treated a Hookshark's toothache. But his wild stunts were also what had led to his death. Last Summer, after the betrayal of his partner, Soren Reiker, Conley had been swallowed by Lochmordra, the Legendary Beast of the Sea.

Conley Murdock was also Tadg's father.

"I've read it a few times, but there's just so much to learn," Viola said. "And I need to learn a lot if I'm going to be elected Grand Keeper one day. But I can put it away, if it bothers you."

"It doesn't bother me." Tadg hugged his knees to his chest and grimaced at the water.

Barclay considered reading too. He still had to finish the textbook Runa had lent him, titled *The Nine Most Crucial Events of Lore Keeper History (They Really Did Happen!)* by Grusha Dudnik. But he wasn't feeling up to homework right now. Instead, like Tadg, he stared grimly over the ship's side, wondering when the gulf's gray waters would become the Sea.

"Rather than lazing around like a bunch of Slothmonkees," Runa told the three of them, her hands on her hips, "I've thought of some training for each of you. You did a good job defending Knunx from the Sleábeaks, but all of your Lore has room for improvement."

Barclay perked up, eager for Lore Keeper training that used actual *Lore*.

"Viola," Runa started. "You had trouble today because you're not used to facing so many fast-moving targets at once."

Viola swallowed and fiddled with her pins. "I—I didn't have *that* much trouble. I could've—"

"Right now, you can shine light from your hands," Runa continued, paying no mind to Viola's discomfort, "but they're focused beams. You have a harder time lighting up an entire room or space, especially for longer than a few minutes. So I'd like to work on your strength and endurance. That way, you'll soon be able to strike all nearby targets simultaneously, instead of one at a time."

Seeming to find her nerve, Viola slid *A Traveler's Log* into her backpack and nodded fiercely. "All right."

"Tadg," Runa said next. "You can—"

"Why should I have to train?" he demanded. "I'm already the strongest one here."

Runa raised her eyebrows. "Funny. I thought *I* was the strongest one here."

This made Tadg cross his arms—and Barclay snort. Obviously Runa was right.

"You can use your water Lore by itself," Runa said, "but you can't use your electric Lore without something to conduct it. I want you to work on conjuring sparks without water or metal. Try to start with your fingers. Position them like this." She pointed her index fingers at each other, with a small gap between them. "See if you can—"

"Yeah, yeah, I get it." Tadg stood up and trudged to the opposite end of the *Bewlah* to practice.

"Just because I've known him since before he could walk doesn't mean he gets to talk to me like that." Runa shook her head and turned to Barclay. "And you. You have a slightly different task. You need to work on a sense of control. That way you'll be able to stop your Lore before things get out of hand like they did today."

"But wind *is wild*." Barclay realized he'd argued with her almost as rudely as Tadg, and Barclay didn't normally talk back to grown-ups. "I mean—I don't think wind *can* be controlled. It's not like light or water or ice."

"All Lore Keepers can learn to control their Lore. It just takes practice." Runa peered around the ship and scooped up a loose bottle cap from the deck. She handed it to him. "Take this. See if you can suspend it over your hand, using wind to keep it in place."

"B-but wind doesn't just *stay still*," Barclay sputtered. "There's no way I can do that!"

"Would I give you an impossible assignment?" Runa asked him pointedly.

"No, but—"

"Would I give you an assignment I didn't think you could handle?"

Barclay sighed. "No."

"Then get to work. The storm is coming soon."

Above, the clouds had darkened from gray to deep purple, like one big bruise across the sky. And the waves around them had gone choppy and jagged.

Frustrated before he'd even begun, Barclay slinked to the upper deck, where Edwyn was fast asleep on a wooden bench beneath a wool blanket. Clearly the run-in with the Sleábeaks had tired him out.

Barclay squeezed the cap in his fist. He still thought wind Lore was too wild to control, but if it *could* be controlled, then Knunx deserved to be angry with him. He was a terrible excuse for a Guardian apprentice—or for any sort of Lore Keeper, really.

He peeked over his shoulder to where Viola and Tadg were practicing. Viola had managed to grow her Lore from a beam to a small dome of light, and sparks already crackled between Tadg's fingertips.

Barclay turned back around and stared at Root, who had joined him on the top deck. "Do you think I can do this?" he asked nervously.

Root barked and twirled in a circle. And so, gathering his nerve, Barclay summoned his Lore to lift the cap off his palm and hold it in the air.

Instead, the cap shot into the blustery winds and pattered across the wooden floorboards.

"Bad luck," the captain said while Barclay scrabbled to grab it.

Barclay nodded, embarrassed to have an audience. But he hadn't summoned wind on his first try either. He only needed practice.

But the second attempt was no different. And the third time, the cap went flying so high, Barclay had to scramble to catch it before it could plunk into the ocean.

Bewlah sang all the while:

There once was a wee little chap
Trying his Lore on a beer bottle cap.
The girl could conjure a flash.
His friend could zap men to ash,
But the little one's attempts were all—

"Bewlah!" the captain bellowed. "Be nice." While Barclay's cheeks burned, the captain told him kindly, "You got tricky Lore, is all. What kinda Beast is he?"

Root puffed his chest out at being addressed.

"A Lufthund," Barclay said.

"So he's Prime class, then?"

Lore Keepers categorized Beasts into five classes, depending on how strong their Lore and how rare they were to find.

"Root is Mythic class, actually," Barclay answered.

Mythic class included the most powerful creatures, second only to the six Legendary Beasts. No doubt the captain thought an apprentice who couldn't control their Lore must only have a Beast that was Prime or Familiar class.

But the captain whistled. "That's impressive, especially for a kid your age. But I shouldn't be too surprised, if the Fang of Dusk is your teacher. Bewlah is just Familiar class, and I never studied hard enough when I was young to get a Guild license myself." He reached his hand out to shake. "My name's Ulick O'Hara. I transport goods from the mainland to the islands of the Sea."

"Like the Isle of Munsey?" Barclay asked, remembering what Viola had called the Sea's capital.

"Yes, sir. Munsey, Dunsey, Coad, Glannock—all of 'em, really. But it's Munsey where we're headed now."

Barclay wondered why Tadg had claimed Ulick was nutty. He didn't seem like it.

"How long until we get there?" asked Barclay.

"It's about three hours, once we pass the Shifts."

"The Shifts?"

"That's the beginning of the Sea. Should be coming up on it any— Oh! It's in sight now." He pointed out past the bow, and chills prickled up Barclay's spine when he saw what Ulick meant.

A long divide stretched across the ocean. On one side— the side where they sailed now—the water was a greenish gray, the waves rough but far from dangerous. But on the other, it was a blue so dark it looked nearly black, and the crests of the waves were massive, rising and falling like the breathing of a great creature beneath the surface. Barclay's heart fluttered with fear.

Below, Yasha looked up from where he slumped over the rail and groaned.

"Might wanna pause your training," Ulick told Barclay. "The Sea always gets rowdy, but with the storm, I'm gonna need a few hands on deck."

"All right," Barclay squeaked. He should've guessed the Sea would look as haunting as the Woods, and he shuddered as the *Bewlah* approached its inky water. The waves thrashed. He'd heard of ships capsizing in adventure books, but he'd never dreamed such a fate could happen to him.

"Stand over here," Ulick ordered him, his massive hands positioning Barclay and Root beneath the sails. "You're gonna use your wind Lore to help us. And you—dragon girl!"

Viola stopped her training with Mitzi. "My name is Viola!" she called, affronted.

"It's gonna get dark out there, so go stand by the bow. Now you—the Frown."

Tadg, realizing Ulick meant him, frowned deeper. "Don't call me—"

"Keep a look out for Beasts. They can get excited during storms. And you, uh . . . Seasick."

Yasha wiped his mouth on his sleeve, as though prepared to fight despite being ill.

"Well, just don't puke all over my deck," Ulick told him. "And you, Miss Fang Lady, you can . . ."

Runa shot Ulick a glare so lethal that Barclay was surprised Ulick didn't freeze into a block of ice. "I don't take orders. But I'll keep watch up front."

For such a huge man, Ulick seemed to shrink several inches at Runa's tone. "Y-yes, ma'am," he stuttered.

While they each took to their positions, the *Bewlah* gave a violent lurch as it crossed the Shifts and sailed out to Sea.

FOUR

Instantly, the voyage changed.

The waves, which already battered the *Bewlah* from side to side, gained strength. The ship whipped back and forth, the mast swinging like a pendulum. Crates and burlap sacks skidded across the bottom deck, forcing Tadg and Yasha to lunge out of their paths. Barclay clung to the closest railing to hold himself upright. Salty spray splashed up from the sides of the ship, stinging his eyes.

Beside him, Root whimpered, and Barclay hastily returned him to his Mark.

"Here we go!" Ulick roared. He gave a great, bellowing laugh and then spun the wheel, sending the *Bewlah* careening up a wave's back. As they launched off the peak, Barclay's heart dropped to his toes. He was beginning to see what Tadg had meant about Ulick now.

Overhead, thunder rumbled, like the growl of an empty stomach. Barclay's Mark stung, as if he needed a reminder that he was once again face-to-face with danger.

"The sails, my boy!" Ulick shouted.

Barclay, still clinging to the railing with all his might, didn't realize Ulick meant him until Ulick reached over and shook Barclay's shoulder. Bracing his feet for balance, Barclay carefully let go and looked up at the sails. The wind roared, whipping his hair across his face.

He raised his arms, preparing to summon a wind of his own. But then an image flashed through his mind—the ruined house in Knunx. If Barclay's Lore went out of control this time, they were all doomed.

"Now! Now!" Ulick yelled.

Heart hammering, Barclay squeezed his eyes shut and thought, *Wind!* Gusts spun out of his hands, and the sails stretched taut—too taut. The ship heaved forward violently. Viola shrieked. Barclay collided with Ulick, which felt no different from smacking into a brick wall. The bench Edwyn slept on went slewing across the deck from port to starboard. Edwyn, still snoring, didn't stir.

Runa climbed up the quarterdeck to Ulick and Barclay. "If the storm gets worse, should we turn back to—"

"Turn back? The *Bewlah* has seen worse than this! Haven't sunk her yet!" Ulick declared, and Bewlah squawked in agreement on his arm. Then Ulick braced his shoulders, a wild look in his eyes, and hollered, "Hold on to your backsides!"

The *Bewlah* vaulted over the crest of another wave, and Runa grabbed the edge of the ship to keep from falling. "Listen. If we turn around now, we can still make it back to Knunx, and—"

"Oi! Frown!" Ulick shouted at Tadg, pointing ahead and ignoring Runa. "Got ourselves a live one!"

Barclay squinted, trying to see what Ulick meant. Then he spotted a large, scaly tail emerge from the water and slink back below the surface.

"What is that?" Barclay squeaked. "A shark?"

Ulick chuckled. "There are Beasts worse than sharks in these waters. That's a Slanntramór. An armored whale. It won't bother us if we don't bother it. But you'll keep an eye on it, won't ya, Frown?"

"Only if you don't call me that!" Tadg yelled back. Regardless, he stationed himself by the bow, where a wooden carving of Bewlah looked out to sea.

Suddenly a geyserlike stream of water burst from the surface, raining droplets over the ship. Barclay watched in a mixture of awe and terror as the Slanntramór's massive body leapt out of the water. It was the largest creature he'd ever seen—even bigger than the treelike Styerwurms of the Woods. Its body was covered in thousands of scaly plates, iridescent like mother-of-pearl.

Barclay's wonder was short-lived.

"Well, that's not good," Ulick breathed.

The Slanntramór collapsed back into the water, creating

a humongous wave that swept over the ship. Barclay's boots and pants were instantly soaked, and empty crates bobbed like apples across the deck.

Worse, another crack of thunder boomed amid the clouds. It was as though the sky split open, because rain began to pour, dumping buckets.

"We're going to need more light," Ulick said, and Viola stretched her arms out in either direction. Light burst from her palms, flooding the ship like a lighthouse's beacon.

Barclay gaped. How had Viola mastered her assignment so quickly?

"Time for more wind," Ulick told him. But when Barclay tried, the result was no different from before. Though the *Bewlah* gained a little speed, it heeled so hard to the side that it took in more water from an oncoming wave. Tadg used his Lore to cast some of it out, but if the storm carried on like this, they would surely sink.

"I'm s-sorry," Barclay stammered, his teeth chattering from the cold. "I'm trying to do better! I don't know why—"

"Never mind that. Just keep trying." Then Ulick nodded to Edwyn behind him, still asleep on the bench. "Is he dead?"

"He's just asleep," Yasha answered, standing at the foot of the stairs below them. He clutched his bucket with both hands. "It's his healing Lore. He got hurt earlier with the Sleábeaks. He'll be out for hours."

"Lot of use that does," Runa muttered.

"Let me help. My fire Lore can make it as bright as Viola's, or maybe I can—"

"Don't just talk, then!" Ulick said. "Come up to the poop deck!"

Yasha clambered up the stairs. When he saw Barclay shivering, Yasha shrugged off his fur coat. "Here. Take this. It's waterproof."

"Won't you be cold?" asked Barclay, who wasn't used to accepting favors. Especially from someone who had spent the entire voyage seasick.

"I'm never cold." He thrust his coat into Barclay's hands. While Barclay pulled it on, grateful for clothing that wasn't drenched, Yasha lit a fire that hovered over his palm. It might've been weak from the rain, but it still was warm. "Now listen to me. To control your Lore, you need to be in control of yourself. Just think about whatever makes you relax. Then—"

"Oi! Don't just stand around!" Ulick told Yasha. "If you can't make us go faster, then use that bucket of yours to help Frown clear some water off the deck."

Yasha nodded at Barclay seriously, as if he had full faith that Barclay could do this. Then Yasha trudged through the water to the stern, where he began scooping as much of it as he could and dumping it over the rail. He mustn't have been feeling much better, though, because he stopped midway through his third scoop to hurl into the bucket.

Barclay took a deep breath to compose himself. It didn't work well—he inhaled a mouthful of rain, and it was hard to calm down when there was only endless ocean in every direction. So he took Yasha's advice. He tried to think of something that made him relax.

The first thing that came to his mind was mushrooms.

Button, he thought. *Chaga. Mourningtide Morel . . .*

He cut himself off. This was Lore, not mushroom farming. He'd never become a better Lore Keeper if he kept thinking like an Elsie. So he switched subjects to his most recent homework.

The Great Capamoo War, he recited, which was one of the nine most crucial events of Lore Keeper history, according to his textbook. *The Man-Eating Hasifuss. The . . . The . . .* He struggled to come up with a third. *The Assassination of—*

"I don't know what you're waiting on!" Ulick shouted at him. "But now's not the time to—"

Giving up on his list, Barclay finally thought, *Wind!*

It was worse than last time. The gusts Barclay conjured blew twice as fierce, no matter how hard he fought to control them. The ship dipped forward. The mast groaned like it might snap. And the deck shifted from flat to diagonal, sending Barclay falling onto his side . . . and Yasha toppling over the stern into the water.

"Man the wheel!" Ulick shouted at no one in particular, then dove over the side of the *Bewlah.* Without someone to steer, the helm spun aimlessly, making the ship veer this way and that.

Barclay rushed to the wheel and grasped it with both

hands. The force of it spinning nearly knocked him over a second time. But he planted his feet and held it steady.

"Look out!" Viola shrieked.

Barclay barely had time to see what she meant before something wet and slimy slapped him across the cheek. He sputtered. Then something else whacked his shoulder. Then his side. Many somethings splashed into the water at his feet, and Barclay realized with a start that they were *fish*.

"Lepinfish!" Tadg called. "Flying fish!"

"Flying" seemed the right word for them. Dozens of Lepinfish leaped out of the Sea, so high they reached the ship's sails. Those already on the ship jumped again, splashing more water into Barclay's eyes. From the mast above, Bewlah squawked in horror as one smacked her wing.

"Don't panic," Runa told them, though Barclay felt a great deal past panic. They were all going to drown, and it was his fault.

"Lepinfish only jump like this if they're running from something!" Tadg yelled. "That means there's—"

His voice was drowned out as something low and menacing groaned beneath the water.

"What was that?" Viola shouted.

Runa rushed to the stern and looked out over the waves. "Ulick! Are you—"

"Oi!" came Ulick's voice. "I've got the boy, but there's something else out here! Toss us the life buoy!"

Runa hoisted the circular raft from the wall and hurled

it to him. While the seconds passed, she hollered, "What do you mean 'something else'?"

At that, the roar sounded again, closer and louder this time. Viola's light flickered as she shook with fear. At the bow, Tadg was frozen, his mouth open in a small, petrified O.

"Something big!" Ulick called back.

Runa slammed her fist on the stern's rail. "Ulick! Don't tell me this is Loch—" She glanced over her shoulder at her apprentices, and a tremor of terror shot through Barclay. Did she mean the sound came from Lochmordra, the Legendary Beast of the Sea? "What Orla warned—"

"No," Ulick answered, appearing at the rail on a ladder. Yasha was slung limply over his shoulder like the day's fresh catch. "I don't think it's that." He dropped Yasha to the flooded deck, and Yasha gasped and choked out lungfuls of water. Then Ulick marched to the wheel, which Barclay was all too happy to return to him.

"We're really gonna need that wind, my boy," Ulick said darkly and, for the first time, quietly. He didn't want anyone else to hear. "I don't care if ya snap the ship in two, so long as we *move*."

"What is it?" Barclay rasped.

"Take a look over port side."

Heart pounding, Barclay dashed to the edge of the *Bewlah* and peered into the shadowy waters.

An eye the size of the entire ship stared back at him.

Barclay screamed and floundered away from the rail. The

Sea was *not* the adventure he'd been waiting for. The Sea was a nightmare.

Barclay raced back below the mast. *Wind!* he thought, but he was so frightened that he might've actually shouted it. Like Ulick had said, he didn't bother trying to control the wind this time. He blew them forward with all the power he had, no matter how much the rickety ship could take.

"That's it! Well done!" Ulick called.

Suddenly, whatever was below them began to emerge from the ocean's depths. The *Bewlah* was swept out of its path as it rose, rose, and *rose*. Barclay stifled a second scream as the monster's face appeared. It had coarse, gray skin covered in bumps, and its head was long and narrow, almost beak shaped. It looked as large as a mountain.

Its hungry white eyes roamed over their ship to where Viola's coat glimmered in the light of her Lore.

"It's a Silberwal!" Ulick exclaimed.

Silberwals were famous for being the largest Beasts in the world.

Tadg, seeming to regain himself, shouted at Viola, "Put out your light! It's a whale dragon! It likes shiny—"

The Silberwal opened its mouth endlessly wide, until the *Bewlah* stared down a vast, dark tunnel lined with bristly teeth.

"Oh, that can't be good," Ulick said, spinning the wheel faster and faster.

Viola extinguished her light, and everything slipped into

darkness. Still, Barclay desperately raised his arms in the direction of the sails to summon more wind. The Silberwal roared behind them, the noise so loud, Barclay had to pause his Lore to cover his ears with his hands. Even Edwyn, still slumbering on his bench, seemed to rouse—then he rolled onto his side and drifted back asleep.

Lightning flashed overhead, illuminating glimpses of gums and teeth and throat.

Then there was a crackling sound and a brighter light. Tadg shot a blast of electricity at the Silberwal. The bolt struck its right eye, and it roared in pain.

Seeming to think better of this meal, the Beast collapsed back into the water. The force of it sent the *Bewlah* hurtling away from its wake.

Before the Silberwal fully retreated, however, it got its vengeance. It splashed its tail—*hard*. A gigantic wave sped out in all directions, larger than the ship. Larger than twelve ships. Larger than a whole fleet.

"Not good. Not good," Ulick muttered, and Barclay braced himself for what would surely be their doom.

Then Runa stretched her arms out, and an icy mist sprayed from her fingertips. It reached the wave, spreading up to its peak. The tsunami froze solid only heartbeats before it could crash onto the *Bewlah*.

Barclay gaped up at the tidal wave that had nearly killed them, that Runa had stopped in an instant. From the way the other Lore Keepers had gossiped about Runa in the

Woods, Barclay had always known that she was powerful. But he'd never imagined *anyone* capable of Lore like that.

And he couldn't even control his.

Runa lowered her arms, her chest heaving. "We are *not* dying tonight," she declared, and even if they still had two hours of sailing ahead, she sounded so confident that Barclay couldn't help but believe her.

And she was right. Long after sunset, when the *Bewlah* spotted the shadow of land on the horizon, each member of the crew—except for Edwyn—hollered in victory. They'd made it through the voyage alive.

But despite his relief, a miserable voice in Barclay's head taunted that their survival was no thanks to him.

FIVE

Edwyn yawned and stretched as their group staggered onto the beach of the Isle of Munsey. "I can't believe we faced such an ordeal! Absolutely incredible!"

"You mean the six of *us* faced an ordeal," Tadg grumbled, tearing a piece of seaweed out of his wavy, light brown hair. "You slept the whole time."

Edwyn hardly seemed bothered by Tadg's grumpiness. "I'm afraid I wouldn't have been much help anyway. What would healing Lore have done against a Silberwal?"

"Are you a Guardian Keeper or aren't you?" Tadg shot back, earning him a warning look from Runa. "I just don't get it. I've sailed over the Shifts a million times, even in a storm. But I've *never* seen that many Beasts attack a ship."

Feeling rather grumpy himself, Barclay trudged ahead across the pebbly sand. It was dark except for scattered flashes of lightning. Rain continued to pelt down, and beneath Yasha's coat, Barclay was so drenched that his socks squish-squished with every step.

Ulick, however, seemed refreshed by their close encounter with doom. He wrung out his magnificent beard, laughed, and winked at the docked *Bewlah* behind them, as though he and his ship had shared a great joke.

"Invigorating!" he bellowed. "A few more of those and we'll be ready to take on Shipwreck Stretch!"

Barclay didn't know what Shipwreck Stretch was, but the only things he felt ready for were a warm bath and a deep sleep.

"We docked on the north of the island," Ulick told them. "It's about a mile to town."

"A mile?" Barclay choked.

Runa sighed. "Well, I guess we better get walking. How are you doing, Viola? You've been using your Lore for almost three hours, and—"

"No, I'm . . ." Viola panted heavily. "I'm fine. I can . . . do it." She held out her hands and emitted a feeble, flickering light over the dunes.

"Here, let me," Yasha offered. A flame erupted over his palm like a torch, and he cradled it in his arms to keep it from getting wet. Viola extinguished her light with a tired thank-you.

Slinging their satchels and backpacks over their shoulders, the group started down a stone path winding through tall grass. Barclay kept to the back, wanting to be alone with his thoughts. Even if they'd escaped the storm alive, he couldn't help but feel like he'd failed everyone when they'd counted on him most.

When Barclay had accepted Runa's offer to be her apprentice, he'd been thrilled. He'd finally found a place where he belonged.

But what if he never caught up to everyone else? What if he didn't have what it took to be a Lore Keeper after all?

Barclay didn't have a chance to dwell on that gloomy notion, however, because a new light appeared in the distance, bobbing down the trail toward them.

Whoever it was walked slowly—*very* slowly. As they neared, Barclay realized they were an old woman, possibly the oldest person he'd ever seen. Her fair skin was wrinkled like a raisin, and her frizzy white hair was tied loosely behind her with twine and hung down to her hips. She wore a rain jacket and, beneath it, a brown shawl that could've been mistaken for a fishing net.

"Well, you've all certainly looked better," the woman spoke. She had a coarse voice, as though she'd swallowed sand. "Edwyn and Yasha, lovely to see you both. And thank you for coming back to the Sea so soon. I hope I'm not keeping you from pleasanter travels."

"Nonsense. We're happy to be of service," Edwyn said brightly, while Tadg still glared at him for his good mood.

"And Runa," the woman huffed, "it took you long enough!

Don't you know better than to keep an old woman waiting?"

Runa rested her hands on Barclay's and Viola's shoulders. "Orla, these are my three apprentices—Viola Dumont, Barclay Thorne, and you know Tadg."

Orla smiled. She was missing half her teeth. "Of course, the grouchy Murdock boy. And Viola, I've heard a lot about you from your father."

"You have?" Viola said nervously.

"Mostly good things, I promise— And Barclay. I don't know you at all. Where are you from?"

Barclay's face went hot. "Um . . ."

"Barclay is from an Elsewheres village near the Woods," Runa answered for him. Feeling the curious eyes of Ulick, Yasha, and Edwyn on him, Barclay flushed all the fiercer.

"Quite a journey!" Orla said. "And Barclay, you have a little something on your face."

Barclay had forgotten that the Gunkwort was still stuck to his cheek like a giant silver zit.

"No, don't fuss with it. It'll let go when it's ready. And believe me, no one around here is a stranger to Gunkwort. You can take my word for that! I'm Orla Scudder, the High Keeper of the Sea."

Barclay had only ever met one High Keeper, Kasimir Erhart from the Woods. Erhart had been so desperate for money that he'd ignored his benefactor Soren Reiker's crimes . . . like the two times Soren had attacked Barclay and tried to steal Root. Erhart had only punished Soren for his wrongdoings after Soren had tried to bond with Gravaldor and almost destroyed the entire Woods in the process.

After all that, Barclay wasn't sure he should trust Orla. But Runa, who despised Erhart, seemed pleased to see her, so Orla must've been a better High Keeper.

"Nice to meet you," Barclay said politely.

"Let's get you all inside and fed," Orla said. "Death could catch you out here, you know."

"You mean that we could 'catch our deaths,'" corrected Viola.

Orla shrugged. "That too."

Then, very slowly, they followed Orla down the trail until they reached the town of Munsey. Despite feeling tired and sorry for himself, Barclay was eager to get a glimpse of this new, exciting place. But it was dark except for the lampposts, which, strangely, had no fire in them. Instead, they were filled with water that glowed with dreamy blue speckles of light.

Orla led them to a massive tower at the outskirts of town, one even bigger than the clocktower in Dullshire. She swung open the door and ushered them into the welcoming warmth. Inside was a comfortable and spacious hall, with numerous rocking chairs, tables, and couches. A fire burned in the hearth that smelled strangely earthy, like fresh mud. Fishing nets, rusty anchors, and shells decorated the walls, and at the room's center, a spiral staircase rose, disappearing far above toward the tower—as well as down to a cellar below.

"Welcome to the Sea's Guild House," Orla said. "And that's Murph. He keeps watch over the place while I'm gone."

Barclay expected Murph to be a man, but the room was empty except for a massive tortoiselike Beast warming himself by the fire. His shell was decorated in vibrant swirl designs, and he had a dignified gray mustache that hung down to the floor.

While they made themselves comfortable, Orla fetched them several blankets and mugs of warm milk. Soon Barclay, Viola, Tadg, and Yasha were buried together on a couch beneath a heap of quilts, Barclay still shivering, Yasha sneezing, Tadg gulping down his drink, and Viola fast asleep. Root, Mitzi, and Yasha's Beast—a white catlike creature with pointy ears—joined Murph by the fire.

"I'm sorry you had such a treacherous journey," Orla told them all, taking a seat on one of the rocking chairs. "I'm afraid this has been a difficult time for the Sea."

"In your letter, you told me there had been attacks," Runa said. "What exactly has been going on?"

Barclay elbowed Viola awake, knowing she'd want to hear this.

"Since the start of the Winter," Orla explained, "Lochmordra has been rising at random and targeting ships and islands. Most recently—"

"Lochmordra's been attacking?" Tadg asked sharply.

"I'm afraid so. Apart from a few ships, he destroyed

much of the Isle of Kelligree. And before that, we lost the Isles of Slakey and Coad."

Tadg went silent. It must've been a shock to hear that the Beast who'd killed his father was now terrorizing his home.

"Kelligree was the second most populated island after Munsey," Orla continued. "Thousands of people lost their homes and have had to relocate to other islands. All our inns here are full. Sailors are wary of long voyages in case they encounter Lochmordra. Except, of course, Ulick."

Ulick beamed. "Nothing keeps me and Bewlah off the water."

"But it's not just Lochmordra, is it?" Runa pressed. "A flock of Sleábeaks attacked Knunx while we were there. And Tadg and I have both traveled the Sea in a storm without encountering half the Beasts that we did tonight."

Orla nodded. "All of the Beasts have become more aggressive, and we don't know why. Lochmordra never used to rise except for Midsummer and Midwinter, but even then, I've never known him to attack an island."

"I'm sorry we didn't stay," Edwyn said somberly. "If we'd known that Kelligree would also be hit, we never would've left."

"It's hardly your fault," Orla assured him. "And I've been trying to summon as many Guardians as I can. Karina Severnaya arrived a few days ago. There's Crumpe, of course. He never leaves. And—"

"What has the Grand Keeper done?" Runa asked.

"Oh, you know Dumont. He promised me kritters that still haven't arrived. But even with all the money in the Argentisaurus Bank, we can't start rebuilding until we understand why Lochmordra and these Beasts are attacking in the first place."

"And there's been nothing strange or unusual leading up to this?"

"I'm afraid not. Or, if so, not that we noticed."

If they don't know why this is happening, Barclay thought, *that means that we're not safe here. No one is.* After the dangers of simply reaching the Sea, Barclay had little desire to throw himself back into harm's way.

But this was the job of a Guardian Keeper, to protect people even when it meant risking yourself.

In Dullshire, Barclay had tried so hard to follow their rules. He'd had to beg for his apprenticeship. And he'd worked day and night just to prove that he belonged.

But they'd banished him anyway.

Barclay refused to fail this time. He didn't care if he had to study and train twice as hard as Viola and Tadg to catch up. He didn't care if it meant facing ten more Silberwals to protect the Sea. He *had* to prove himself as a Guardian Keeper, no matter what.

"If all the inns are full, where will we be staying?" asked Runa.

"Most of the other Guardians are staying here in the Guild House, and there's still one room left for you," Orla answered. "As for the apprentices, the boys can share the loft over Ansley MacGannon's shop. Viola, you can stay with my friend Lifen Hao. She has a guest cottage."

"And Edwyn, you can stay with me," Ulick told him cheerily. "I've got a shack on the beach where I keep some supplies. And you'll have it to yourself most of the time—I come and go. Normally I sleep on my boat."

If Edwyn was less than thrilled to be staying in a shack, he didn't show it. And even if Barclay didn't know Yasha well, he was happy to have someone else to distract him from Tadg's sour moods.

An hour later, Ulick led the three boys and their Beasts to Ansley MacGannon's shop, where bells above their heads chimed as they opened the door. There, a short, middle-aged woman with fair skin greeted them. She wore a nightgown and a thick cardigan, and her spectacles were tinted bluish green, like sea glass.

"Hello, Ulick," she said. "I'm always surprised to find you in one piece."

"And I'm surprised to see ya at all! You're always cooped up here with all your beakers and fancy equipment."

"Oh, I don't mind. Though I admit I'm eager for the company." She examined the three apprentices, whose hair and clothes were all still damp. "Don't tell me you were sailing in this weather?"

"What, this?" Ulick asked, as a roar of thunder boomed behind him. "Just a bit breezy, is all."

Ansley pursed her lips and motioned for the boys. "Come in out of the cold, all of you."

Wearily muttering good night to Ulick, the three apprentices stepped inside. With the shop unlit, Barclay couldn't see what sort of merchandise it sold, but it smelled strongly medicinal. Behind them, Root shook the rain out of his fur, and Yasha's catlike Beast turned her head in disgust.

Ansley ushered them all up a narrow, rickety stairwell to an attic, where there were three beds made up for them to sleep on. It was a cramped room for one person, let alone three kids and two Beasts, but Barclay was so eager for rest that he would've slept beside Murph on the Guild House floor.

"You'll want to wash up, I'm sure," Ansley said. "I can draw up some hot water for a bath. But I'm not sure I have enough for all—"

"I think we'd just like to sleep, if that's all right," Barclay said drowsily.

He set his satchel down by the windowsill. The view outside was dark except for the blue lamp posts that lined the street.

Suddenly, a shadow loomed behind one post in the distance. It stood on two legs, but it was far too large to be human.

It disappeared. Barclay blinked. He must've been so tired that he was imagining things.

"Of course, of course," Ansley chirped. "I'll leave you all to—"

The ground began to tremble, much like it had in Knunx—only stronger. The furniture wobbled and thumped on the floor, and Ansley would've fallen had Barclay not caught her by the shoulder. There was the crash of something shattering downstairs.

"What's happening?" Tadg asked, bracing himself against a wall. Yasha's Beast darted beneath one of the beds, and Root's ears went flat with fear.

"It's another one!" Ansley gasped. "Everyone—everyone stay calm! We need to hurry—"

But no sooner had Ansley gotten the words out than the shaking stopped. They all stared at one another with wide-eyed alarm.

"That's the second one since Spring began," Ansley muttered, readjusting her crooked glasses.

"Are earthquakes common at the Sea?" Barclay asked.

"No," Tadg answered.

"These are troubled times," Ansley said. "I hope your teachers know what they're doing. I don't care how famous Runa Rasgar is. It's not wise to tow a bunch of kids along on a dangerous assignment. . . . Oh, that'll be the Ripple-weed pots that shattered, I just know it. . . ." With a huff, she marched down the steps.

For several moments the boys stood in ominous silence.

Then Tadg grunted, "I call the bed in the corner."

Yasha looked at Barclay and shrugged. "I don't care. Pick whichever you like."

Before Barclay could choose, Root leapt onto the middle bed—choosing for him.

"You're going to make the blankets all damp," Barclay scolded, but Root ignored him. He nestled at the foot of the bed, gave his ears a good scratch, and closed his eyes.

Remembering his manners, Barclay tugged off the fur coat and handed it back to Yasha. "Thanks for letting me borrow this. Do you feel any better?"

"Now that I'm off the water, yes. But I'm not happy you all had to work so hard while I did practically nothing. Worse than nothing, since Ulick had to save me."

"You can't help that you were seasick."

Yasha clenched his fist. "Maybe not. But I should be stronger than that. I *am* stronger than that."

Barclay didn't know what to say. It struck him as odd that Edwyn was so charming but his apprentice was so stern.

But Barclay forgot all about a response as he rifled through his satchel—all his belongings were soaked. Groaning, he dumped out everything in his bag. A soggy clump of clothes, *The Nine Most Crucial Events of Lore Keeper History*, and the conch toppled to the floor.

Before Barclay could hide the shell or kick it beneath his bed, Tadg snorted loudly. "You must really like that shell, don't you? It's no wonder you can't use your Lore right. You pretend otherwise, but you're still an Elsie."

His face burning, Barclay shoved the shell back into his bag and slid into bed, damp clothes and all. He was so mortified that he regretted not being skewered by a Sleábeak.

If Yasha wanted to laugh, he hid it well. Or maybe Yasha just never laughed, same as he rarely smiled. He set out a bowl on the floor and filled it with food pellets. The sound made Root look up with interest.

"Here, Motya," Yasha whispered, and the Beast poked her head out from beneath the bed. She crept to the food bowl, then, a moment before taking a bite, heaved out a great breath of air. The food caught fire, making Barclay and Root startle. Only then did Motya deign to touch her flambéed meal.

Tadg groaned at the noise and rolled over to face the wall.

Yasha glanced at Barclay. "Is he always like that?" When Barclay nodded, the other boy rolled his eyes, and Barclay felt a bit better. Maybe Yasha didn't actually think him strange for being an Elsie.

All Lore Keepers can learn to control their Lore, Runa had assured Barclay while on the *Bewlah.* But the words meant to comfort him now seized him with fear.

If Barclay couldn't learn to control his Lore, then he wouldn't just fail at being a Guardian Keeper—he would be no Lore Keeper at all.

SIX

Something slammed, and Barclay and Root jolted awake, making the Gunkwort on Barclay's cheek slip off and land on his pillow with a wet splat. Barclay blinked bleary eyes at Edwyn, who loomed in their doorway with an unusually serious expression. Despite all his sleeping, Edwyn looked as haggard as ever, his gray-peppered hair disheveled, and dark circles ringing his eyes.

"What is it?" Yasha mumbled. On Barclay's other side, Tadg pressed his pillow over his head.

"Lochmordra attacked another island last night during the storm," Edwyn told them. "We've only just gotten word. Some survivors from the Isle of Glannock have arrived. There will be more—"

"The Isle of Glannock?" Tadg threw off his pillow and sat up with a start. "Are you sure?"

"That's what I've been hearing. So come on. We have work to do."

The boys bolted out of bed. Root stretched and gave a wide, toothy yawn, and Motya, who looked to have been awake for some time, stared down regally from her perch atop the bookshelf while the boys staggered and tripped over themselves in a sleepy rush. Not ten minutes later, they raced downstairs and out of the shop.

In the daylight, Barclay got a far better look at Munsey, and it didn't resemble Sycomore from the Woods as much as he'd expected. It was *huge*. And very, very gray. Its stone buildings blended into the bleak cloudy sky. Brittle bits of shell were caked between the cobblestones. And at this time of year, all the trees were bare. However, Munsey made up for this by painting all of its doors in bright, cheery colors, like yellows and reds and greens.

And the bustling streets were anything but boring. Pelican-like Beasts with ruffly black plumage soared overhead, letters and parcels for delivery clutched in their beaks. (Root barked at all of them.) Lore Keepers of all sorts passed by, with every variety of dress and features. Barclay noticed a man with very dark skin hauling a cart filled with mollusk Beasts that squirmed and crawled about with their long, slimy tongues. A pale and freckly woman trod past with a horned otter riding in her backpack. Up ahead, Barclay spotted Ansley tending to one of the streetlamps, feeding whatever it was that glowed blue inside.

But of all the sights, the most incredible by far was the Guild House. It towered over Munsey, and no matter how exhausted he'd been, Barclay didn't understand how he hadn't realized yesterday that it was a lighthouse. Then he realized the beacon wasn't lit.

Inside, numerous Lore Keepers and Beasts gathered amid the tables and rocking chairs, including Runa and Viola.

"Who are all these people?" Barclay whispered to Yasha.

"Guardians," he answered. "Orla summoned them here from all across the world."

Barclay examined them in awe. He had never seen so many Guardians in one place. He recognized Edwyn and Ulick, who sat side by side on the bottom steps of the spiral staircase. Next to Orla stood an old, cross-eyed man with a cane crusted with barnacles. A woman paced near the fire, wearing the most interesting cloak Barclay had ever seen, embroidered with shimmering designs of all sorts of Beasts. Another woman lounged at the feet of her massive brown-and-gold dragon.

They all looked as fierce and impressive as Barclay imagined Guardians should be—though none had a presence as fearsome as Runa's.

While the Lore Masters spoke, Viola motioned the boys to join her at a table in the back.

"This is the fourth island," the woman with the cloak said heatedly. "That leaves only five remaining. You've already turned off the lighthouse beacon out of fear of catching the

Beast's notice. This has gone too far. We must evacuate."

"And go where?" growled someone else. "The Woods is a long journey away. And we all know Erhart can't accommodate—"

"Have the Grand Keeper send carrier dragons. Send a fleet of them—"

"It's dragon breeding season!" hissed the woman beside her, who stroked a chameleonlike Beast on her lap. Its scales rippled in an array of colors to blend into her tan skin, long black hair, and red leather jacket. "You can't expect him to—"

"Enough," Orla said sharply. "We of the Sea are a proud people. We won't be abandoning our homes just yet."

Then Orla began calling off a roster of names, separating the Guardians into groups. To the first several, she ordered, "I'd like us to interview the refugees from Glannock. We'll see if there's anything they saw last night that could be enlightening." And then: "You two. You can take your ship out with Runa and Edwyn. I need you four investigating the area where Lochmordra reportedly rose. Ansley will give you Polypops in case you dive. But be careful—the Jawbasks are fond of the waters near Glannock. And you six . . . there were also reports of Muirmarú destruction from the Isle of Orn. See what you can find there."

All of the Lore Keepers and Beasts shuffled out of the Guild House. One Beast, a massive serpent that was nothing but skeleton, lingered behind. It slithered across the floor to the sounds of *click click click.*

"What about us?" Tadg demanded of Orla.

Runa clicked her tongue. "Show more respect for the High Keeper."

"Fine. What about us, *ma'am*?" Tadg corrected, sounding no less irritated.

Orla didn't look offended. She even smiled. She had a bit of seaweed caught on her lone front tooth. "You four will be going with Ulick to investigate the wreckage in Glannock for any clues. I don't expect you'll find much—the reports say there's little left."

Despite the grimness of it all, excitement fluttered in Barclay's chest. This was their first true assignment as Guardian apprentices. And that meant it was his first chance to prove himself.

"What kind of clues will we be looking for?" he asked eagerly.

"Anything that seems out of the ordinary," Orla answered.

"But most of us won't know what ordinary here looks like," Viola pointed out. "We haven't been to the Sea before."

"Tadg and Ulick will be able to help with that," said Runa. Her eyes flickered to Tadg, who stared off in the distance. He didn't seem to have heard. "You'll be up to it, right, Tadg?"

"Sure," he said softly.

Barclay realized that the Isle of Glannock must've been Tadg's home. And though he rarely felt anything but annoyed at Tadg, now he felt a bit sorry.

"Because I don't like to send you without a licensed Guardian Keeper," Runa told them, "you can take Goath."

"Goath?" Barclay repeated.

At that, the massive bone serpent slithered up Runa's back and propped its head on her shoulder. Though it had no eyes, only empty sockets, it stared intently at the apprentices. Barclay's skin broke out in chills.

"My Haddisss," Runa said, drawing out the word like a long hiss. Despite weeks and weeks on the road, Barclay had never met any of Runa's Beasts. She'd kept them to their Marks so they wouldn't draw unwanted attention in the Elsewheres.

"Why can't we take Klava?" Tadg asked. "Goath is creepy."

Goath rattled, as though flattered. Runa scratched him beneath his jawbone.

"Trust me—Goath is far friendlier than Klava. And besides, Klava doesn't like to be away from me."

Barclay and Viola exchanged glances, and he could tell she was as keen to learn more about Runa's Beasts as he was. But before they could ask more questions, Edwyn called for Runa to hurry up, and Runa left with the rest of the Guardian Keepers.

At that, Barclay and the other apprentices, plus Goath, followed Ulick back to the *Bewlah*. Their journey took them through a street of shops. A window display advertised a Spring sale on all magical Beast antiques of reptilian and marsupial varieties. Barclay spotted a Draconis Emporium, which he recognized from Sycomore. One storefront, Fillitot's Gourmet Beast Treats, was painted in glossy stripes of red and yellow, with ribbons hanging like streamers over its awning.

"Munsey is so *big*," Barclay said.

"That's because the Sea has over twenty times as many people as the Woods," Viola told him.

Barclay's eyes widened. He'd known that the Woods was small—after all, Sycomore was its only settlement, and the Sea had *nine* islands. But twenty times seemed impossibly large. "Is it the biggest of all the Wilderlands?"

Viola laughed. "No. Well, the Sea is the biggest in size, but in people, the Mountains is the biggest. The capital city, Halois, has over three hundred thousand people. That's where I grew up."

Soon Barclay had dozens of questions for Viola. Which Wilderland was the smallest in size? (The Tundra.) How many Wilderlands had she been to? (Five—the Mountains, the Desert, the Woods, the Jungle, and now the Sea). Which Wilderland was the closest to here? (The Woods, which shocked Barclay, since it had taken them thirteen weeks to travel here).

Barclay pestered Viola with so many questions that he still had her talking by the time they set sail on the *Bewlah*.

Now that the storm had cleared, the Sea looked far less threatening than the night before. Its waters were a sapphire blue instead of inky black, and when Barclay peered over the ship's side, he spotted colorful fish flitting about beneath the surface. The wind blew fiercely, but he didn't mind. It reminded him of running, even though he was standing still.

Mitzi squawked behind him and flew up the mast, where she got into a squabble with Bewlah for the prize of the tip-top perch. Goath, who'd taken a liking to Tadg, slithered after him wherever he walked. Root ran in excited circles around the deck. Then he noticed Motya prowling near the ship's stern, and he padded closer and sniffed the Beast's butt. Motya huffed and scampered away.

"Sorry," Barclay told Yasha, who sat clutching another bucket—and did not look happy about it. "Root is just being friendly."

"Nothing is friendlier than a good butt sniff!" Ulick declared from the helm.

Yasha pet his Beast behind her pointed ears. "Motya is just shy, but most Smynxes are."

"Aren't Smynxes Mythic class Beasts?" Viola asked.

"They are. Motya is very powerful. But she can be a bit self-important."

Motya lifted her chin high, like a queen. Yasha obediently scratched her neck.

Viola frowned, then quicky dug into her satchel and pulled out a notebook. When Barclay opened his mouth to ask if something was bothering her, she cut him off.

"I know you have a lot to learn about the Wilderlands,

Barclay. But *I* have work too. And I can't afford to fall behind." Then she buried her face in her notes.

Barclay was used to Tadg making him feel clueless, but not Viola, too. Maybe he should've brought his own book to study. But so far it hadn't taught him any Lore Keeper basics like this. In the last chapter he'd finished, the author had rambled for thirty pages insisting that the Ickypox Plague hadn't been caused by Ickies at all, but rather by a solar eclipse.

Leaving Viola to her reading, Barclay scooted closer to Yasha, whose skin was now the shade of sea kelp.

"I hate sailing," Yasha mumbled. "Even at home."

"Do people sail there, too?" Barclay didn't mean to badger Yasha with his questions either, but he was too curious to hold his tongue.

"Some do. The Tundra has a few islands, but most people live on the mainland. It's also very cold most of the year. And during the Winter, there's no daylight—it's always dark."

Barclay gaped. "But how do you go out? How do you do anything?"

"We use fire and Lore. But during certain times, there are colorful lights that appear in the sky. They make our Lore stronger. And some Beasts can only be found when the lights are out."

Now that Barclay had reached the Sea, he'd seen far more of the world. But hearing Yasha's and Viola's stories made him feel oddly small. The world was bigger and stranger than he'd ever imagined, and he wanted to see all of it.

An hour later, they sighted the Isle of Glannock—not by the shape of it in the distance but by the dark pillar of smoke that billowed into the sky. As they neared, Barclay expected to spot the skyline of another town. But all he could see was rubble.

Tadg sucked in a breath but said nothing.

Suddenly Barclay had the flash of an unhappy memory—the ruins of Dullshire after Gravaldor had attacked. Barclay had been four years old at the time, and even though he no longer blamed Gravaldor for what happened, he still didn't like to think about it. And for Tadg, that same pain must've felt fresh.

"Looks like the pier was destroyed," Ulick said. "We better take the rowboat out. Barclay, will ya drop the anchor? Just turn the lever there." Ulick pointed at a handle on the *Bewlah*'s port side.

Once the anchor was secure, the five of them returned their Beasts to their Marks and clambered into the rowboat. Goath stretched out over their laps, his many vertebrae digging uncomfortably into Barclay's thighs.

Around them, strange, frothy speckles of white floated on the ocean's surface. Barclay didn't think much of it—not until they rowed toward the beach, where there were so many speckles that the water was more white than blue. It reminded him of pouring two colors of paint into the same cup, the way they swirled together. Goath writhed and squirmed away from it.

"What is this?" Barclay asked, reaching down to dip his fingers in it.

Tadg grabbed Barclay by the wrist and wrenched his hand away. "Don't touch that," he snarled. "It's a weeping tide."

Barclay shivered at the spooky name. "What's that?"

"It's an algae bloom," Ulick explained. "Algae is a type of plant that grows in the water, like seaweed. When there's too much of it, it creates what we call a bloom. This kind here, the white kind, is actually caused by a Trite class Beast. And it's carnivorous. Put your fingers in, and all you'll be pulling out is bones."

Barclay scooted nervously to the center of the boat.

"I thought weeping tides only occur twice a year?" Viola asked.

Of course Viola had heard of the weeping tide. Which meant, once again, Barclay was the odd one out.

Ulick nodded. "Normally they only come on Midsummer and Midwinter. Because that's when Lochmordra rises. He's what causes the blooms."

Viola whipped her notebook back out of her bag and jotted down Ulick's words. Barclay *really* wished he'd brought his books now.

They rowed until they reached the beach; then Ulick carefully climbed onto the sand and dragged the boat—with the four of them still inside—far from the eerie white water. Fish bones were scattered across the shoreline, picked clean of any meat.

Once they'd all safely disembarked, they trekked across the dunes to town. Or, at least, what was left of it. Glannock was snuggled on a field of lush green grass, though the streets were mostly flooded now. Tiny water-bug and minnow Beasts swam in the puddles, and a few buildings still smoldered slightly.

"It looks like there was a tidal wave," said Yasha. He pointed to a trenchlike divot that sliced through part of town, then to another farther down the road. "And those are the spots where Lochmordra struck down the buildings."

Barclay examined the trenches in surprise. They didn't look like the tracks or claw marks of any animal he'd seen before. They were long and snakelike. But Lochmordra couldn't have been a snake, because the trenches didn't connect to one another.

"What does Lochmordra look like?" he asked.

"He's a kraken. A giant squid," Tadg answered darkly, and he didn't bother to jeer at Barclay for not knowing that. Instead, he sped down the road, leaving the others to lag behind him. For a while, Barclay didn't know where Tadg was headed, until Tadg stopped before a particular house. The roof and front had been entirely smashed, and wooden splinters and shattered glass littered the lawn. All that remained was a single wall along the building's back.

Again, Barclay was reminded of his own home, when Gravaldor had destroyed it.

"Tadg," Barclay said softly. "I'm sorry—"

But Tadg wasn't listening. He scrambled through the heap of broken walls and ruined furniture.

"Now wait a moment," Ulick told him. "You could get hurt if ya—"

"Dad kept papers here. Maps, notes. About the Sea, about Lochmordra, about the Isle of Roane . . . They could help us. They should still be here, in his room." Tadg climbed toward the far end of the house, where his father's bedroom must've once been.

"But everything is wet, Tadg," Viola said gently. "The papers were probably destroyed."

"No," he snapped. "No, they'd still be here."

Viola sighed. "Well, then we'll all go on ahead and keep looking for clues."

Yasha and Ulick nodded, but as the three of them set off with Goath, Barclay lingered behind. Tadg was rarely nice to him. But Barclay had never owned anything that belonged to his parents, and he would've liked it if someone had searched *his* broken house and saved something for him.

Barclay knew that Tadg's situation was different. Tadg had far more than a few foggy memories of his father. But the world didn't give out trophies to whoever had the saddest story. And Tadg shouldn't have to sift through his ruined home alone.

Barclay scaled the rubble to where Tadg was yanking up fallen roof tiles and planks of wood. Tadg looked up at him and frowned, as if he didn't know why Barclay was there.

But instead of sneering at him like Tadg normally would, he pointed at a nearby beam. "Help me lift that."

The two grabbed it from either end and hoisted it up. Beneath it was a dirty, damp fabric that might've once been a bed quilt. Then Tadg threw it to the side, revealing a metal lockbox.

"This is it! This is where . . ." Tadg trailed off as he knelt in front of it. The safe's door hung ajar. It was empty. "I don't understand. Why would he have taken the papers out?"

"Would he have kept them somewhere else in the house?"

"No, no. We'll just . . ." Tadg's voice hitched. "We'll keep looking."

"Okay," Barclay agreed.

They searched for twenty minutes, by which time Barclay's fingers had blistered and his muscles ached. The others had certainly reached the other side of town by now. Maybe they'd found something important. He hoped they had, because he and Tadg definitely hadn't.

"I don't get it!" Tadg seethed. "He and I were the only ones who knew the safe's combination. And he kept all his work in his room."

But all that remained of the room was a small stretch of wall and nothing else. They'd cleared away most of the debris except for the heaviest beams, and everything was damp. Puddles pooled in between stones. Dust and dirt smothered every surface.

"It has to be here," Tadg breathed.

"*Croak.*"

"What did you say?" Tadg growled at him.

Barclay held his hands up. "I didn't say anything." But he'd heard the sound too. It reminded him of a stomach rumbling, or maybe a belch.

"We'll keep looking." Tadg bent down to try to pick up a beam that Barclay could already tell was too heavy to lift, but Barclay squatted to help him anyway.

"*Croak.*"

"All right, what is that?" Tadg let go of the beam and whipped around.

Then Barclay spotted it. On a wet stone only a few feet away from them sat a toad. It had bumpy green skin and a large gem at the center of its head.

"Is it a Beast?" Barclay asked. He'd never seen a toad with a stone in it before.

"Not like one I've ever heard of." Tadg bent down to get a closer look, then the toad leapt at him and landed on the back of his hand. Tadg tried to shake it off, but it was as though the creature had suctioned itself to his skin. Then Tadg let out a loud yelp. "*Ow!* It—it bit me or something! Get it off me!"

Indeed, something dark and purple began to seep across Tadg's hand.

"Here—stay still—I can't—" Barclay reached forward to grab the toad, but a moment before he touched it, it disappeared. "Huh? Where did it go?"

Tadg searched the puddle where they stood. "Probably fell."

"I didn't hear a splash."

"Yeah, but . . . No. You have got to be kidding me."

"What is it?" Barclay asked.

Tadg showed him the back of his right hand, and below the purple mark the toad had left behind, Barclay saw another mark, this one metallic and golden. A Beast Mark, in the shape of the toad.

"You *bonded* with it?" Barclay asked. "Why would you do that?"

"I didn't mean to! You think I'd want a weird toad that—"

"Croak!"

At that, the toad appeared on Tadg's shoulder, though Barclay guessed Tadg hadn't meant to summon it. Tadg screamed and fell into the puddle, soaking his clothes.

"What's going on?" a voice asked, and Barclay turned and spotted Viola running down the road, Ulick, Yasha, and Goath charging after her. "We heard shouting! Are you both—"

"Tadg bonded with a toad," Barclay told her. And he couldn't help it—he snickered.

Tadg shot him a furious look. "I did not—"

"A Beast? I want to see!" Viola cooed.

Grumbling under his breath, Tadg stood up, wrung out his dripping sweater, and climbed out to the street. Viola peered at the toad on his shoulder.

"Oh," she said, disappointed. "It's so ugly."

"It was an accident," Tadg muttered. He tried to shake it off his shoulder, but it didn't budge. "I'll make Runa show me how to get rid of it."

"Breaking a Mark takes a Beast of a higher class," Viola told him. She reached into her satchel and pulled out *A Traveler's Log*, then flipped furiously through the pages. "There's no mention of a toad with a stone in its head in the Beast glossary. Or maybe it's a frog?"

Ulick frowned at it. "I've lived here my whole life, and I've never seen a Beast like that before."

"Not that this isn't important," Barclay said impatiently, "but did you all find any clues about the attack?"

"No," Yasha answered bitterly. "There isn't anything *to* find. Everything's ruined! What about the papers you were looking for?"

Tadg gritted his teeth. "They're gone. But I *swear* they were here. Maybe someone took them recently, or—"

"Viola?" came a smug voice behind them, one that definitely belonged to a girl.

They all turned around, to where not one but *three* girls stood at the edge of the street.

The one in the center was the one who'd spoken, and her arms were crossed. She had light brown skin, and one of her pants legs was bunched around the thigh. Below it was a sleek metal contraption that replaced everything from her knee down. A large scorpion Beast with plates like steel stood beside her, its tail as sharp and menacing as her expression.

On her right was a girl with long black hair, brown skin, and a heavy build. A small beelike Beast rested on the point of her nose, but she didn't seem worried about getting stung. She gave them a dimpled smile and even waved, though Barclay had never met her before.

The last girl slouched, as though trying not to be noticed. Her skin was very pale, and her dark brown hair was tied back at the nape of her neck. Perched on her forearm was a black-and-white magpie with big, clever eyes. Both her and her Beast's shadows danced below them, though they were each standing still.

"What are *you* doing here?" the first girl demanded.

When Viola didn't respond—only stared with her mouth hanging open—Barclay whispered, "Who are they, Viola?"

"They're my . . ." Viola shook her head and swallowed. "They're Cyril Harlow's apprentices."

SEVEN

That evening, the seven apprentices returned to the Guild House, waiting for the other Guardians to arrive.

Across the room, Cyril Harlow silently paced by the fireplace.

He looked as Barclay remembered, pale and very slender, with brown hair cut blunt and short and wearing clothes spangled in medals and adornments. His forehead glistened with sweat. If Barclay didn't know better, he'd guess that Cyril might be sick.

"Why would the High Keeper hire both Cyril *and* the Fang of Dusk?" one of the new girls whispered beside him—the friendly one with the dimples. According to Viola, her name was Hasu Mayani, and the girl with the metal prosthetic was Shazi Essam. "Doesn't she know they hate each other?"

"Maybe she didn't care," said the slouchy girl with the

magpie Beast. Viola hadn't known her name. "If Lochmordra is attacking the islands of the Sea, it sounds like she could use all the help she can get."

"Well, whatever it is, I don't want to have to leave," grumbled Shazi, who was busy polishing one of her sabers. Barclay had never met a kid who carried around a sword, but Shazi had *two* of them. "It took us *ages* to travel here."

"Where did you travel—?" Barclay started to ask, but Viola immediately shushed him. Just because the seven of them were sitting at the same table didn't mean they were speaking. In fact, Viola seemed determined not to look at the three girls, not once. For twenty minutes, she'd buried her face in *A Traveler's Log*, but Barclay had yet to see her turn a page.

It must've been hard for Viola to see Cyril again. Barclay still never understood why Cyril would've fired Viola as a student. She was the hardest-working and smartest person he knew.

But what he was *really* nervous about was what would happen when Runa returned. The last time Runa and Cyril had seen each other, Cyril had testified against Runa for a crime she hadn't committed. And even before that, it was no secret that the Fang of Dusk and the Horn of Dawn loathed each other.

Mitzi, however, was delighted to be reunited with old friends. She flew around the spiral staircase with the bee-like Beast.

Beneath their table, Root also ignored Viola's no-speaking

rule and curiously padded over to the scorpion Beast, who was almost as large as he was. But when he bent down for a butt sniff, the scorpion jerked its pointy tail. Root growled at it, then scampered back to Barclay's side.

"You're all right, boy," Barclay told him, scratching Root behind the ear.

Once Root had settled down, Barclay pulled the bottle cap Runa had given him out of his pocket. Tadg and Viola had already mastered their assignments, and Barclay didn't want to fall any further behind. But each time he tried to make the cap hover, it sputtered off in a different direction, sending him reaching across the tabletop and floor.

On the fifth attempt, it landed in one of the girl's laps— the slouchy girl with the magpie Beast. The bird reached down to peck it, but the girl snatched it up.

"Practicing some kind of trick?" she asked Barclay.

"Not exactly," he muttered, reddening. Beside him, Viola jabbed him with her elbow.

"What's your name?" the girl asked. "I know those two. That's Conley Murdock's son, and she's, well . . ." She leaned in and lowered her voice to a whisper. "I think I'm her replacement."

At this, Viola elbowed Barclay again, harder. He winced. Just because Runa and Cyril hated each other didn't mean their apprentices had to as well. And Viola hadn't exactly been nice to him today.

"I'm Barclay Thorne," he told the girl. "What about you?"

"I'm Cecily Lloris. This is Oudie. He's a Tenepie." She pet her Beast's shiny feathers, and Oudie's shadow along her lap puckered up in pleasure.

The Guild House door opened, and several Guardian Keepers entered, including Orla, Runa, and Edwyn. At first they didn't notice the newcomers, as they were deep in conversation.

"—a waste," Orla said bitterly. "If Lochmordra rises at a different place each time, then—"

"But surely you must have some idea where Lochmordra *lives*?" Edwyn asked.

One of the others snorted. "Not from the Sea, are you, Lusk?" This made Edwyn's charming smile go crooked.

"Conley . . ." Runa's voice hitched, and she cleared her throat. "Conley claimed he had an idea where Lochmordra lived, but I don't think he—"

Her voice died abruptly when she sighted Cyril by the fire. He'd stopped his pacing to face her with a lethal glare.

"What in the six lands are *you* doing here?" Runa hissed.

"Orla asked me here," he answered tightly. "I wasn't told you'd be here too."

For several moments, the only sounds in the Guild House were the squawks of Mitzi playing with the bumblebee Beast, the clicks of Goath slithering back toward Runa, and the taps of Oudie pecking at the stale bread crumbs on the table. Barclay held his breath, bracing himself for an explosive argument, maybe even a battle—he'd heard rumors

Runa and Cyril had once fought each other in an unfinished duel to the death. Around them, the other Guardians retreated awkwardly into the room's corners. Edwyn's face had gone weeping-tide white.

Orla, meanwhile, cleared her throat. "At my age, we know what a treat it is to see old friends—"

"Leave," Runa snapped at Cyril, ignoring the High Keeper. "I don't want to look at you."

"My apprentices and I traveled all the way here from Halois," Cyril told her dryly. "I have no intention of making them repeat the same—"

"Then you should've arrived before I did." Runa stormed toward him and jabbed her finger into his chest. Barclay shuddered. In a choice between facing another Silberwal or Runa Rasgar, he'd take the Silberwal. But Cyril didn't even flinch.

"Really, Runa," Orla said with a tsk. "I don't think—"

"I might've arrived first," Cyril growled at Runa, "had I not been forced to travel to the Woods last Winter because you'd gotten yourself into trouble."

Runa barked out a laugh. "Oh please. You couldn't *wait* to tell Erhart whatever lies you—"

"Lies? I'm the only one who knows what you've done—me and Leopold. You might've squandered the past eight years playing your Dooling games and doing who knows what else, but I have worked directly with Leopold—"

"Yes, I see you and our old teacher are on a first name

basis now," Runa said coldly. "That must've been the most exciting day of your life, when he finally learned your name."

Cyril's ears burned crimson. "I—I—" he blustered. "At least he has one student to be proud of. You know what he says when *your* name comes up? You know what he told me when he learned that *you* are his daughter's new mentor? He said that you—"

Orla grew increasingly flustered. "Cyril—Runa—"

"—were a lost cause from the moment he started teaching the three of us," Cyril continued, seething. "And that if any of us were going to be the one to betray him, he would've guessed it was *you*."

Runa and Cyril had clearly forgotten anyone else was in the room. Barclay felt bad for eavesdropping on a private conversation, but he couldn't help being curious. Viola had told him that Runa and Cyril had once been the Grand Keeper's apprentices, but Cyril had said "the three of us." Who had been the third?

An icy mist shimmered around Runa's fingertips. "Then go back to doing all *Leopold's* paperwork and errands for him, since that's what obviously makes the both of you so happy."

Beside Cyril, the closest rocking chair began to warp. The wood bent into sharper, thornier shapes, making the chair wobble and crash to the floor.

"Really?" Orla placed her hands on her hips. "My furniture? That is an *antique*."

But the two of them didn't listen. Goath had slithered up Runa's shoulder and down her arm, as though a skeletal armor, ready for battle. And the floorboards beneath Cyril's feet peeled back and curled like fingernails.

"Come on," Edwyn told the apprentices, his voice shaking slightly. "I'm sure we all have somewhere else we could be. I, for one, spotted a pub this morning with plumberry mead that—"

"Why should *I* leave?" Cyril shouted. At that, one of the boards sprang out from the floor and launched across the room. Then a second. Then a third—that one came close to whacking Tadg in the head. "You act as though I came here to make you angry! I came here for an assignment—"

The apprentices and their Beasts scrambled out the door, which Edwyn slammed behind them. Barclay was stunned into silence. He'd known that Runa and Cyril hated each other, but he hadn't realized that they *really* hated each other. He half expected one of them to murder the other before sunset.

The others must've felt the same way, because none of them spoke.

It was Edwyn who broke the silence with an eerie laugh. "Funny, the way that fate brings people together." Then, without bothering to tell any of the apprentices where they should go, he stalked off. Probably to that pub.

"Who was that guy?" Cecily asked.

"That's my—" Yasha started.

"Never mind him, did you *see* the scar on Runa's face? And her Haddisss?" Hasu shuddered. "She's way scarier in person than I thought she'd be!"

"Runa isn't scary. And she's a very good teacher," Viola shot back. She might've sounded more persuasive if Mitzi wasn't latched onto her arm poking at the pins on her coat.

"Oh, is that why you decided to be *her* student?" Shazi demanded. She was still clutching her sabers. "Is that why you left me and Hasu behind?"

Hasu shushed her. "You don't have to—"

"If anyone was left behind it was me," Viola hissed. "And Runa is just as respected as Cyril—"

Shazi snorted. "Is that what your father said when you told him?"

Viola flinched. "I . . . I . . . Mitzi, stop!" She pried the baby dragon from her forearm, then she glared back at Shazi. "Yes. That's exactly what he said."

"Ha! I knew it! You haven't told him."

At this, Viola gave a loud *hmph*, seized Barclay and Tadg by their wrists, and dragged them with her down the street. Yasha, looking torn, set off on his own into town.

"Your friends seem great," Tadg said flatly.

Viola's nostrils flared. "They're *not* my friends. Well, not anymore, at least. And I don't even know Cecily. When did Cyril have time to find a new apprentice since we spoke in the Woods? There hasn't been another Exhibition—"

"Just stop, okay?" Tadg wrenched his arm out of Viola's grip. "So Cyril thought you were a useless apprentice. Get over it!"

With that, he stormed away—in the direction of Ansley MacGannon's shop.

By the time Barclay swiveled around to assure Viola that Tadg didn't really mean it, Viola had huffed and stomped away too.

Barclay looked down at Root. He had an unpleasant flash of the three of them eight years in the future, except instead of Runa and Cyril dueling one another, it was Viola and Tadg.

"They'll come around, right, buddy?" Barclay asked.

Root only hung his head.

But if grown-up Viola and Tadg famously hated each other, where would that leave Barclay? An anxious voice warned him that he wouldn't be a Lore Keeper at all. He'd live in a grimy cave in a place not on any maps. Never able to control his Lore. Belonging nowhere.

"Do you want to go for a run?" Barclay asked Root, eager for a chance to clear his head.

Root wagged his tail. He never said no to a run.

"Then let's go."

They started off walking. Then, before they even reached the edge of town, they began to jog. As soon as the cobblestones faded into dirt roads, they broke out in a sprint. Faster and faster, until Munsey lay far behind them, and there was nothing but sheep and cattle and grass stretching on and on.

Even before Barclay had bonded with Root, he'd been a fast runner. But now that he was a Lore Keeper, he was capable of so much more.

Soon the breeze rushing past went soft and still as a whisper. Beside Barclay, Root's black fur wisped around him in smoky coils. Like if you reached out to touch him, you'd be grasping at air.

Barclay was no different. His sweater blurred. His body felt lighter, as though his boots barely grazed the ground. And his hands had gone slightly see-through.

Barclay hollered, and Root howled next to him.

They were running so fast, they had become the wind.

In minutes they reached the Isle of Munsey's beaches, and they raced along the edge of the water, where the sand was firm. They passed dunes and fences, buoys and fishing boats. Sleábeaks nested in the grass, far calmer than the ones that had attacked Knunx. The waves rippled with every color to match the sunset—red and blue and orange, as though the Sea was aglow; then gradually everything darkened into the black of night.

Only then did the two of them slow. They were both tired. And they'd spotted a figure in the distance, surrounded by flashes of bright light.

"What is that?" Barclay asked.

Root strode ahead, and Barclay followed, panting to

catch his breath. They climbed to the peak of a hill and watched the figure below. It took Barclay a few moments to recognize the blond hair as Yasha's, and the flashes of light as fire dancing around his chest and fingertips. Beside Yasha, Motya watched, her tail entirely transformed into flames.

Barclay did not mean to spy, but Yasha's Lore was mesmerizing. It was as though the fire behaved entirely how it wished, and all Yasha did was guide it through the air. Occasionally it changed into new shapes, like a rope or an arrow. Sometimes Yasha sent the embers skyward, where they fizzled out dozens of feet above.

"I'm never going to be able to use my Lore like that," Barclay said miserably. Yasha had been an apprentice longer than Barclay, but only a year longer. Maybe because Yasha had grown up around Lore, he was already more advanced than Barclay would ever be.

Root placed his paw on Barclay's leg and pushed, making Barclay stumble back.

"Hey! I mean it. The only reason I placed top in my Exhibition was luck. If fewer people had cheated on the first exam, if Tadg hadn't given me the item I was missing in the scavenger hunt, then—"

Root barked at him, cutting him off. Then, apparently fed up with Barclay's bout of self-pity, Root strutted back toward town.

Barclay sighed and trailed after him. He'd better spend

the rest of his night studying *The Nine Most Crucial Events of Lore Keeper History*.

Twenty minutes later, they retraced their steps to Ansley's shop. Barclay had been so tired last night and in such a rush this morning that he hadn't noticed the building was an Apothecary store—the Planty Shanty, according to the sign. The bells above the door chimed as they entered. The place was a mess. Clay pots were scattered across the tables and shelves, none of them labeled. Tinctures bubbled in glass beakers, and plants grew wild from their pots. Even the sales desk wasn't clear. It was piled high with craft supplies: balls of yarn, squid ink glitter pens, an embroidery hoop, and dozens of cutouts of the crosswords from the *Keeper's Khronicle*.

Despite the chaos, Barclay instantly liked the shop. It smelled good in here, like earth.

By the windowsill, Ansley hunched over a large tank filled with green seaweed, all thin and tangled like a hair ball. She sprinkled some dust overtop it. The algae wiggled.

Ansley caught Barclay watching her. She was wearing an even fluffier cardigan than the night before, which Barclay guessed she'd knitted herself. "It's called Siggykelp, very common—and useful for tonics that heal Gruignad rash. That's the Gruignad, right over there. Helps cure Siggykelp blisters."

She nodded down the table, where a spiderwebby black seaweed drifted on the water's surface.

Curious, Root stood up on his hind legs to sniff one of the other tanks, this one filled with a curly yellow algae.

"Your Lufthund has good taste," Ansley said. "Ripple-weed is considered a delicacy here. Some people eat it as a snack. I personally like to dry it and use the flavored salt that it leaves behind."

Barclay scanned the collection. Some of the algae resembled seaweed, but others looked like little more than speckles of color in the water, all clumped together. Her trove struck him as pleasantly familiar. Then he realized it reminded him of Master Pilzmann's mushroom caves in Dullshire. He scolded himself. That was in the past now.

"Do all these plants have special uses?" he asked.

"Most do. I'm sure you recognize all the jars of Gunkwort that we use for healing. But some other specimens I keep for study. Like the Fire Coral. That one's dead rare. Took me almost a year to find it." She pointed to a tank at the very end. The dull gray coral inside didn't seem to deserve such an interesting name. "And of course, you might also recognize this one next to it."

She nodded at the tank filled with white, foamy seaweed, which rose up and down as though breathing.

Root whimpered and backed away, and Barclay shivered. "That's the weeping tide."

"Yes. I keep it in the shop, but it's not like the rest of my collection. For one, it's a Trite class Beast—it has Lore to it, but not enough for anyone to bond with it. Not that you'd want to!" She chuckled, and Barclay tried not to look disturbed. "It also doesn't seem to consume sunlight like other algae. As far as I can tell, it only eats meat."

Ansley pulled out a dried sardine from her apron pocket and waved it at Barclay. "Would you like to feed it?"

Barclay hesitated. "I don't know if . . ."

"Oh, it's all right. I know not everyone finds my work interesting." With slumped shoulders, she tossed the sardine into the tank. The weeping tide foamed and gurgled. A moment later, the bones of the sardine drifted to the water's surface.

The front door burst open, and Barclay slammed into the weeping tide's tank. He watched in horror as it wobbled and knocked into the one beside it. One at a time, the tanks teetered and crashed to the floor. Glass shattered everywhere, and water and algae swept across their feet.

Most shockingly, the Fire Coral—no longer submerged—burst into flames.

Barclay yelped and lunged out of the way of the weeping tide, not wanting to lose his toes. "I'm sorry! I didn't— I just—"

"I'll get my oven mitts!" Ansley shouted, rushing to her desk.

Root barked at the weeping tide seeping across the floorboards. For a plant, it moved *fast*. The white froth on its top swelled, like a rabid animal.

"What was that?" Tadg called from upstairs.

"Nothing, dear!" Ansley yelled, brandishing a pair of pink oven mitts.

From the front door, Runa dashed over and yanked Barclay out of Ansley's way. However, Ansley was still blocked by Root, who raced around the edge of the weeping tide, barking louder and louder. He had a strange, panicked gleam in his eyes.

"Root!" Barclay said. "Calm down. You need to—"

"Call him back to his Mark," Runa said. "He's had a fright."

Obediently, Barclay returned Root to his Mark, and he felt his skin prickle as Root continued to thrash around on his shoulder.

But Ansley still didn't move.

"What are you waiting for?" Runa asked her, coughing from the smoke. "If you don't hurry, the fire will—"

"Look at this," Ansley said breathlessly. She crouched down, so close to the weeping tide that Barclay squeezed one eye shut, certain she was about to lose a foot. The white algae had crowded around the Fire Coral, growing taller and taller into a writhing, foamy hedge. "It likes the fire."

"Is something burning?" Tadg shouted.

At that, Ansley finally picked up the flaming Fire Coral and thrust it into the Siggykelp's tank, one of the few Barclay hadn't managed to destroy. The mound of the weeping tide sagged back down into a sudsy puddle.

Barclay looked at all the mess and moaned, "I'm sorry. I'm so sorry."

"Don't be!" Ansley told him giddily. "That was the most excitement I've had in a long time! And we might've made a very interesting discovery just now. You'd make a great Apothecary, Barclay."

Despite her compliment, Barclay had never felt a worse excuse for a Lore Keeper than he did in that moment.

While Ansley slipped into the closet to fetch a broom, Barclay turned to Runa. Judging from her tangled braid and angry scowl, he didn't have to ask to know that her argument with Cyril had gone nowhere good.

"Are we leaving?" Barclay asked nervously.

"No one is leaving," Runa said. "Orla is right—the Sea needs all the help it can get. Even if it's from that pompous fool."

Runa stormed back to the door.

"You're heading out already?" Ansley asked, returning with a broom, a mop, and a whole tin of sardines in her hands. "I rarely get visitors who aren't customers. I could brew some tea!" Her eyes, already magnified by her glasses, went wide with excitement. Behind her, one of the beakers burped out a puff of smoke. It smelled like cheese.

Runa hesitated awkwardly. "That's generous, but no thank you, Ms. MacGannon. I'm in a hurry, and I only came to make sure the boys don't spend their night packing. But I'll gladly pay to replace the tanks—"

Ansley tsked. "It's no trouble. Really!"

"I insist," Runa said, making Barclay's ears redden.

Being an orphan, money had always been hard for Barclay to come by. Even if that wasn't true for Runa, he hated to make Runa pay for his clumsiness. "Besides, I already have a running tab. Orla is making Cyril and me pay her for a few . . . repairs."

Barclay frowned, wondering exactly what state the Guild House was in now.

"You don't have to . . ." Barclay swallowed. He didn't have many kritters to his name. "I mean, I could try to—"

"Don't fuss over it," Runa told him. "You and Tadg should rest tonight. We have another day of work tomorrow. All of us! For who knows how long!" And with that, she threw up her hands and left, while the white of the weeping tide continued to seep across the floor.

EIGHT

UNDER TEMPORARY RECONSTRUCTION

Reconstruction'?" Yasha read. The next morning, the seven apprentices gathered outside the Guild House, where a wooden sign hung on the door. The writing on it was etched in scratchy Lore script. "What are they building?"

"They're not building," Tadg told him, "they're fixing. Runa and Cyril probably tore the place to shreds."

Shazi crossed her arms. "That isn't a surprise, given the rumors about Runa's temper."

"Oh, just admit it!" Viola snapped. "You're jealous of Runa because *you've* always wanted to be a Dooling champion."

"And you're jealous because *you* know that Cyril is a better teacher."

While the two of them bickered, Hasu yawned and cast

the others a weary look. "They've been at this all night. Cecily and I barely got any sleep!" Even her Beast was exhausted. The bumblebee slumbered on the tip of Hasu's nose.

"You're all staying together?" Barclay asked.

"Yeah. One of the inns gave Cyril a special room because he's the assistant to the Grand Keeper. But the three of us and Viola are stuck at Lifen's guest cottage."

"I like it there," Cecily said cheerily.

"It smells like manure."

"That's why I like it!"

Barclay almost felt bad for Viola being crammed up with her ex-friends. But after Tadg had made fun of him all night for nearly destroying the Planty Shanty, Barclay felt worse for himself.

The door to the Guild House swung open, whacking Viola in the back. She whipped around, but her grimace dropped when she saw Runa standing at the threshold. Runa had borrowed Ansley's apron, which looked almost as ridiculous on her as an apron on a Styerwurm.

Runa frowned deeply. "As Cyril and I are busy, you all have the day off to do whatever you like."

"Nice apron," Tadg joked. "I like the polka dots."

Runa moved to slam the door, but before she could, Tadg wedged his elbow in front of it.

"Wait—wait! I need to show you something. It's important."

A crash thundered from within the Guild House, followed by shouts and muffled grunts. "Klava! My shoes are not food! Give them—*uff*— Those are genuine leather—*Runa!*"

Runa smiled at Tadg. "On second thought, why rush things? What is this important thing you need to show me?"

"Croak!"

As if on cue, the toad Beast appeared atop Tadg's head, nestled in his hair. It slapped its sticky fingers on Tadg's ears.

"You bonded with another Beast?" Runa asked. "You should've told me before—"

"It was an accident," Tadg fumed. "I want to get rid of it."

Curiously, Runa poked the stone at the center of the toad's forehead. The toad gave a loud, defiant croak.

"Hm, I have no idea what sort of Beast it is," Runa murmured. "It must be powerful if it forged the bond with you itself."

"Powerful?" Tadg echoed. "Does it *look* powerful to you?"

"You shouldn't judge a Beast by its appearance. Take Goath, for instance. He's unnerving to look at, but he's one of the sweetest, most charming Beasts I've ever met."

Goath, who slithered around Runa's boots, was staring at the toad Beast like he was contemplating eating it.

"Well, I don't care how powerful it is," Tadg said. "I want you to remove the Mark."

Runa shrugged and gave Barclay a sly smile. It wasn't

that long ago that Barclay had asked her to get rid of *his* Mark.

Inside the Guild House, Cyril's shouts grew louder and more frantic. "Klava! No—I command you to— That was personally given to me by High Keeper Mayani!"

"As you can see," Runa told Tadg, "I'm afraid I'm very busy today saving the esteemed Horn of Dawn from becoming Klava's chew toy. I can't possibly—"

"Wait! No! Don't—"

Runa slammed the door shut, leaving the seven apprentices on the street.

"I thought she'd throw you from the lighthouse tower when you joked about her apron!" Hasu told Tadg, sounding impressed.

"That would've been neat," Cecily agreed.

"Well, if we have the day to ourselves," Viola said, "then I want to run errands. It's been *ages* since I've been to a proper Lore city." She pulled a bulging leather pouch from her pocket, and it jangled when she shook it.

Hasu brightened and clapped her hands. "Yes! Let's all go shopping!"

Shazi scoffed. "We're not going shopping with *them*! We're going separately." She hooked her arms around Hasu and Cecily on either side and, ignoring their protests, hauled them off down the street.

"I don't think I meant to choose sides," Yasha said. "But I guess I'm on yours."

"Don't you think all the fighting is getting out of hand?" Barclay asked Viola.

"Do *you* think Runa deserves being called a sneak?" Violet demanded. "Or a liar? Or some kind of . . . of . . . *scoundrel*?"

Tadg snickered. "I actually think she'd like that last one."

Viola groaned. Since Barclay knew the past day had been hard for her, he didn't say anything. Not when she ushered them into a clothing store to buy waterproof socks made of Jabershark hide. Or the Maritime Merchants of Munsey, who sold everything from astrolabes to wooden chests filled with fool's gold. Or even the Draconis Emporium, to buy a dragon-grade nail clipper for Mitzi's claws.

The whole morning, they avoided Cyril's apprentices. Barclay caught a glimpse of them in a store selling Beast toys. (SCRATCHPROOF! FIREPROOF! WATERPROOF! TOXIC SLUDGE–PROOF! claimed the sign.) Then he saw them coming out of a bakery, carrying humongous golden pastries that made his mouth water. Once, they passed the other group on the street. Everyone averted their eyes.

"Ooh," Viola cooed, just as it was nearing lunchtime. "They have a Fillitot's! We have to—"

"How can you have any kritters left?" Barclay asked, exasperated.

Viola paused. "Hm, I suppose we could stop by the Argentisaurus Bank before . . ."

And that was how Barclay was dragged to the Lore

Keeper bank, where Viola convinced him to open a meager savings account of four kritters.

"That was nearly all the kritters I have," Barclay complained. He glanced at Tadg, who was usually the one in the foul mood. "Aren't you tired of this?"

In response, Tadg held up the assortment of purchases *he'd* made, including three new cable-knit sweaters and a pack of hexagonal champion cards. Each one depicted a famous Dooling player or their Beast, and they were popular collector's items among young Lore Keepers.

"In case you forgot, all my stuff was destroyed," Tadg said, which shut Barclay up.

"Why is that one shiny?" Yasha said, studying Tadg's champion card of Sanjit Varma. The only thing Yasha had bought was a weird, frosty silver stone he called Starglass. He claimed it had some kind of light Lore properties and that it was very rare. Barclay just thought it looked like junk.

"Because it's a special edition. I haggled with the shopkeeper for it," Tadg said proudly, though Barclay would've described it as bullying, as the shopkeeper had been reduced to tears. "Don't you collect champion cards?"

"I don't play games," Yasha answered flatly.

"Champion cards are not just a *game*—"

"How about we go into Fillitot's?" Barclay suggested, pointing at the gaudy red-and-yellow-striped store that he'd spotted yesterday. Beast treats seemed to be something they could all agree on. Inside was every type of delicacy, from

Gluppyfish liver snacks to rare-cooked Watermoose steaks and jelly taffy flavored like apple, hazelnut, or squid.

While Viola wandered to the displays of sugared fruits for Mitzi, the three boys made for the section labeled CARNIVORE. The treats came in all sorts of designs, including bones and fish. There were even ones shaped like brains.

"No, those *are* brains," Tadg said after Barclay pointed them out. He scooped several sopping ones into a bag. "Mar-Mar loves them."

Barclay was dismayed to find that the treats were expensive, but he felt Root deserved something special after being cooped up in his Mark while they traveled. So, on Yasha's recommendation, Barclay paid three kritters for a small pouch of Bristlebuck knuckles.

"They're Motya's favorites," Yasha said. "And Motya has a very refined palette."

Unfortunately, that was not the last of their errands. But, Viola assured them, this next stop really was the "last place" she had to visit.

They entered a small building wedged between a fishmonger and a magical-wig boutique. The walls behind the counter were covered in wooden cubbies, and within each one, a Beast rested. Some were the pelican Beasts Barclay had seen delivering parcels. The others were dragons. They might've been small, but they didn't look much like Mitzi. These were adults, judging by the wrinkles around their snouts and graying feathers. They wore tiny, brown uniforms with red neckerchiefs.

"What is this place?" Barclay asked.

"It's a post office," answered Tadg. "Didn't you visit the one in Sycomore?"

Then Barclay noticed the birds and dragons along the far wall being prepped for departure, with leather backpacks tucked behind their wings. A miniature runway stretched out the window.

"The Fwishts deliver goods around the nine Isles," Yasha explained to Barclay. "The dragons specialize in long distance delivery. They can zap all across the world."

No sooner did he finish speaking than one postal dragon took off down the runway. It flapped its wings once, twice, and then—*boom!* It launched outside and into the sky, leaving behind a wispy ring of smoke.

Viola approached the woman at the counter, who wore aviator goggles ringed with soot. She asked Viola for her name.

"Hm . . . Dumont . . . Yes, I think we received some parcels for you." The woman's goggly eyes fell on Tadg. "Ah! Murdock boy!" she screeched. "At last!"

Startled, Tadg collided with a display of phoenix feather quills labeled FOR SECRET MESSAGES. JUST ADD HEAT! "What? Me?"

"I have *three seasons worth* of letters for you. Yes, yes, our whole supply closet is full of them!" She cackled, then scurried into the back room.

"Why would you have that many letters?" Barclay asked him.

"I have no idea," Tadg answered.

The woman returned with a small package and letter in her arms . . . and a sack the size of a baby Slanntramór hauled over her shoulder. Groaning, she thrust the package and letter into Viola's hands; then she hoisted the sack onto the counter. Dozens of letters spilled out onto the floor.

All of them were addressed to Conley Murdock.

"What are all these?" asked Barclay. He'd never seen so much mail for one person.

"Dad's fan mail. And I don't want them!" Tadg barked, but the mailwoman wouldn't take no for an answer. Even when he tried to shove the sack back over the counter, she began pelting him with letters, forcing him to duck for cover behind the quill stand.

Meanwhile, Viola grimaced over her delivery.

"What is it?" Barclay asked.

"Oh." She threw on a smile. "Mom sent me a birthday present! She couldn't reach me while I was in the Elsewheres, obviously, but look!" Viola showed him a collection of dazzling, gold pins—twelve for her twelfth birthday. Her coat was already so covered that Barclay had no idea where she would put new ones, but she seemed pleased.

"What about the letter?" The back of the envelope gleamed with a wax seal of a three-headed dragon. It looked very official.

Viola quickly tucked it behind her back. "It's nothing."

"That's the Grand Keeper's seal, isn't it?" Yasha asked. "What did your dad write?"

"Probably the same thing he's been writing ever since he heard rumors I was in the Woods. That he's disappointed that I left Cyril—as if it's *my* fault. That he's worried about me. That I shouldn't trust Runa."

At that, she tore the letter into strips.

"*Hmph*. At least Mom remembered my birthday!"

As they left the shop, the four of them awkwardly helped lug Tadg's fifty-pound sack of fan mail back to the Planty Shanty.

Tadg groaned louder with every few steps. "I say we just dump it out at sea."

"That's polluting," Barclay told him. Polluting was highly illegal in Dullshire.

"And it's a shame!" Viola said. "These are letters for your *dad*. Don't you want to read them?"

"What for? It's not like these people even knew him. All they say are—*oof!*"

The four of them, too focused on carrying the sack to pay attention to where they were stepping, knocked into someone. Barclay and Viola both tumbled to the ground, the sack toppling onto their laps.

"There you all are," Shazi said impatiently. "We've been looking everywhere for you. We've come up with an idea."

"For the record," Hasu said, twiddling her fingers, "this was Shazi's idea."

"I helped!" Cecily added cheerfully.

"What kind of idea?" Tadg asked.

"If we want to know whether Runa or Cyril is a better teacher, then the answer is obvious." Shazi licked her lips. "A competition."

"Competition?" Viola repeated, shoving her side of the heavy sack onto Barclay.

Barclay groaned and squirmed out from beneath it. "That doesn't sound like a good—"

"I think it's a great idea," Viola cut in.

"So do I," Tadg said hotly, which stunned Barclay. Not just because Tadg was willing to break the rules, but because both of them were *happy* to. No, Runa hadn't *forbidden* them from wandering out of town . . . but Barclay still knew she wouldn't approve of this. "What sort of competition?"

"You'll see," Cecily said, an unnerving glint in her dark eyes. "Come on."

"But what are we supposed to do with all the letters?" asked Barclay.

"Here." Cecily snapped her fingers. All at once, the sack vanished, replaced by a tiny black orb. It floated up into Cecily's outstretched hand, and she caught it and stowed it in her pocket.

Everyone gaped. Even Yasha looked impressed. "How did you do that?" he asked.

"Shadow Lore," she answered. "Now let's go."

They followed Cecily down the streets of Munsey. Cecily was especially sneaky, darting from wall to wall, careful not to be seen—even though no one was bothering to pay attention to seven kids strolling around in broad daylight. She led them to the stony beach below the lighthouse.

"According to this map," Cecily declared, wielding *A Traveler's Log*, "there are underwater rivers that—"

"Is that my book?" Viola asked, frowning.

"Sure is," Cecily chirped. "I stole it. Now, as you can see on the map—"

"You *stole* it?" Viola repeated angrily.

"You can have it back when we're done. Now look at this map. As you can see, the nine islands of the Sea form an archipelago. And there's an underwater river right here that goes straight to—"

"How can a river be underwater?" asked Yasha.

"The river water is heavier than the ocean water because it's full of sand and sediment. So it sinks and forms currents. And there's a *ton* of these rivers in the Sea."

Cecily showed them the map, which, like all maps of the Wilderlands, was only partially finished. Veinlike squiggles snaked across the ocean and looped around islands. Cecily pointed to one in particular that flowed from Munsey to the reef at the archipelago's center.

"We propose a race," Shazi declared. "The river is mostly straight the whole way to the reef. The first group to make it to the reef is the—"

"But how will we breathe underwater?" Viola asked.

Cecily rubbed her hands together. "I have everything we need."

Then Cecily reached into her pocket and pulled out a handful of those black marble-like spheres. She threw them on the ground. *Splat! Splat! Splat!* Each one burst like eggs cracking open, revealing squishy, phlegmy blobs. They looked like jellyfish without the tentacles.

"These are Polypops," Cecily told them. "Or at least, these are the shed skins of Polypops. I heard the Guardian Keepers mention them this morning, so I stole them from that Apothecary shop you're sleeping in."

"You stole them, too?" Barclay said, aghast.

"Oh, the store had plenty. If you wear these like a mask, you can breathe! *And* we won't have any problem seeing. Underwater is full of Firenekkies, the Trite Beasts that light all the streetlamps."

Hasu hugged her arms to herself. "I don't know. They look gross."

"They do," Shazi agreed. "*I* suggested we just Dool."

Viola rolled her eyes. "Of course you did."

"The race is supposed to make us work as teams," Cecily pointed out.

"So?" Shazi said. "It could be three on three."

"Good, because I want no part of this," Yasha muttered.

"But I haven't even gotten to the best part!" Cecily said brightly. "Here. Come look."

She scampered to the rockiest part of the beach and climbed over the boulders that stretched across the water. *"Look!"*

The others scaled the rocks and stared. Cecily's "best

part" was six very strange-looking Beasts floating in the shallows. They were long and flat, with faces that looked like they'd been smooshed beneath the heel of a boot. They drifted aimlessly on the ocean's surface, and even though they were clearly fish, Barclay was not positive they could actually swim.

"What are they?" Barclay asked.

"They're Sunboards, a Trite class Beast," Tadg explained. "You might be wondering how something so *big* could be Trite class, but trust me—it is physically impossible to bond with them. They're so bony that not even Hooksharks will eat them, though I've heard of Muirmarús playing with them for sport."

"That's so mean!" Hasu said. "I like them. They're cute and pink."

"How did you find them?" asked Viola.

"Lifen—the woman we're staying with—has a Beastiary," Cecily said. "So I took them."

Barclay's jaw dropped. "You can't just go around stealing everything!"

Cecily paid him no mind. "Sunboards are perfect for riding—they'll float on the rivers. So it's decided. We'll spread out over the underwater river between here and the reef, and we'll each get a Sunboard to ride. To make it fair, no other Beasts allowed—"

"But that's—" Tadg started.

"But then I can't—" Hasu cut in.

"It's *fair*," Cecily said firmly. "Hasu and Viola can start. Then Barclay and I can wait for them a third of the way down the river, and Tadg and Shazi can wait on the last third."

"And I'll go train," Yasha said, but before he could leave, Shazi grabbed him by his collar.

"No you don't," she told him. "You're the judge. Oh, don't look so grumpy. It's easy. Just wait by the reef, and the first team there wins the relay race."

Viola nodded vigorously. After three months of her playing teacher's pet to Runa, Barclay couldn't believe she'd be willing to break so many rules. Even for Runa's sake.

"Let's do this," Viola breathed. "We'll *prove* that Runa is the better teacher."

But Barclay wasn't convinced. Maybe it was from living in Dullshire, but he didn't like breaking rules. Runa already felt that Barclay lagged behind Tadg and Viola, which meant if all three of them were punished, he'd probably be punished the worst. If Barclay was banished from Munsey, he had nowhere else to go.

But he didn't want to voice *that* to the others. Instead, he said, "But what if we encounter dangerous Beasts?"

"You want to be a Guardian, don't you?" Tadg taunted. "You should be able to handle it."

He *should* be. But Barclay couldn't control his Lore like the rest of them.

The others didn't give Barclay a chance to change their minds. Within five minutes, they had each kicked off their boots. Cecily used her shadow Lore to swallow up the Sun-boards and stow the black marbles in her pocket. Shazi removed her prosthetic. And Viola untied her hair from her buns and braided it into two pigtails.

Cecily slapped one of the stolen Polypops in Barclay's hand. He grimaced. It was cold and slimy. And it was even grosser when he looped it around his ears like the others. He felt like he was breathing through a booger.

Each of the apprentices trekked into the ocean. It was frigid, and it would certainly be colder the deeper they dove.

This was going to be miserable.

Once the water reached their waists, Tadg summoned Mar-Mar, the terrifying Nathermara that he'd inherited from his father. Mar-Mar looked like a lamprey, and his fleshy gray body was lit from within by lightninglike sparks that sizzled through his veins. He was also massive, over a hundred feet long. And when he lifted his head out of the water, baring a hideous circular mouth of teeth, Barclay cowered, expecting to be eaten.

Instead, Mar-Mar just shrieked. Hasu and Viola both covered their ears, but Tadg, face-to-face with the Beast, rolled his eyes as though bored. "Yes, I know you're happy to be home. We need a ride."

"That's a *happy* noise?" Hasu asked. "He sounds like he wants to kill us!"

"Oh, he does. But I keep reminding him that killing people is rude."

"Maybe he gets his rudeness from you," Viola muttered.

Ignoring her, Tadg hoisted himself onto Mar-Mar's back. "Well, come on," he told everyone.

After such a description, Barclay hardly wanted to pet Mar-Mar, let alone ride him. But the others all did as Tadg instructed, so he had no choice. Barclay clutched the Beast's side, wishing Mar-Mar had fins or scales he could grab onto. Knowing his luck, he'd be thrown off Mar-Mar's back and lost out at Sea.

"This better not make me sick," Yasha grumbled.

Then, before Barclay could even muster up his nerve, Mar-Mar dove.

The water was *freezing*. And unlike what Cecily had promised, it was dark. So dark that Barclay couldn't see, and the deeper they descended into the blackness, the more panic clawed up Barclay's throat. He squeezed his eyes shut and pressed his forehead against Mar-Mar's slippery back, and he didn't dare even to breathe.

"Whoa!" came a voice ahead of him—one of the girls.

"It's beautiful!" said another.

"I've never seen anything like it!" That voice was Viola's.

Finally, Barclay peeled his eyes open. All around them, blue speckles glimmered, as though Mar-Mar was surrounded by floating starlight. They must've been Firenekkies, which Hasu claimed lit the Munsey streetlamps. Their glow made it bright enough to spot the river below, which truly did look like a current winding across the ocean floor.

Its sludgy water reminded Barclay of a mudslide.

The Sea was also growing warmer than he'd expected, and the farther they dove, the warmer it became. Then he spotted the source of the heat. Clustered around the edges of the river were vents, spewing up smoke and streams of bubbles. It was so warm that Barclay's skin flushed pink.

"Hasu and I will get off here," Viola said, her voice sounding muffled and distant through the water. "The rest of you keep going."

She and Hasu climbed off and floated at the edge of the river. Then Cecily grabbed two of the black marbles from her pocket. She tossed them, and the marbles *popped*! Out sprang a pair of Sunboards. If the Beasts had been surprised to be held as shadow prisoners, they didn't show it. They drifted upside down, eyes blank, their mouths bobbing open and shut.

Mar-Mar took off again, following the riverbank until they'd traveled far enough to satisfy Cecily.

"This little bend looks like it's a third of the way, from the map," Cecily said. She handed her map to Shazi and two of the shadow marbles to Tadg. "Swim down until you reach the lumpy lichen rock—that marks the last third. Just give the marbles a toss when you're ready. Come on, Barclay!"

Barclay climbed off. He *still* thought this plan was a bad idea, but he had to admit—it was amazing down here. While on the surface, all Barclay could see of the Sea was endless dark water, but underneath, it was beautiful. Countless strange plants sprouted along the ocean floor, seaweed bushes and nettles and colorful blooming flowers. Tiny Beasts swam among them. There were whole schools of fish that vanished and reappeared at random. Crustaceans drilled tunnels into the sand. Crowded around the vents, the Firenekkies glowed like aquatic lightning bugs.

"It's incredible, isn't it?" Cecily said. Then she stretched her muscles, preparing for the race. "But I won't be distracted. My Lore might be no good down here, but I'm not taking it easy on you."

Barclay didn't see how his Lore would fare any better. It wasn't as though there was wind underneath the water.

But then he glanced behind him, back at the vents. If there were bubbles, that meant there must've been air.

As a test, he summoned a gentle breeze from his hand, and bubbles flitted from his fingertips. His hopes soared. He could use his Lore to propel himself forward. And Tadg's water Lore could do the same.

They were going to win this.

The thought bolstered his mood. Even if Barclay didn't like Cecily's reckless, rule-breaking idea, he wanted to prove he could keep up with the other apprentices—even if he was an Elsie.

All he needed was to stop his Lore from going out of control.

Like it always did.

Barclay stretched, trying to mirror Cecily's confidence.

"I won't be taking it easy on you, either. We'll win this for Runa."

Cecily looked at him curiously. "*Is* Runa as terrible as Cyril says she is?"

"Runa isn't terrible at all. Is . . . Cyril also terrible?"

"He thinks very highly of himself, but no, I like Cyril."

"Do you know why Runa and Cyril hate each other?"

Cecily shook her head. "Hasu said she asked once, but Cyril refuses to talk about it."

That was no different from when they'd asked Runa in the Woods.

"What could anyone do to make someone else hate them like that?" asked Barclay.

"I don't know. But it must've been something really awful."

Her words led them into silence. Barclay sensed that Cecily was also trying to guess what that really awful thing was. The only hatred Barclay had ever known was Dullshire's hatred of Beasts, but that was because Beasts had hurt them. He wondered if that was what happened with Runa and Cyril, if somehow one of them had hurt the other. Or maybe it didn't always work like that.

Then a figure came hurtling down the river—Hasu. She clung to her Sunboard like a life raft as the current swept her forward. Suddenly, a golden light formed around her in the shape of a hexagon, and she vanished. She reappeared fifty feet ahead of where she'd been.

"How did she—?" Barclay started, but then Hasu reached out for Cecily and slapped her hand.

Cecily leapt into the river, clutching her own Sunboard. She waved as the stream carried her and the Beast away. "Bye, Barclay!" she called, laughing.

After another hexagon of light, Hasu and her Sunboard appeared at Barclay's side. He yelped, a few bubbles shooting out of his Polypop. "How did you do that?"

"I have spatial Lore," Hasu told him brightly. "I can zap myself to anyplace I've been before. Or that I can see. But without Bitti—she's my Madhuchabee—I can't go very far."

Barclay was about to tell her how amazing her Lore sounded before he remembered that they were on opposing teams. "How far behind is Viola?"

"Not very. But her light Lore doesn't do much underwater."

A minute or so later, Viola appeared upstream. Barclay reached out his hand for her, and as soon as she slapped it, he grabbed his Sunboard and jumped into the river.

It didn't feel like regular water—it was thick and mucky. All the sand and pebbles within it prickled like needles against his skin. Even so, he didn't let go of his Sunboard. The Beast, which clearly never moved fast, seemed to be enjoying this unexpected rush of speed. Its mouth gaped open in a lopsided smile.

Once Barclay got used to the river's current, he pointed one arm behind him and thought, *Wind!*

Bubbles plumed from his hand, and the Sunboard lurched forward. It rocketed around each bend in the river, smiling wider and even more lopsidedly. Barclay hollered in victory. His Lore wasn't going out of control. He could do this.

In a matter of minutes, he caught up to Cecily.

Cecily's eyes bulged when she spotted him. "Is that wind Lore? No fair!"

Barclay grinned as he passed her. This was almost as fun as running with Root.

But a moment later, a fork came into view up ahead. Barclay stopped using his Lore. "Which direction do we take?"

"The, um, right one!" Cecily called back.

He narrowed his eyes. Cecily was sneaky. She might purposefully give him the wrong direction so that she'd reach Tadg and Shazi first. Using his wind Lore as a brake, he slowed his pace until Cecily caught up.

"We're taking the *same* direction," he told her.

"But . . ." She whipped her head from side to side. "I don't remember which direction *is* the right one!"

Barclay's stomach sank. Cecily had claimed that these rivers ran all across the Sea. If they took the wrong turn, they could end up in a far-off part of the Wilderland.

"Make a guess!" He wished he'd given the map a closer look himself.

"Left!" she blurted, and the two of them swerved to the left side of the fork.

As soon as they did, the current sped up. Barclay realized it was because the ocean floor was dropping—they were hurtling down a hill.

Cecily desperately hugged her Sunboard. "I can't—this is too fast! Help me—" Her head bobbed in and out of the sandy water.

Barclay reached out and hooked his arm around Cecily's, propping her up. The faces of their Sunboards smooshed together. "I thought you said the river was straight all the way to the reef!"

"I thought it was!"

"Well, hold tight, okay?"

"Holding tight," she squeaked.

Awkwardly, he lifted his hand and pointed it in front of them. *Wind!* he thought.

A torrent of bubbles shot out from his fingertips, but even when Barclay tried with all his might, the wind wasn't strong enough to push them backward against the flow of the river. They continued speeding forward. Around them, the blue Firenekkies were growing sparser, making the world horribly dark.

Then, up ahead, the river looked like it stopped.

"Does it end?" Barclay asked.

"I . . . I think it falls," Cecily breathed.

Terror seizing him, Barclay summoned more wind, but it was little use. They plunged off the river into a drop. And not just any drop, but a *trench*, so deep and so black, it seemed to dip into the very center of the earth. Barclay and Cecily screamed as their Sunboards careened out of the waterfall's current. When they finally stilled, they floated in the midst of darkness.

"Let go! Swim up!" Cecily said, though Barclay was so dizzy that he could hardly tell which way *was* up. But Cecily tugged him, and he followed, letting go of his Sunboard so Cecily could swallow it up again with her shadow Lore. Barclay kicked his legs and flapped his arms as hard as he could. He'd learned to swim in the creek that snaked around Dullshire, but that hadn't prepared him for swimming at the bottom of the ocean.

They swam and swam and swam, the only light a sliver of blue up above. The water around them was extremely cold, and in the darkness, Barclay worried any number of Beasts could be stalking them. They were easy prey.

His wind Lore propelled them up until they reached the top of the trench, which was—thankfully—warmer. Barclay squinted to make out their surroundings. The waterfall had hurtled them so deep that they'd emerged far down the trench. If the river was still close by, he couldn't see it.

"We're lost," he said, stricken.

"Don't panic," Cecily said, but it was too late. Barclay was already panicking. Then she reached into her pocket and drew out another black shadow marble. She clapped her hands together, squashing it with a *pop!* In its place was a glass jar of the shimmering Firenekkies. It glowed dimly, but it was better than nothing.

"Did you steal that from Ansley too?" he accused.

"We all have our talents."

"It's not a talent! Stealing is wrong. And Ansley doesn't deserve it."

"I'll return it when we get back. *If* we get back."

Barclay shivered. Then he spotted something in the light—a swirl carved into the rocky seafloor by the trench's mouth. It was as big as Barclay's head, with each of its lines so thin and precise that it had to have been carved by a person. But who would bother to etch anything into the bottom of the Sea?

"What should we do?" he asked, focusing on the problem at hand. "We could swim to the surface."

"If we do that, we'll be just as lost in the middle of the ocean," Cecily answered. "Let's find the river. Come on—I think it was this way."

They swam along the mouth of the trench, and Barclay was careful not to look inside. Its darkness frightened him. They kept moving until they heard the familiar roar of the river, and then Barclay was relieved to spot more Firenek-kies ahead, lighting their way.

Unfortunately, at least an hour had passed since they'd taken the wrong turn down the stream. The others were certainly wondering where they were.

"This was a bad idea," Barclay groaned.

"At least we didn't die," said Cecily cheerily.

"Is that supposed to make me feel better?"

Then a light appeared in the distance, and Cecily nearly

leapt beside him, waving. "That must be Viola!"

But it wasn't Viola. It was Runa, clutching a Firenekkie lantern similar to Cecily's. She wore a Polypop across her mouth, but even so, Barclay could see her furious frown.

"Have you ever heard the expression 'hot water'?" she asked. "Because you are all in a *heap* of trouble."

NINE

The next morning, the seven apprentices gathered solemnly in the Guild House.

It had been a dreadful night, and Barclay hadn't slept a second of it. He'd been too petrified over what judgment their teachers would dole out in the morning. In Dullshire, rulebreakers were punished with hours locked in the pillory or—for the gravest offenses—banished entirely. What if Runa fired them all as apprentices? Or worse, what if Runa fired just *him*?

Barclay could feel the disapproving stares of all the Guardians in the Guild House, and he guessed the other apprentices could too. Beside him, Hasu hung her head miserably. Tadg had his arms crossed. And Viola had fiddled with the baubles on her coat so much that several had popped off.

Finally, Runa and Cyril entered. It was strange to see them side by side without arguing. Probably because they were angrier at their students than they were at each other.

"What you did," Cyril told them seriously, "was reckless, irresponsible, and immeasurably dangerous. You could've each been killed."

Cyril's gaze dragged over them one by one, and it was so dour that, despite not knowing Cyril at all, Barclay felt that he had personally and grievously offended him.

"What would I have told each of your parents?" Cyril continued. "What would the Chancellor of the University of Al Faradh say to learn his only child had snuck out for the sake of some contest?"

Shazi looked down shamefully at her lap.

"Or High Keeper Mayani of the Jungle, that her daughter could've drowned last night at the bottom of the Sea?"

Hasu anxiously bit her fingernails.

The daughters of a university chancellor, a High Keeper, and the Grand Keeper? Apparently Cyril only taught the children of important people.

But he hadn't brought up Cecily's parents. Barclay wondered if they were famous too.

"Not to mention the way your actions reflect on us as mentors," Cyril said. "We had to rally all the other Guardians to search for you. If not for one of their tracking Lore, I don't think we'd ever have found you. I am shocked. And incredibly disappointed."

"That being said," added Runa, "the two of us understand how our own behavior may have contributed to your . . . competition."

Looking sheepish, Cyril and Runa both took a step away from each other.

"Does that mean we won't be punished?" asked Hasu hopefully.

Cyril laughed darkly. "Oh, no. You'll each be punished. Hasu and Viola will be helping Orla with her paperwork. Shazi and Barclay, you'll be assisting Ansley with her research. And Tadg, Cecily, and Yasha will be cleaning out Ulick's ship."

Barclay's mood soared. Assisting Ansley with her research didn't sound so terrible—even if Shazi was scowling over it.

"So you're not . . ." Viola's voice trembled like she might cry. "You're not firing us?"

Cyril's face bunched up into an expression Barclay didn't recognize—annoyance, maybe, or nervousness. Runa's, however, softened.

"Of course not," Runa told her, and Viola let out a deep sigh of relief.

"Now wait just a moment," Edwyn cut in, walking over with his breakfast toast clutched in his hand. "I never said you could punish *my* apprentice."

"Do you permit your student to sneak off and throw himself in harm's way?" demanded Cyril.

Edwyn gave Yasha a sideways smile. "I'm only disappointed he didn't invite me. I'd like to see these underwater rivers myself."

Cyril flushed scarlet. "You should not *encourage* such ill behavior—"

"I think it's a fair punishment," Yasha said, despite not wanting to join the competition in the first place. "And I owe Ulick for helping me when I . . ." He grimaced, clearly remembering his tumble off the *Bewlah*. "I don't mind cleaning the ship."

"I mind," Tadg grumbled.

Runa cleared her throat. "Because Orla, Ansley, and Ulick all have important business to attend to, the punishments will be postponed until next week. So you can squabble about it some other time."

"Yes," Cyril said. "What's more important is that—since you each betrayed our trust—we now feel obligated to keep an eye on you. So moving forward, the three of us have *all* agreed"—he looked pointedly at Edwyn, who didn't object— "that one of us will stay behind each day as an instructor, while the others continue to study Lochmordra."

"You mean we won't be able to help you?" Barclay asked, downcast.

"I think you've helped quite enough," Cyril said coolly.

It wasn't that Barclay wasn't interested in lessons from each of the teachers—he knew he needed them—but he also wanted to help with Lochmordra. And Barclay still hadn't mastered his last assignment. What if these lessons were just more chances for him to fall behind?

Tadg elbowed Barclay in the ribs. "This never would've happened if you and Cecily hadn't gotten lost."

"Or if we hadn't all done the contest to begin with," Barclay countered, shooting Viola a glare. "I thought it was a bad idea from the start."

Viola let out a *"Hmph!"* and turned her back to him. But Barclay wasn't sorry. Shazi and Cecily might've suggested the competition, but it was Viola who had dragged them into it.

Maybe that wasn't fair. Obviously Viola still held a grudge against Cyril and her old friends. But if any of them deserved to worry about being cast out, it was him. He was the Elsie. He was the one who couldn't control his Lore.

He was the one who didn't belong.

An hour later, Cyril led the seven apprentices across the mossy stone causeway to the Isle of Dunsey, Munsey's brother island. They trekked through the quiet town to a bog at the island's center.

Barclay opened to a fresh page in his notebook. "What is a bog?" he asked.

"It's like a swamp," Hasu replied, since neither Viola nor Tadg were speaking to him. "Apparently most of the Sea's islands are covered in them."

Barclay had never seen a swamp up close, but to him, the

bog looked like a muddy field. Pools of water formed tiny rivulets that wormed through the scraggly grass, and the air smelled strongly of mud. Workers dug up clumps of dirt and grass and piled them in tall stacks.

"Why are they collecting . . . dirt?" asked Shazi.

"Bog peat makes good fuel for fires," Cyril answered, and Barclay realized this explained why the hearth in the Guild House always smelled so earthy. He quickly jotted that down in his notes. "But that isn't why I brought you here today. The bogs are home to all sorts of Beasts, and I thought we could study them. In particular, the bogs are famous for preserving the bodies and fossils of long extinct species that roamed the world thousands of years ago. Wouldn't it be fascinating if we were to discover one?"

"Discover an old body? Like *bones*?" Hasu asked, horrified.

"I want to find bones!" Cecily said giddily. She leapt into the bog, splashing water on Barclay and Yasha behind her, and rubbed her hands together. "I bet I could find a good skull. Maybe a femur or two."

Shazi rolled her eyes. "You're so weird."

Cyril bunched up his pant legs and stepped into the bog next. "Come on." He motioned to them. "There are a few types of Beasts in particular I want to show you."

Barclay shivered as he waded into the water. It was frigid, but he was too determined to be a model student to turn back. And it was no grosser than the grimy mushroom caves in Dullshire.

"Even though the Sea is obviously known for the ocean itself, there are all sorts of animals and Beasts native to this Wilderland," Cyril said. His eyes glimmered almost as brightly as the many medals pinned to his shirt. He clearly loved studying Beasts. "Some are land-dwellers who live on the islands. Others live in freshwater, like the lake on the Isle of Orn, the rivers, and the bogs."

At this, something darted through the grass ahead of them.

"What was that?" Viola asked nervously.

Cecily crept forward. "I'm gonna catch it!"

Barclay squinted at the small furry creature crouched in the reeds. He made out two long ears—two *very* long ears, as tall as antlers. It must've been a rabbit sort of Beast.

"Croak!"

Suddenly Tadg let out a strangled shout. He flailed his arms then fell into the bog, splashing mud, once again, on Barclay's coat. If Barclay was going to stay at the Sea for a while, then he'd better save up his kritters to buy a more waterproof wardrobe.

At the commotion, the rabbit Beast took off running—before Barclay even had a chance to sketch it.

"You scared it away," Cecily complained.

"What happened?" Cyril asked Tadg. "Are you all right?"

Tadg scowled and stood up, his clothes dripping. On his shoulder perched the toad Beast. "It just comes out whenever it wants!" In response, the toad croaked defiantly.

"Ooh, you have a *second* Beast?" Hasu asked, peering

at the toad. She reached forward to pet it, then wrenched her hand back. Dark purple bled up her fingertips. "Ow! It's poisonous!"

"It won't kill you. It just stings a bit," Tadg assured her. "But the Beast is a menace. I'm not keeping it, whatever it is."

Cyril studied the Beast, careful not to get too close. "Interesting that its poison Lore also affects you, the Keeper." He pointed to the bottom of Tadg's ear, where a splotch of purple bloomed that matched Hasu's.

Tadg grimaced. "Yep. Fascinating."

"I've never seen a Beast that— Hm, I wonder what the stone is on its forehead. . . . Maybe it's— No, that doesn't make any sense . . . ," Cyril murmured to himself, so fast he was hard to understand.

"There's nothing in his dad's book about it," Viola said. "I already checked."

"You should ask Orla," Cyril told him.

"I don't care what kind of Beast it is," Tadg snapped. "I want to get rid of it. Mar-Mar is difficult enough. I don't need this one just popping out whenever it feels like it. Can't you remove the Mark? You have two Mythic class Beasts."

Cyril hesitated. "I imagine Codric and Tati are higher class, but I don't think I should . . . You should ask Runa. . . ."

Cecily groaned. "I'm bored. I'm going to find myself a skull." Then she scampered farther into the bog.

To her right, Hasu had wrenched a long reed from the ground and wielded it like a sword, its roots dripping mud all over her clothes. Across from her, Shazi drew one of her *actual* swords. She swiped it, slicing Hasu's reed in two.

"No fair!" Hasu whined. "I don't have metal Lore."

Shazi ignored her and continued practicing her swordsmanship. She was very good, her movements graceful and quick. If she controlled her prosthetic using Lore, that meant she was using her powers all the time, which must've taken a lot of skill and concentration.

Cyril rubbed his temples. "Leopold assured me girls would be better behaved. But *look* at them."

While Shazi hacked at the reeds with her saber and Hasu squeezed the mud out of her pants, far in the distance, Cecily shouted, "I found some bones! I found some bones!"

"Gross!" Hasu called back, but then that same golden, hexagonal light glowed around her, and she vanished and reappeared at Cecily's side in the distance.

Maybe Cyril is right, Barclay thought. *Girls are terrifying*.

"It's a skull!" Cecily yelled gleefully.

"It's not a skull! It's a box!" Hasu called.

"Now w-wait a moment," Cyril blustered. "I've prepared an entire lesson on Thunderlarks, Keelinewts, and Moorbits. There are some very interesting Beasts that only exist in these bogs. Fossils that Scholar Keepers travel from all across the world to study—"

"There's *goo* inside it!" Cecily shouted. She didn't seem at all disappointed that it wasn't full of ancient Beast skeletons. "It's yellow!"

"That's not goo," Tadg said. "It's butter."

"Butter? Like for bread?" Barclay asked. "Does the bog keep it . . . fresh or something?"

"No, it just gives it a boggy flavor."

While Shazi and Yasha went off to investigate the bog butter, Tadg, Viola, and Barclay lingered with Cyril. Cyril looked like he'd given up on corralling all the apprentices, so he launched into his lesson just for the three of them. Barclay paid close attention and took careful notes, knowing he needed to learn as much as possible. Viola kept glancing at the girls across the bog, probably because she was curious about their goopy discovery but didn't want to admit that. Tadg, meanwhile, was distracted by his toad Beast. Whenever he ordered it to return to its Mark, it croaked at him louder.

"In the Spring, the Thunderlark is found only on the Isle of Dunsey, where it goes to lay eggs," Cyril told them. "But during the colder seasons, it flies south. No one is certain where it ends up—the nine islands of the archipelago are the only islands in the Sea—but explorers have been interested in mapping their flight patterns for generations. They fly in swirl shapes instead of Vs—"

"Swirls?" Barclay said. Then he cleared his throat, realizing he'd interrupted a teacher. "I just mean . . . like the symbol I saw carved into the trench?"

Cyril frowned. "I doubt it. Thunderlarks fly in swirls due to the magnetic pulls of their Lore—"

"You saw a swirl carved into a trench?" Tadg demanded.

"Yeah. Do you know what that means?" Barclay asked.

"It's the symbol for the Isle of Roane. My father was obsessed with finding it. That's what his maps were full of— the ones I was looking for at our house. He charted as much of the Sea as he could searching for it, but he never—"

"The Isle of Roane?" Yasha asked, the others returning behind him. "I thought that was just a myth."

"It *is* just a myth," Cyril said haughtily. "And it should hardly be taking time away from our *real* studies."

Barclay hesitated. "But I really saw the symbol on the trench. Cecily saw it too. Didn't you, Cecily?"

Cecily was busy peering into the box, which Barclay saw was indeed full of butter. She dipped her finger in it, tasted it, and scrunched her nose. "Tastes like mud."

"That was some family's butter you stole," Tadg said.

Cyril raised his eyebrows at her. "I thought we talked about the stealing."

Barclay had never seen Cecily look guilty for her thieving, but for the first time, her expression went shameful. Pouting, she said, "I'll go back and bury it where I found it."

"Now that you stuck your fingers in it," Tadg muttered.

"But wait," Barclay cut in. "You saw the symbol too, right, Cecily?"

She nodded. "There was a swirl carved into the trench by a knife or something. It definitely wasn't natural."

Yasha turned to Cyril. "What does this mean, then?"

"If you all must know." Cyril jutted his chin up high, as though to emphasize that he was above this silly discussion. "The Isle of Roane is a mythical island that the people of the Sea once believed existed. It's rumored that if you find the Isle, it will lead you to where Lochmordra lives."

"Then shouldn't we all be looking for it?" Barclay asked. "That way we'll find Lochmordra."

"It's not real," Cyril snapped. "It's just a fable. If Guardians spent their time chasing after every myth in the Wilderlands, they'd waste their whole lives doing it. Not every rumor and story is true."

"My father believed it was real," Tadg pointed out.

"And I respect your father's work very much," Cyril said. "Which goes to show . . . if he couldn't find it, then it doesn't exist. Now let's get back to *real* study."

But Barclay knew what he'd seen. The trench had been so deep within the Sea, so dark and terrifying. For someone to go through all the effort to carve the symbol in the rock . . . it must've been for an important reason.

He and Tadg shared a suspicious look. Just because no one knew where the Isle of Roane was didn't mean that it didn't exist.

The next day was Runa's lesson. The seven apprentices and their Beasts staggered out of the water onto the sand. Cecily gave a low moan and lay down while Oudie pecked at her like a vulture. Viola was so exhausted, she didn't even scold Mitzi for nibbling her ears. Motya miserably shook the water from her fur, then her entire body erupted into flames. After they burned out, she was perfectly dry. Yasha stared at her enviously.

Barclay, however, hadn't minded the strenuous lesson. Because it hadn't relied on Lore, he'd had no chance to mess it up.

Panting heavily, Barclay wrung out his hair. He turned to Root and burst out laughing. "You look ridiculous."

Root huffed. His drenched fur hung down like a mop.

"Refreshing, wasn't it?" Runa asked, striding briskly ahead of them. Goath slithered behind her, water leaking through his bones.

"I could nap for a thousand years," Hasu complained. Exhausted, Bitti was *already* napping on Hasu's nose.

"I could nap for a million," Shazi echoed. Beside her, her scorpion Beast Saif must've disagreed. He stretched out his pointy metal tail, as though ready for a Dooling match.

"My back hurts," Tadg grumbled. "I'm too old for obstacle courses."

Runa smirked. "Clearly the weeks out on the road have made you all soft. *I* didn't have any trouble completing the obstacle course with you. Now buck up. We do it again in ten minutes!"

While the others rested, Tadg glanced at Barclay and jerked his head toward Runa. Barclay ushered Root off to play with Oudie and Mitzi while he and Tadg left to speak to their teacher.

"We were wondering if we could ask you something," Barclay started.

"Ask away," Runa said.

"Why aren't the Guardians looking for the Isle of Roane?" Tadg asked.

Runa blinked. "The Isle of Roane? You sound like your father."

Tadg crossed his arms. "Yeah, well, it could be important, couldn't it? If we find the island, then we'll find Lochmordra. And then we could stop all these attacks."

"Orla has summoned some of the best Guardians in the world here—more arrive every day. And we've decided to team up to investigate *real* questions, like the Muirmarú pod attacking any ship that goes near the Isle of Orn. Or the different sites where Lochmordra has been rising. Now what brought all these questions on?"

"I found a swirl carved onto the ocean floor beside the trench," Barclay said. "That's the Isle of Roane's symbol, isn't it?"

"It is," Runa agreed.

"Well, why would anyone take the time to carve it all the way down there if it wasn't important?"

Runa sighed. "I don't know, and I think it's great that you're all trying to help. But I'm afraid this leads to a dead end."

"Then let us *really* help," Tadg growled. "We could be working with the other Guardians! We'll learn more from them than obstacle courses."

"I'll tell you what—if either of you can beat me in the next obstacle course, I'll consider letting you come with us."

Tadg's eyes lit up. "Fine. I was taking it easy on everyone last time, anyway."

Except it wasn't Tadg who'd been taking it easy—it was Runa. During the second obstacle course, she froze the waves below her feet and skated across them in a frosty blur. She made it back to the beach before the apprentices even passed the first ice buoy in the water.

"I thought we weren't supposed to use Lore," Tadg said afterward.

Runa smirked. "You thought you'd beat me without it?"

And even though Barclay told Tadg that he'd never beat Runa, with or without his powers, Tadg grouched about the race for the rest of the afternoon.

By the third day, Barclay had nearly given up hope of learning more about the Isle of Roane. The same couldn't be said for Tadg. Luckily, Edwyn didn't seem to mind someone interrupting his lesson.

"Now, there are a few items I think all Lore Keepers should carry on them," Edwyn said, spilling the contents of his backpack over their table in the Guild House. Jars, vials, and bottles rolled across the surface. "A good Mendijuice is a must. Even better, Gunkwort, if you can get your hands on it. Maybe not so much for me as I've got Lira here."

Edwyn looked up the spiral staircase, where his Caladrius perched atop the railing. The white dovelike Beast was far more timid than her Keeper, preferring to keep her distance.

"But for anyone without healing Lore," Edwyn continued, "Gunkwort is a good idea—"

"Excuse me," Tadg said so politely that Barclay could hardly believe he'd heard him right. "I was wondering if we could ask you a question."

"Not this again," Shazi muttered. Beside her, Cecily had grabbed two glass jars and placed them over her eyes, magnifying them to three times their normal size like a Dungwasp.

"Ask me whatever you'd like," Edwyn told Tadg.

"We were wondering what you knew about the Isle of Roane."

At this, Cecily lowered the jars. Yasha spilled a vial of Mendijuice all over the table. And even Murph, the only other occupant in the Guild House, stirred from his napping spot by the fire to listen.

"Ah! The Isle of Roane is one of my favorite stories," Edwyn said. "The mythical island where Lochmordra lives. Sailors and locals have spoken about it for centuries, but it's been a long time since anyone has actually found it."

"People *have* found it?" Viola asked.

"Of course! How else would the story come to be? But the

last person was over four hundred years ago, and wherever she said the island was has been forgotten."

"So do *you* think it's real?" asked Barclay.

"Absolutely. But . . ." Even though the Guild House was practically empty, Edwyn leaned forward and lowered his voice. Barclay suspected this was just for dramatic effect. "The legend is that it's guarded."

"Guarded?" Hasu squeaked.

"By monstrous Beasts. And there's a saying: 'Not even the sun knows where it lies, and the stars won't spill the secret.'"

Chills crept up Barclay's spine. He couldn't tell if the phrase was beautiful or creepy.

"But what does that mean?" Barclay pressed.

"It means that it's all a great mystery. Maybe it will remain a mystery forever." Then Edwyn's eyes roamed over each of them theatrically—as though they all had a secret to hide. "Or maybe it won't."

TEN

Within a week, the apprentices had fallen into a routine in Munsey. Days spent with Cyril were usually followed by nights bogged down with homework, while Runa's lessons meant achy muscles the next morning. By far, everyone's favorite teacher was Edwyn, who had now twice amazed them with thrilling tales of adventure.

"Do you think he *really* found an Óirscale?" Hasu asked. "They're really rare!"

"And expensive!" Cecily said, twiddling her fingers like a pickpocket.

"I don't see how he could do that with only healing Lore," Shazi said. When Viola shot her a warning look, she added, "What? It just doesn't make sense to me. You'd have to jump off a waterfall!"

When everyone turned to Yasha for an explanation of

his teacher's dazzling feats, Yasha asked, "Haven't you been listening? He uses Lore-enhanced tools. The dorsal fin of a Hookshark makes a great grappling hook, and the vines of a Cordigourd are impossible to break."

"Dad used tools like that all the time," Tadg pointed out. "They're normal for Surveyors."

Looking disgruntled, Shazi picked at her bread. "Well, I want to go on a dangerous adventure. It's boring here. And the food is awful. The sailors keep saying the fish are all dead and gross now, so every meal is just potatoes and seaweed and twelve different types of milk."

Shazi wasn't wrong. On their table alone were four different pitchers, full of what Tadg had described as sweet milk, sour milk, thick milk, and thick sour milk. Barclay missed the pear cider from Sycomore's famous Ironwood Inn.

"Actually, there are sixteen types of milk," Tadg corrected, eagerly reaching for his second cup.

"Yeah, and they all make my stomach hurt," Viola muttered.

Even Mitzi, who normally thrilled in tipping over their glasses, steered clear of the sour milk ever since she'd sniffed it for the first time. She tried to play at the end of the table with Motya, who was far less interested in wrestling than she was in grooming her luscious white fur.

"Um, Tadg?" Yasha asked. "Will that cream still be good to drink?"

He pointed to Tadg's toad Beast, who squatted in a dish of sweet cream as though it was a pond.

"I wouldn't," Tadg said flatly.

"I thought that you weren't going to keep him," Viola said. "Weren't you—"

"Runa won't let me get rid of him in case he's a major discovery or something. Like he's a trophy." He pointed his spoon at the toad Beast. "You are the *worst* trophy."

The Beast croaked in response.

"Then you should name him!" Cecily said eagerly. "I like Toadles."

"There's no way I'm naming him Toadles," Tadg said. "I should name him Yuckywart. Or Dungfart."

"Oh, you're no fun," Hasu whined. "You don't deserve Toadles."

At that, Toadles leapt out of the cream across the table, making the bowl topple over and spill. A puddle of it soaked through the envelope resting beside Viola.

Barclay hurriedly fished it out of the cream. "Here, before it gets all—"

Viola snatched it from his hands and glanced at Cyril's apprentices to make sure they hadn't seen. Even though Viola spoke to the other girls now, she wasn't ready to call them friends again. No matter how much Barclay tried to change her mind.

"It doesn't matter," she said quietly. "I'm not reading it anyway."

When she went to shove the envelope into her bag, Barclay caught a flash of the official purple seal on the back.

"But it's from your dad," Barclay said. "He sent you another letter?"

Viola stiffened. "He sent me five, actually."

"You're not going to at least read what he has to say?"

"Why bother? I already know what he'll say. He'll say that I made a great mistake letting Runa be my teacher. And that he's very disappointed in me."

Barclay didn't see how she could know that, seeing as the letter was unopened. But he didn't want to press her while she was upset. Instead, he turned to Hasu on his other side, but Hasu also looked downcast. "I miss my parents. And the food from home. I haven't been home in over a year."

"What kind of food do you eat in the Jungle?" Barclay asked.

Hasu brightened. "The best kind. Cardamom rice, fresh mangoes . . ." She trailed off, poking her fork around her colorless plate. "Do you ever get homesick?"

Barclay's thoughts instantly veered to the earthy smell of mushroom caves. To the peaceful quiet in the graveyard where his parents were buried. To Master Pilzmann gossiping about the town's latest rules and scandalous rule-breakers. His heart gave a painful tug.

"Not really," he answered, his face flushing.

Viola raised her eyebrows. "Your cheeks only get red like that when you're lying. But why would you be homesick for your Elsewheres town? They kicked you out."

"I'm not l-lying," Barclay stammered, flushing all the fiercer.

"You're an Elsie?" Cecily asked with surprise. "I thought all Elsies were terrified of Beasts."

"I'm *not* lying," Barclay repeated, firmer this time. "You can't be an Elsie and a Lore Keeper, so that makes me a Lore Keeper—"

The door to the Guild House swung open, and Cyril and Runa trudged inside. Their dour expressions must've meant that their hunt for Lochmordra had led nowhere—again.

"Where's Edwyn?" Runa asked the seven of them. "I'd like him to come with us to the reef. Maybe he can spot a clue we can't."

"Or he'll spend the whole time cracking jokes," Cyril mumbled.

"Oh, cheer up, Cee-Cee," Runa said. "You used to have a sense of humor."

Barclay swore he saw steam blow out of Cyril's ears.

"Edwyn went to wash up," answered Yasha. "During our lesson, he accidentally got covered in sea jelly."

"We'll find him," Runa said. "But since the three of us will be gone tonight, we decided this is the perfect opportunity for you to perform your punishments for sneaking out. Orla, Ulick, and Ansley are all expecting you."

And so, unhappily, the seven apprentices split up, and Barclay and Shazi trekked across Munsey to the Planty

Shanty. Ansley waited for them by the front door. She held a slimy clump of Polypops, and she'd replaced her sea-glass spectacles with matching goggles.

"I hope you're ready for another journey under the Sea," she told them brightly. "I think you might actually enjoy this, Barclay. And I . . ." She trailed off, studying Shazi's prosthetic leg. "Are you going to be all right swimming?"

Shazi crossed her arms. "I'll be fine."

"All right, then. The three of us have a tough task ahead of us. We're diving deep to the ocean floor to study the thermal vents."

"The vents?" Barclay asked. "Why?"

"The Sea is getting warmer. It's causing fish to die, Beasts to migrate where they don't normally belong—and I can't prove anything, but I have a hunch it's creating even more problems that we haven't figured out yet." Ansley beamed. "So we're going to investigate, Apothecary-style!"

Without Mar-Mar to ride, the swim down to the ocean's bottom was long and exhausting. But the slower pace also made it easier to appreciate the Sea's beauty. Coarse stone and stringy seaweed covered the floor, with all sorts of animals and Beasts crawling or swimming or floating about. The vents rose up from pillars of craggy rock. Bubbles and dark sand teemed out of them, and glowing blue Firenekkies clustered around their edges.

Ansley drew a bunch of jars from her knapsack and

handed several to Barclay and Shazi. "We're going to collect as many specimens as we can find. Just scoop up whatever seems unusual or out of the ordinary."

"But we don't know what looks ordinary down here," Shazi said.

"Oh, that's why you have me! Grab what you can, and then I'll decide if it's worth bringing up to the shop."

For the next twenty minutes, they each worked in silence. Barclay swam as close to the vents as he could, but it was hard because they were *hot*. Boiling hot. So instead, he drifted below them, paying special attention to any Beasts. The brown seaweed clumped here was so thin and ticklish that it reminded him of human hair. Beastly minnows with two heads burrowed deep into the grasses. Broken shells and sand dollars littered the floor like a treasure trove, and Barclay stuck several strange ones into his jars.

Though the work was far from exciting, Barclay liked it. In many ways, it reminded him of mushroom foraging.

He scolded himself. He was never going to be a proper Lore Keeper if he couldn't stop thinking about Dullshire.

But his thoughts of homesickness vanished when he stumbled across an interesting find—the shed skin of some type of sea snake. Cringing, he pinched it between two fingers and picked it up. The bottom of it was coated in strange black dust.

"That's weird," Barclay muttered. He parted the hairy grass to get a better look at the ocean floor, revealing a jagged line of bubbly black rock. He tried to yank a piece of it off, but it wouldn't budge. So he stuffed the snakeskin into his jar and swam to Ansley.

"Yes?" she asked. She had spent so much time near the vents that her skin was flushed. Her eyes fell on the smooshed snakeskin in his jar. "Ooh! Reptilly scales! Excellent find, Barclay!"

"Are they important?" he asked hopefully.

"No, but they're delicious on a piece of toast. And what did you find, Shazi?"

Shazi held up her jars, which, like Barclay's, were full of shells and algae. "This one is special-looking." She pointed to a clump of seaweed with a silver metallic glint to it.

"Ah, I'm afraid that's not as unusual as it looks. That's Gunkwort. You can find it all over these parts." Ansley tapped her own jars. "I took a sample of the Firenekkies down here. They're the bioluminescent plankton that light our streetlamps. I could study the ones in Munsey, but I thought a wild sample might be useful. As you can see from how they crowd the vents, they're quite fond of extreme heat."

Barclay cleared his throat. "I also found something else. Can I show you?"

"Of course," Ansley answered, and Barclay led them back to the bubbly black rock.

"Do you know what this is?" he asked.

Ansley's eyes widened. "I should've expected to find something like this! Yes, this explains quite a lot. What we're looking at here is hardened volcanic lava. The ocean floor has shifted a tiny bit, and the lava seeped out the crack. Do you know what might've caused that?"

Barclay thought for a minute, wondering what could change the ground itself. But then he realized that was exactly what he had felt his first night in Munsey.

"An earthquake," he said.

"That's exactly right. It's possible that the earthquakes have shifted some of the floor here, making the vents stronger—and making the Sea hotter."

"But what's causing the earthquakes?"

"Unfortunately, that's a question we can't answer tonight. But this is a tremendous find! I said it before, and I'll say it again—you'd make a good Apothecary, Barclay."

She was smiling, but Barclay didn't know whether or not to take her words as a compliment. Because Barclay didn't want to be an Apothecary; what he wanted was to be a Guardian. And it had been a long time since he had felt good at that.

After they returned to the surface, Ansley let them end their "punishments" early.

She winked. "Just don't tell Runa or Cyril." Then she left to haul their findings back to the Planty Shanty.

"What do you want to do?" Shazi asked Barclay. She sat on the sand beside the collection of sabers she'd left behind while they dove. With a swipe of her finger, the metal of one of her blades warped and reformed into her prosthetic. Barclay imagined she had done this a thousand times before, but the Lore was so quick and precise that he couldn't help but be amazed. "We could go back to the Guild House, or—"

"I want to practice," Barclay told her, fishing the bottle cap from his pocket.

At first, Shazi winced, then her expression brightened into a wide smile. "Yeah, that's fine. We can practice. Here on the beach?" She fastened her prosthetic back into place, the metal of the socket molding around her thigh until it was snug and comfortable.

"Sure," Barclay answered. "Why not?"

While Shazi stood and drew a new saber to practice her footwork, Barclay summoned Root from his Mark. Root padded around on the sand, occasionally stopping to dig.

Barclay squeezed the bottle cap in his fist. "I need to figure this out," he told Root. "Can you help me?"

Root wagged his tail eagerly. And so Barclay tried it. *Wind!* he thought, summoning a gentle breeze to hold the cap in place. Except no matter how hard he focused, the wind was anything but gentle. The bottle cap flew into the air and plopped in the sand at his feet.

"It's just one mistake," Barclay said, trying to calm himself. "I can still do this."

Root barked in agreement, and so Barclay tried again. And again and again and again. The final time, the cap hovered for a moment, then it jolted and smacked Barclay in the face.

He groaned. "I don't get it! There's no way to keep it still. That is the whole *point* of wind. It's never still!"

Root barked again, and Barclay narrowed his eyes. "I'm

beginning to think you're no help at all. You're just agreeing with everything I say."

This time, Root stood on his hind legs and rested his paws against Barclay's chest. Then he looked at Barclay expectantly, his mouth open and tongue flopped out.

Barclay sighed. "You just want to play. But I can't right now. If I don't figure this out . . ." Then he didn't deserve to be a Guardian apprentice anymore.

Maybe he was being too hard on himself. But Guardians had a crucial job to protect those around them. And if Barclay wasn't up to that, then maybe he should just quit.

He switched tactics, back to the advice Yasha had given them when they'd sailed on the *Bewlah*. Barclay needed to think about something that made him relax.

Once again, he listed the facts he'd memorized in his homework. *The Man-Eating Hasifuss. The Ickypox Plague. The Great Capamoo War . . .*

Even when he scrunched his face up tight in concentration, he still failed. He had the urge to kick up sand, or to throw the cap as far as he could into the Sea.

Instead, he stole a glance at Shazi. She was so confident and tough. Barclay bet *she* never failed to measure up.

But to Barclay's surprise, Shazi looked less graceful than usual. Normally, the metal pylon bent and shifted like an anklebone, thanks to Shazi's Lore. But something had broken her focus. She stumbled as she stepped, and she winced as though she'd been hurt.

"Are you all right?" he asked her.

"Oh," she said, pausing her practice. She stood awkwardly, all her weight on her right leg instead of her prosthetic. "Are you stopping already?" When she leaned to the other side, she winced again.

"Is your leg bothering you?"

She grimaced. "I'm fine."

"But it looks like . . . It's okay if you want to stop." He stuffed the bottle cap in his pocket. "I want to stop too. Come on, let's go back to the Guild House."

At this, Shazi sheathed her sword, looking relieved. But when she moved to take a step, she stumbled and fell onto the sand.

"Are you sure you're all right?" Barclay asked hurriedly. Root padded to Shazi's side with concern.

"I said I'm fine," she snapped, sounding as prickly as Tadg. Her expression softened as Root rested his head on her lap, and she scratched him behind the ear. "Let's just take a break. I'm going to sit for a moment."

Barclay nodded and sat beside her. He watched as Shazi traced her finger over the edge of her prosthetic as she had done only minutes before, making the metal bend and unclasp from her thigh. Barclay tried not to stare—he didn't want to be rude—but this close, he could see a sliver of an old scar along her skin. He guessed that Shazi must've lost her lower leg at some point, rather than been born without it.

Catching him looking, Shazi said, "It was bitten off by a Werelion."

"Really?" Barclay asked, aghast. He didn't know what a Werelion was, but that sounded awful.

She chuckled. "No. It was an accident when I was seven. There was a sandstorm, and a Karkadann got spooked—they're like angry unicorns. There's lots of them in the Desert. Anyway, it landed on my leg, and my calf and knee had to go."

"I'm sorry," Barclay told her.

"It's fine. But it hurts every day—not because it's still healing or anything, but because my brain sometimes thinks my foot is still there. Even if I can control my prosthetic with Lore, the sand . . . it's so uneven. It makes it harder to focus on the million things I need to focus on, like keeping my balance or bending the metal like regular joints. Especially when I'm having one of my bad days." She shifted her position to stretch better, making Root whine. She grinned and returned to petting him. "I'm really lucky that I can still walk with my Lore, even if it took years of training to learn how. But that doesn't mean it's easy. I feel like I have to work twice as hard as everyone else just doing normal things, which means I'm always twice as tired."

Barclay was shocked into silence. He'd just been complaining to himself that his assignment was impossible, but it would be that much harder if he was hurting from an old injury, too. And if he'd been less focused on himself and paying better attention to Shazi, he might've realized that her leg was bothering her as soon as they reached the shore.

"We can sit here for as long as you like—then we'll go back to the Guild House," he told her.

She looked at him gratefully. "Thanks. And thank you, too," she told Root, who wagged his tail happily.

"Can I ask you something?" Barclay hoped he wasn't about to spoil the moment. "Why are you so hard on Viola? I thought you used to be friends."

"Friends don't run off without telling you," Shazi said fiercely. "They don't just leave without saying goodbye." She sounded no less pained than when she'd told Barclay that her leg was bothering her. It must've hurt to wake up one morning and realize your friend was gone.

Once Shazi regained her strength, they walked together to the lighthouse, where they were surprised to find Viola and Hasu already waiting for them.

"Barclay! Shazi!" Viola called, waving them over. After they sat down, Viola leaned across the table, her voice hushed. "You'll never guess what we found in Orla's apartment!"

"What?" Barclay asked.

Viola reached into her bag and pulled out a leather-bound box. She opened it, revealing a pile of loose parchment, scribbled with maps of the Sea.

"It's the papers Tadg was trying to find. Conley Murdock's maps to the Isle of Roane!"

ELEVEN

What is this place?" Hasu whispered. In the near darkness, she clutched Shazi with one hand and Barclay with the other. Her grip was so tight that Barclay's fingers had gone numb and tingly.

"This is Maedigan Cove," Tadg answered.

Viola strengthened her light Lore, sending it sweeping across the beach in a shimmering, golden dome. After finishing their punishments, the seven apprentices had followed Tadg to a far corner of Munsey. The sand here was uneven and rocky, and the water of the small bay sat eerily still.

"I don't like this," Barclay said. "You remember what happened last time we snuck out."

"We're not sneaking out," Yasha reminded him. "We told Ansley and Lifen where we're going."

"And it's not like we can talk about my dad's papers in

the Guild House," Tadg said. "We still don't know why Orla kept them secret."

"You don't think Orla is hiding something, do you?" Viola asked.

"I doubt it. Orla has been High Keeper here for over a hundred years. But I do think she must've had a reason."

They stopped at the mouth of a cave. It was tiny and snug, the perfect size for the seven of them to sit in a circle while Yasha lit a cozy fire in their center.

Tadg passed around his father's papers, starting with Shazi and Hasu on his right.

Shazi studied them and frowned. "I don't see the Isle of Roane on the map."

"That's because Dad never found it," Tadg said. "But he spent years searching for it."

Hasu groaned. "But the Sea is the biggest of all the Wilderlands! Even if you rode a flying Beast, it would be almost impossible to spot a single island amid all this ocean."

Sighing, Shazi handed the papers to Barclay and Viola. "This proves it, then. If Conley Murdock couldn't find it, then the Isle of Roane really is just a myth."

Even so, as Barclay inspected the hand-drawn maps, a mixture of thrill and frustration welled up in his stomach. His gaze darted across the nine islands of the Sea, as though expecting one of them to be labeled *Roane*. That swirl near the trench *had* to mean something.

"What if we tried this?" Viola spread the yellowed parchment across the ground and traced out a path with her fingertip. "These are all the islands Lochmordra has already attacked. Maybe if we map them out, we can find a connection between them. Here's Glannock. Kelligree. Slakey. Coad—"

"That's just a random zigzag," Cecily said. "It doesn't make any sense."

Yasha wrung out his hands. "But if the papers don't tell us anything, why would Orla keep them secret?"

Barclay, Viola, and Tadg met one another's eyes. They knew firsthand why someone would hide information about Legendary Beasts.

"What if someone is trying to wake Lochmordra up on purpose?" Barclay asked. "What if someone is trying to bond with him?"

Hasu shuddered and scooted closer to Shazi. "B-but it's almost impossible to bond with a Legendary Beast. Only a few people have *ever*. In all of history."

"That doesn't stop people from trying," Barclay told her darkly.

"So you think Orla was hiding the maps for their protection," Shazi said. "You think she doesn't trust the other Lore Keepers."

"But there isn't anything useful on these maps in the first place," said Yasha.

Barclay peered at Tadg, who was acting unusually quiet.

"These are your dad's maps," Barclay said to him. "There must be more that you can tell us about them."

Tadg folded his arms across his chest. "Dad didn't exactly share all his work with me. He was gone most of the time, and even when he was home, he was busy studying deepwater Beasts or writing his book."

"But you also know the Sea better than us," Viola pressed. "Like these symbols. What do they mean?" She pointed at various scribbles on the maps. Even if Barclay had held the maps sideways or upside down, he wouldn't have been able to make any sense of them.

"Well, they're obvious, aren't they? This one with the fins marks the Zapray territory—you don't want to sail out there."

"Fins?" Shazi muttered. "They're just triangles—"

"The curvy lines mark underwater rivers," Tadg continued, ignoring her. "Those squiggles there are the algae forest. . . . The tornado things are whirlpools—there's a whole region full of them called Shipwreck Stretch. . . . The little mountains over there are the cave systems, and that V is the trench—"

"Wait a minute," Viola said. "Even if we *knew* where the Isle of Roane was, we're all forgetting one very important detail."

"What?" Barclay asked.

"In order to bond with any Beast, including a Legendary one, you need its six bonding items to build its snare, which is what summons and traps the Beast. The snares of Legendary Beasts include the rarest, most difficult items to find in their Wilderland. And of all six Beasts, Scholars only know the full list of bonding items for two: Dimondaise, from the Mountains, and Gravaldor, from the Woods."

Suddenly, Barclay understood something about Viola he never had before. "That's why you went to the Woods. You could've gone anywhere after Cyril—"

"Yes," Viola cut him off, looking embarrassed. "But if Orla was hiding the papers, maybe that's because . . ."

"Because Conley Murdock wrote down ingredients," Yasha finished for her, his eyes wide.

All at once, the seven apprentices scrambled to divide up the stack of papers. Barclay snatched a bunch and hurriedly flipped through them. There were dozens of sketches of the moon, in every phase from waxing to waning. Several papers featured smaller, messier versions of the map, as though Conley had scribbled it all in an excited rush. With these, Barclay couldn't even tell which *way* was right-side up.

"I found it! I found it!" Cecily brandished a sheet of parchment so long that it dragged across the stony ground. "Oh." Her smile fell. "Almost everything is crossed out."

"Except for two items," Tadg read over her shoulder. "Polypop bells and Fire Coral."

"Polypops?" Shazi repeated. "Like the goopy things that let you breathe underwater?"

Viola frantically flipped through the pages of *A Traveler's Log* until she found the right entry. Then she slid the book around and showed them the image of a smack of Polypops soaring through the air like a Midsummer parade. She read: "'Though Polypops are a Familiar class Beast and very common, only one in every one thousand is born with bells in its tentacles, which ring when it takes to the air. Legend goes that hearing the chime brings good luck—and a warning that you will need it.'"

"And what about Fire Coral?" Hasu asked.

"Ansley has one in her shop," said Barclay. "She said they're really rare."

"So what should we do with these papers, now that we have them?" Yasha asked.

"I think we should tell the Guardian Keepers about them," Hasu said.

"But Orla had the papers, so she already knows all this stuff," Shazi pointed out. "And for all *we* know, if we told the Guardian Keepers, we could be helping whoever is trying to bond with Lochmordra. We could be playing right into their hands."

The idea that one of the other Guardian Keepers was behind this was a very unpleasant thought. Guardians were supposed to protect people from dangerous Beasts, not set a Legendary one loose on islands and ships. But then again, Soren had been a Guardian too.

"We should try to learn more about Lochmordra," Barclay

said firmly. "Maybe if we do, we'll find some clues about who is behind all this."

"*If* someone is behind all this," Viola said. "We still can't be sure."

"I agree with Barclay," Tadg said. "We have to try."

"But where are we going to learn more about Lochmordra by ourselves?" Cecily asked. "None of the Lore Masters will teach us that in our lessons."

Tadg shot a wary look at Barclay and Viola.

"What?" Barclay asked.

"Don't get too excited. I know how you both love books and everything. But Munsey has a *huge* library."

Tadg had not been wrong. The next day, after their lesson with Runa, the seven apprentices gathered in the atrium of a grand building. It was nothing like the libraries Barclay knew, like the small and cozy one in Dullshire, or the dark and dusty one in Sycomore. It was magnificent, its domed ceiling painted to resemble the morning sky, its massive stone shelves smattered with barnacles and coral.

"We should split up," Tadg said. "Shazi and Cecily, you should go look up maps and compare them to my dad's. Viola and Yasha, you two research bonding items. Barclay and Hasu, you both find whatever you can about Lochmordra."

"What about you?" Barclay asked.

"I can't help today. Runa is making me report the toad Beast to the Surveyors in case it's a newly discovered species."

Hasu clapped her hands together. "But that's so exciting!"

Tadg glared at her, making it clear *he* didn't think so. Then he stormed off toward the reference desk.

"I think Toadles is kind of cute," Hasu whispered to Barclay.

Barclay didn't see what was so cute about it, since it was all warty, with big bulging eyes that looked like someone had poked it too hard in the stomach. But Hasu also thought Bitti was cute, and Bitti was a bug.

"Where do you think we should start?" Barclay asked her.

"Maybe in the history section? We could look at old editions of the *Keeper's Khronicle*. Oh! And the fiction section might have some good stories. Maybe they shelve some fables there. . . ."

An hour later the pair of them had found several promising tomes. As they roamed the adventure section searching for more books of legend and myth, Barclay couldn't help but think of Mrs. Havener, the librarian in Dullshire. He felt a fresh tug of homesickness in his gut. It seemed the more he swore *not* to think about Dullshire, the more everything reminded him of it.

"What's wrong?" Hasu asked, noticing his gloomy expression.

"Oh, nothing. I just used to go to the library a lot, back home—I mean, back where I grew up."

Hasu gave him a sad smile. "I'm sorry you miss it. I miss my home too."

"I don't miss it." Then, hoping she didn't spot the telltale heat creeping up his neck, he asked, "When was the last time you were home?"

"Since before our Exhibition, which was a year ago. My parents send me letters, but I still miss them a lot. I wasn't so sure I wanted to go to an Exhibition in the first place."

"You weren't?" Barclay thought everyone who grew up in the Wilderlands dreamed of becoming a Guild apprentice.

Hasu shook her head. "Shazi, Viola, Cecily . . . they're all so different from me. Shazi spent a *year* planning on bonding with a Scormoddin like Saif. Viola is the smartest person I've ever met, and she's always wanted to be Grand Keeper one day. And Cecily is really powerful even though she never had formal training until after Midwinter."

"You're really powerful too. Your spatial Lore is amazing."

"Thanks. But it was my parents who convinced me to bond with a Beast as strong as Bitti, and who wanted me to become Cyril's apprentice. My mom especially—she's the High Keeper of the Jungle."

"It wasn't what you wanted too?" Barclay asked, surprised. Hasu always seemed to enjoy their lessons, and she was proud to have the Horn of Dawn as a teacher.

"I don't know. I love Bitti, even if she's the opposite of a busy bee and spends all day napping. But I'm not very good at being sure of things. I get scared too easily. And I'm most scared that I'll never be good enough." She met Barclay's eyes, biting her lip. "What did your parents think about you becoming Runa's student?"

Barclay cleared his throat and made a show of scanning the shelves of books. "My parents died a long time ago."

"Oh, I'm sorry. I didn't know. You must really miss them."

Barclay had been so little when they died that he only had foggy memories of them. Usually, when he thought about his parents, he imagined what his life would've been like if they'd been alive. If they would've had dinner together every night as a family. If he would've had younger siblings. If he would've grown up always feeling like he belonged.

He knew he shouldn't miss Dullshire, but missing his parents didn't have anything to do with being a Lore Keeper or an Elsie. They had loved him. And they would've still loved him no matter what future he chose for himself.

"Yeah," Barclay answered. "A lot." Then, not wanting to make himself sad, he said, "Come on. Let's find a place to read all these books."

They teetered through the shelves in search of a table or a comfy set of chairs. As they turned the corner, Barclay spotted an archway sealed off with a blue velvet curtain.

"Where do you think that goes?" he whispered.

"Let's go see."

They both peeked inside, where a narrow stairwell led up into darkness.

"It's spooky." Hasu nodded at a spiderweb clinging to the ceiling's corner. "I don't know if we should—"

"Come on," Barclay said, feeling braver from all the adventure books in his arms. "Let's just see where this leads."

The pair climbed the stairs until they emerged in another domed room. This ceiling, however, wasn't just painted like the sky—it *was* the sky, the glass radiant with the orange and scarlet hues of dusk.

"Are you supposed to be here?" a man asked sharply, making Barclay and Hasu jolt. The man wore important-looking golden robes that trailed across the floor, and the pendant on his necklace was shaped like a crescent moon overlapping a sun.

"W-we got lost," Barclay lied, making his face flush hot. "Are you a librarian? I want to check out these books."

"Ask someone downstairs," the man said dismissively. "This place is for Scholars." Barclay knew from the Exhibition that Scholars were another kind of Lore Keeper, who studied the history and science of Beasts. It was the fourth profession licensed by the Guild, along with Guardians, Surveyors, and Apothecaries.

"We're very sorry," Hasu squeaked. "We'll just be leaving—"

"What is this place?" Barclay asked. His gaze dropped from the ceiling to the huge bronze telescope in the room's center.

"It's an observatory. Perhaps not as grand as those of the Mountains, but we see our fair share of Scholars nonetheless. There is no better place in the world to study the celestial bodies and their effects on Lore." The Scholar's chest swelled with pride like a puffer fish.

"Celestial bodies? You mean like the moon?" The man's

pendant *did* remind Barclay a little of Conley Murdock's papers.

The man gaped as though Barclay's words were incredibly foolish. "Of course like the moon. This is the Sea—everything is controlled by the moon. The tides, the coral spawning in the reef, even some of the currents. We may divide our year into four solar seasons and celebrate holidays like Midsummer and Midwinter, but the moon also plays a crucial role in nature. And there are many of its mysteries still left to solve. Not that you younger generations appreciate such things."

Barclay was offended—he appreciated knowledge plenty. And he was about to tell him so when the man barked, "Now leave! Without permission from the High Keeper, the observatory is for Scholars only."

At that, Barclay and Hasu fled back down the stairs, and no sooner did they emerge from the curtain than they collided with Viola and Yasha. The towers of books they each carried spilled across the floor.

"Sorry!" Barclay yelped. He knelt to pick up the volumes. "Are you planning on checking out *all* of these?"

"So what if I am?" Viola asked tightly.

"It's just . . ." He scanned the titles. Yasha was carrying the sort of books he'd expect—encyclopedias on rare items of the Sea. But Viola's books were different. There were biographies of past Grand Keepers, scientific papers on various Sea Beasts, histories of the Desert, the

Tundra, and the Jungle. "It's a lot, is all."

"Well, I thought I'd assign myself a little extra reading."

As Barclay lifted another book off the floor, he uncovered a piece of parchment crumpled beneath it. The broken seal of the three-headed dragon glimmered as though gold dust had been stirred into the wax.

"Hasu, Yasha, would you mind catching up with the others?" Barclay asked. "I want to talk to Viola about something."

Hasu and Yasha nodded, then gathered their books and disappeared through the shelves.

Barclay grabbed the letter and its opened envelope. "You read one of your dad's letters. What did he say?"

No different from yesterday, Viola tried to snatch the letter from his hands. But Barclay was ready this time, and he yanked it out of her reach. "Don't look at it. . . ." She sniffled, and Barclay was shocked to see tears glinting in Viola's eyes. "It's not—"

"I won't read it," he promised. "But you're upset. If you let me know why, maybe I can help you."

"What is there to help with? My dad has been writing me letter after letter all to say he's upset that I'm Runa's student. And that he's angry and worried because I'm ignoring him. And that he's been writing to my *mom* about it." Judging from her grave tone, Barclay guessed that her parents speaking to each other meant the situation was dire. It had been a long time since they'd been married. "He said if I don't answer soon, he'll come here himself. And I don't want to see him."

"But once he sees how well you're doing, won't he change his mind?"

"How well I'm doing?" Viola repeated. "Haven't you noticed? I'm the farthest behind of all of us."

Barclay's mouth dropped open. "That's not true—"

"*All* of you have Mythic class Beasts. So you see? I'm the odd one out. I'm the one who doesn't belong."

"If anyone doesn't belong, it's me. I'm the Elsie. I can't even control my Lore right."

Viola scoffed and finally tore the letter out of Barclay's hands. "Don't be ridiculous. You fit in fine. You became friends with Shazi and Hasu right away, even after what they did to me."

"I thought it was Cyril who made you quit, not them."

"He did, but they didn't exactly come find me or write to me or anything. Because everyone thinks I'm a failure."

"Viola, you're not a failure. You're the most brilliant person I know."

"You're lying."

"You know I'm not. You can always tell when I am."

She studied him suspiciously, then finally sighed. "It's just . . . it's been hard to see Shazi and Hasu again. You don't know what it was like to be a student with them. I might've come in first in my Exhibition, but only because Shazi didn't study for the written exam and Hasu fainted during the practical. They're *incredible*. Prodigies. And no matter how hard I pushed myself, I couldn't keep up. Everything came naturally to them, but meanwhile, Cyril had to give me private lessons just so that I wouldn't fall behind."

But Barclay *did* know what that felt like. He felt it every day being a student with Viola and Tadg. Shazi and Hasu might've been extraordinary, but to him, Viola was no different. And from the way Shazi had made it sound, before Viola had left, they hadn't thought her different either.

"You've never had a hard time keeping up since I've known you," Barclay said.

If Viola caught the jealousy in his voice, she didn't show it.

"That's because I . . ." Viola swallowed. "I was nervous. I thought being Cyril's apprentice was exactly what I needed so I could become Grand Keeper one day. But once we started—and Shazi and Hasu were so strong—I just . . . I choked. I could barely control my Lore. Everything I did was a mistake. Until Cyril finally told me he didn't know how to teach me anymore."

Viola wiped her eyes before continuing. "And it seems like Cyril replaced me with Cecily the moment I told him I was Runa's apprentice, like he'd been planning to all along. I've been so scared that if I start falling behind again, Runa will want me gone too."

No wonder Viola was always trying to please Runa. Because like Barclay, Viola knew how much it hurt to be cast out.

Barclay knew he should comfort her, but it bothered him that Viola felt like she didn't belong when she had often made *him* feel that way. And unlike Shazi or Hasu, she'd made him feel that way on purpose.

And there was something else that she'd said that had surprised him. "You couldn't control your Lore?" he asked.

She nodded. "After I became Cyril's apprentice, my Lore never seemed to listen to me. Not until I ran away." She must've understood the thoughtful look on Barclay's face, because she asked, "Do you think the same thing is happening to you?"

"Maybe. Or I'll never be enough of a Lore Keeper to control my powers."

"That doesn't make any sense. Of course you're a Lore Keeper."

"Really? Because you've made fun of me for being an Elsie loads of times."

Viola's expression softened. "I'm sorry. I know I've been a really bad friend lately. I was jealous, and I should never have made you feel bad. You're one of the most amazing Lore Keepers I've ever met."

Now Barclay suspected that *she* was lying. They spent every day surrounded by powerful Guardian Keepers, and with apprentices who were already powerful themselves.

Even so, Barclay's mood brightened. Maybe, like Viola's, his Lore wasn't a lost cause. And it was good to feel like best friends again.

"I'm glad you told me about what happened between you and Cyril," Barclay said, "but you're wrong about Runa. She'd never abandon you. And I'm sure that no matter how your dad feels right now, he's still proud of you."

Viola let out a dry laugh. "Thanks, but I'm not so sure. He's still angry I picked Runa over Cyril. He's so angry that I don't think he'll ever get over it."

Barclay didn't know what to say to that. He didn't have a lot of expertise with parents. In his mind, his parents had been loving and warm and perfect. But that was because all he truly had were hazy memories blended together with his own wishful thinking. Real people, even grown-ups, even parents, were more complicated than that. And sometimes they disappointed you.

After the pair finished cleaning up the mess they'd made, they returned half of Viola's books to the shelves and walked back to the library's checkout desk at the entrance. They found the others waiting there, gathered amid a small crowd. In the center stood Tadg, a medal dangling around his neck and Toadles perched on his shoulder. Several Lore Keepers vigorously shook his hand.

"Just like his father!" one chirped.

"It's been a while since we recorded a new Sea Beast!" said another.

"You *must* write to us often about any developments or Lore," urged the last.

Barclay couldn't tell if the flush on Tadg's cheeks was

from his own annoyance or Toadles's poison. Or maybe, possibly, a little bit of pride.

In typical Spring fashion, it rained that night. But after his conversations with Viola, Shazi, and Hasu, Barclay needed to sort out his thoughts now more than ever. Because no matter how much he might feel otherwise, everyone got nervous. Everyone made mistakes. Everyone faced their own challenges.

So maybe he really could conquer his.

After changing into his thickest sweater, Barclay and Root ran across the hills of Munsey, where the wind blew at its fiercest. His hair quickly got tangled. His clothes, mud splattered. But it was only in the wildest moments that his mind felt calm.

Then Root skidded to a stop. His ears perked up on alert, and Barclay whipped around to see what he was looking at. A dark smudge of a figure loomed in the distance. It stood on two legs, but that was the only humanlike thing about it. It must've been twelve feet tall, and two sharp tusks jutted from its head like crooked spears. It stood still as stone—which was good, because Barclay did *not* want it to notice them.

Then Barclay blinked, and the Beast was gone.

"Do you think we could *both* be seeing things?" Barclay asked Root.

Root still stared at where the Beast had been, then

sniffed the air suspiciously. No, that monster had definitely been real.

Lore Keepers from all across the world traveled to the Sea, so even if the Beast didn't look like it was from here, there was probably a good reason for it.

But the mysterious dread in Barclay's chest warned that the reason wasn't good at all.

TWELVE

Over seven weeks had passed since Barclay came to the Sea, and the first day of Summer had finally arrived. Despite this, it was still far from warm. Barclay, Tadg, and Yasha wore their heaviest wool sweaters and had their window shut tight.

"Jump," Tadg ordered the Stonetoad, which was the extremely boring name that Tadg had dubbed his species. Per Cecily's suggestion, the apprentices had all taken to calling him Toadles. Though sometimes Tadg called him Scatbreath. "Jump!"

Toadles stared blankly at Tadg from atop his bedpost.

Tadg groaned. "He doesn't even blink."

Barclay peeked up from his copy of *The Nine Most Crucial Events of Lore Keeper History*. "Maybe Toadles would be easier to train if you were polite." Beside him, Root huffed in agreement.

In return, Tadg gave Barclay a rude gesture and turned back to his Beast. Yasha snorted but muffled the sound in his elbow.

"Jump," Tadg commanded. *"Jump!"*

Toadles leapt off the bedpost and plopped in the center of Tadg's pillow, then squirted a dark purple liquid onto the white linen.

Barclay fell into hysterics. And even Yasha, who was usually too serious for jokes, let out a surprised howl of laughter.

"That's what he thinks of you," Barclay told him.

"He's not the only one," Yasha added.

Tadg collapsed onto his bed, and the jolt of the mattress made Toadles soar into the air. He landed in Tadg's lap and teetered from side to side, dizzy. Then, gathering himself and looking up at his Keeper, he uttered a loud *"Croak!"*

Barclay and Yasha laughed harder.

"You remember that night Tadg woke up and Toadles was on his face?" Yasha said.

"Tadg screamed so loud that Ansley came to check on us," Barclay said, remembering fondly. "I didn't know your voice could go that high, Tadg."

Tadg jerked his head, and the water in the cup on the nightstand splattered all over Barclay's face and open page.

"Hey!" Barclay sputtered, shaking out the damp pages. "This is Runa's book."

Tadg raised his eyebrows. "Really? I thought that book was a load of phooey."

"What is it?" Yasha asked curiously.

Barclay was about to explain that it was a *textbook* and therefore should be treated with respect. But then Tadg reached over and tore it from his hands.

"Dad told me the author is some Scholar Keeper," Tadg said, "though there's been talk she might lose her Guild license. I mean, have *you* ever heard of the Great Capamoo War? And I thought Ickypox only affected chickens, but she said it once killed half the Lore Keepers in the Woods!"

"Pretty sure it was goats," Yasha said.

Tadg smirked at Barclay. "You're from the Woods. Are you part goat?"

"If it's all nonsense, why would Runa assign it to me?" Barclay asked miserably. He'd memorized most of the book by now.

"Maybe it was a joke—"

"Croak!" Toadles's head shot toward the window.

Tadg peered at Toadles suspiciously. "Maybe it can sense when more earthquakes are coming. That's why it has a weird rock in its head—it has some kind of stone Lore *and* poison Lore. It croaked the whole time during the last one."

The last earthquake had been nine days ago. It'd been far stronger than the one before, destroying half of Ansley's supply of Gunkwort. They'd each crawled for shelter underneath their beds, and Motya kept fearfully nibbling Barclay's toes.

"I think you secretly like Toadles," Barclay told Tadg. "And want him to be really powerful."

"Yeah, right. I'll get Runa to change her mind eventually."

Barclay doubted that. Whenever Tadg asked Runa to remove his Mark, she reminded him that Toadles was a great discovery. But Barclay suspected Runa just thought he was funny.

Suddenly a bell began to toll outside, so loud and heavy that Barclay's ribs seemed to rattle.

"What is that?" he asked sharply.

Yasha rushed to the window and swept aside the lace curtains. "There's people running. I don't know what they're— There's a fire!"

Tadg and Barclay scrambled to the window. Figures darted through the darkness, and screams sounded from the streets. In the distance, a crimson fire engulfed a neighborhood close to the beach.

Ansley burst through the bedroom door. "Brutopods! Dozens of them!" She was so frazzled that she dropped the knitting needles in her hands.

"Are you serious?" Tadg asked.

"I'm afraid so. Caoimhe Byrnes just told me. She nearly broke down my door!"

"What are Brutopods?" asked Barclay.

"Just about the ugliest Beasts you've ever seen," Tadg answered. "Come on. If there are dozens of them, then we need to help."

"Help?" Ansley repeated, scooping up her half-knitted sock. "I think you three should stay put. Let the Guardians—" She was cut off by all three boys dashing past her down the steps. "Or just run *straight* into danger! Very levelheaded of you!"

They barreled out of the Planty Shanty, and the air reeked of smoke. Townsfolk clambered past, knocking into Barclay's shoulders and making him trip over Root and collide with Yasha. The scene reminded him of Knunx—only worse because it was night.

Not wanting to waste time, Barclay told the other boys, "We'll meet you up ahead. Come on, Root. Let's go."

Leaving Tadg and Yasha to chase after them, Barclay and Root took off. They ducked through Munsey's backstreets. It might've been less crowded there, but it was far harder to see. Barclay ran face-first into a pair of lady's knickers hanging on a clothesline, and when he ripped them off, a monster loomed at the end of the alley.

That was the only word for it—a monster. True to Tadg's description, it was the ugliest Beast Barclay had ever seen, and that included the Styerwurm in the Woods that had once swallowed Viola and Mitzi whole.

The Brutopod was some awful version of a crab or lobster, but fifty times as large—so large that one of its pincers could snap Barclay's entire midsection. And Barclay counted four of them. Its shell was red and spiky, and its eyes were milky white.

Barclay threw the underwear aside and scrambled back. The Beast advanced until it towered over him. Its claws and antennae thrashed.

Barclay had never used his Lore on a Beast so big before. But, desperately hoping for the best, he lifted his palm toward the Brutopod and thought, *Wind!*

A gust blasted from his hand down the alley, blowing sand and window shutters and laundry with it. The Brutopod squared its shoulders as it was shoved back, but then its feet caught on the cobblestones, and it held its ground.

Barclay looked behind him, wondering if he should flee and find a new route to the fire. But then someone screamed on the other side of the Brutopod.

"Help!" they called. They sounded like a child.

Barclay's heart pounded. Now was not the time to test out a new type of Lore. Not when he had yet to master simpler moves. Not when there was so much at stake. But someone was in trouble, so there was no time to second-guess himself. Returning Root to his Mark, Barclay turned and backed against one of the alley walls. Then he took a running start and blasted a gust of wind at the ground, propelling himself into the air. His chest landed on the rooftop, making him let out a loud "oof!" He grasped onto a pipe and held tight.

While he flailed his legs trying to hoist himself up, the Brutopod lunged forward. Its claws reached for Barclay's foot and closed with a loud *snap!* But Barclay had just managed to kick himself over the gutter.

He climbed to his feet and raced across the rooftop. Two more Brutopods stalked the street below. Like the first, they thrashed about, smashing all nearby windows and carts.

"Help!" shouted the voice again, and Barclay spotted a small boy cowering behind some trash barrels. Barclay jumped down off the roof, slowing his fall with a bit of wind. But his landing was far from smooth. As soon as he struck the ground, he tumbled into wooden fencing. The line of pickets came down with a crash.

Dizzy but unhurt, Barclay ran to the boy's side.

"Come on," Barclay told him. "I'll help you get out of here."

The boy nodded, and Barclay picked him up in his arms. He wasn't big for his age, but neither was Barclay, and the extra weight slowed him down as he ran. But he was still faster than the Brutopods. He dashed out of their reach and carried the kid several blocks east, where a crowd of Munseyers was evacuating.

No sooner did Barclay hand the boy off to a grown-up than a familiar golden hexagon shone beside him. Hasu appeared, Bitti buzzing beside her face.

"Come with us!" she said, seizing Barclay's hand.

There was another flash of golden light—this time so bright that Barclay had to squeeze his eyes shut. When he reopened them, they were on a different street, one lined with ash trees. Shazi and Viola stood back-to-back in a face-off with two Brutopods.

Viola aimed a red beam of light at the larger one, making steam waft off its shell with a hiss. The Brutopod retreated, writhing in pain.

Shazi took on the smaller one, wielding not one but *two* swords. They clattered against the Brutopod's sturdy pincers.

"Where's Cecily?" Hasu called.

"I don't know!" Shazi shouted back, huffing between breaths. "Oudie just took off, and she ran after him!"

"You help Viola," Hasu commanded Barclay, and then she raced to Shazi's side. For someone who claimed she was always nervous, Hasu kept a level head in battle.

Barclay did as ordered and sprinted to Viola's side.

"Oh good! You're here," Viola said. "Listen. You need to blow the Brutopod onto its back—then it won't be able to get up. Can you do that?"

"I—I think so. Just stand back."

He aimed at the thrashing Brutopod and summoned the strongest wind he could muster. But he missed.

"Look out!" Viola called. She slammed into Barclay, tackling him just before a heap of broken branches rained down where he'd stood. The tree Barclay's Lore had struck groaned, then it snapped and toppled onto the fishing shed beneath it. The building collapsed with a loud crash.

"I'm sorry," Barclay groaned. He hadn't had problems aiming his Lore since they'd been in the Woods. Which meant he wasn't just falling behind the others. He was growing worse. "I don't—"

He didn't have time to finish his sentence. The Brutopod dashed toward them, and—without pausing to think—Barclay aimed a second blast of wind. This one met its mark. The gale swept the Brutopod right off its feet, and it landed with a thunk on its back. Its legs flailed helplessly in the air.

Behind them, Shazi expertly parried the other Brutopod's blows. Then, hollering, she drove her boot down onto the center of its forehead. The Brutopod stumbled back into Hasu's portal, and it vanished.

"Where did you send it?" Viola asked, standing up and panting for breath.

Hasu shrugged. "The middle of the Sea."

Shazi gave her a light punch in the shoulder. "That was great. Now let's go find Cecily."

The four of them took off down the street toward the shore. Dozens of Brutopods rampaged across the beach, and even more emerged from the waves. Much of the water was frothy with white foam—the weeping tide.

"Is Lochmordra coming?" Barclay asked, terrified.

"No," Shazi answered. "The sailors we passed said he attacked a ship. This weeping tide is just left over."

"I don't like this," Hasu said. "I don't see Cecily any-where."

Suddenly, a dark shadow swept overhead, and Shazi and Viola skidded to a halt.

Barclay whipped around. "What are you doing? We need to—"

"I—I can't move!" Viola stuttered. She scrunched up her face and wiggled her fingers, but other than that, she didn't budge. Shazi let out a shout of frustration. She was frozen too.

Meanwhile, several Brutopods on the beach charged toward them.

"Look!" Hasu pointed behind Viola and Shazi, but Barclay didn't see anything. "Look at their shadows! It's Oudie!"

Barclay examined Viola's and Shazi's shadows, which were stretched out skinny and taut. At their ends, a different, twisted shadow grasped them and held them tight. Oudie flew overhead. His wings flapped strangely, like he was flailing about more than flying.

"Why would Oudie attack us?" Viola asked.

"I think he has Cecily, too," Hasu said, pointing at a third shadow—this one without any person attached to it. "She can fade into darkness, but she must be stuck like that."

"Um, guys?" Shazi said anxiously. "The Brutopods—"

"Light, Mitzi!" Viola shouted, and Mitzi appeared on her shoulder. Opening her mouth wide, Mitzi shot a beam of light on the cobblestones, making Viola's and Shazi's shadows snap back to their normal size . . . and making Oudie's shadowy talon wrench away.

Finally free, Shazi lifted her swords just in time as a pincer smashed down over her head.

Shazi grinned at Viola. "Thanks."

Viola tripped, clearly caught off guard from Shazi acting

like her friend again. Then Viola smiled back. "Of course."

Barclay summoned Root once more, and the two braced themselves in front of the second and third Brutopods. Barclay raised both arms out, and two strong winds tore across the beach. The Brutopods teetered over onto their backs.

When he turned around, Viola and Mitzi had freed Cecily, who gradually returned to solid form. She shouted at her Beast, "Oudie! Oudie, what's wrong?"

Oudie only cawed in response. His shadow writhed this way and that.

Shazi elbowed Barclay in the side. She'd summoned Saif beside her, who waved his sharp tail like a sword of his own. "Let's go take out the other Brutopods before they can get to town."

Barclay hesitated. It should've been Viola or Hasu backing her up, not him. But the two other girls were distracted fending off Oudie's shadow, and Shazi had already sprinted headfirst into danger. So, stomach in knots, Barclay followed after her.

His Lore was no more predictable than before. Each gust he called flew in a new direction—up to the sky, out to the ocean, down to the sand. But Barclay never had a moment to pause and focus. The Brutopods stampeded at him one after the other, and Barclay sent out countless bursts of wind, hoping at least a few would hit their marks.

"Ahh!" Shazi shrieked. One of Barclay's gusts had swept her off her feet and flipped her over like an omelet.

"Sorry!" Barclay called, mortified.

"Ugh! Never mind that—what matters is that every time we take down a Brutopod, more just crawl out of the water."

"It's like what happened in Knunx with the Sleábeaks. Except the Brutopods are a lot nastier."

Suddenly a gale of wind struck Barclay from the right, so strong that he was thrown onto the ground. He groaned and lifted his head, searching for the perpetrator. But Shazi looked just as flabbergasted as he did.

"What are you doing?" she asked, struggling to her feet as another Brutopod shuffled near. "Get up! Get up!"

Before Barclay could, another wind blew, making sand pelt his skin. His eyes watered as he spotted Root advancing toward him.

Root looked strange—his head bent low, his black fangs bared. As though preparing to attack.

"Root?" Barclay said hoarsely.

Root didn't seem to have heard. He shook his head about, growling. His eyes had gone an unnatural white.

Then Root pounced.

At *him*.

Before Root's fangs could sink into Barclay's arm, Barclay returned Root to his Mark. Root instantly disappeared, but even so, his golden Mark thrashed across Barclay's shoulder. Like a monster locked inside a cage.

"Hey, I could use some help— Saif?" Shazi said a few yards away. "Saif, what are you doing?!"

Saif whipped toward Shazi, his spearlike tail pointed straight at his Keeper.

Before Saif could impale her, Barclay aimed a gust of wind at him, and thankfully, he didn't miss. Saif skidded back across the beach.

"What are you doing?" Shazi demanded. "He's my Beast! You can't—"

"Look at him! Look at his eyes! Something is wrong with him—just like with Root and Oudie."

"But what's wrong with—"

"I don't know. But send him back to his Mark. *Now*."

Just as Saif prepared to charge at them a second time, he vanished.

Shazi hugged her arms to herself. "I've never seen him like that before. Is . . . is he going to be all right?"

"Barclay! Shazi!" Viola screamed from across the beach. She pointed at the water. "Look out!"

Barclay swiveled around. A fresh wave of Brutopods emerged from the ocean, in between the thin, frothy puddles of the weeping tide. Barclay froze. He would do whatever it took to save Munsey, but he and the others were already tired. How much longer could they fight before one of them got hurt?

Click click click click click.

"Um, Barclay," Shazi choked out.

"I'm sort of busy here." Barclay readied his stance for battle.

Click click click click click.

"Barclay!" Shazi snapped.

Barclay turned—and looked up at the giant, terrifying Beast in front of him, a snake that stretched high in the air, its body made only of its skeleton. Its bones shifted as it moved. Its vertebrae pointed outward like blades, and its jaw opened wider than its whole skull. Even though its eyes were only empty sockets, it bore down on them, preparing to strike.

"Goath," Barclay said, horrified.

"I don't—I don't—" Shazi stammered. "I don't think we can fight one of Runa's Beasts."

Barclay agreed with her. But when Shazi yanked his arms to run, for the first time, his legs were frozen stiff. If all the Beasts of Munsey had gone feral, then the Lore Keepers wouldn't stand a chance.

Goath whipped his tail out, ready to chop Barclay and Shazi into mincemeat. Barclay squeezed his eyes shut. He wished more than anything that he had Root beside him.

"Get back!" a voice shouted. Then a rumble erupted from the ground, and the air around them became unbearably hot. Shazi wrenched Barclay back—so hard the two of them stumbled and splashed into the edge of the water. Barclay's eyes shot open in pain as the foamy remnants of the weeping tide seared his palms.

In front of them, a circle of oozing lava surrounded Goath, trapping him.

Barclay and Shazi bolted out of the water, both furiously wiping their hands on their clothes. Every touch burned.

"Are you all right?" Cyril asked, rushing to their sides. Shazi had fallen, and he knelt beside her and seized her by both shoulders. Frantically he studied her and Barclay's bloody, blistery palms. The weeping tide had eaten away patches of their skin. Barclay could still move all his fingers, but the pain hurt so much that his stomach heaved. "Any other injuries? How many fingers am I holding up?"

"I'm fine," Shazi swore, even though she was wincing.

"Thank goodness. Neither of your wounds look severe, but we'd better have Edwyn heal you up." Finished fussing, Cyril stood and turned to Goath, who thrashed about angrily in his lava prison. "This is what happens when you let your Beasts run wild. Absolutely reprehensible. I don't like to think about what would've happened to you all had I not gotten here in time."

Barclay, who rarely took Cyril's side, had to agree with him there. Without him, he and Shazi would've both been goners.

"Behind you!" Hasu called.

Cyril glanced over his shoulder at the fresh army of Brutopods advancing up the shoreline. With an impatient flick of his wrist, a line of lava barged through the shallows, forming a massive wall between the ocean and beach. Barclay's jaw dropped as he looked down the coast on either side, where the barricade stretched the size of three city blocks.

"It was very good of you all to help," Cyril told them. "But I'm going to take you to the Guild House now. The Guardians will handle the rest."

Normally, Barclay wouldn't want to be left out of Guardian Keepers duties, but he was too shaken and hurt to argue.

"What's wrong with all the Beasts?" Shazi asked.

"They're in a frenzy. It's very similar to the reports we've gotten from the other islands," Cyril said. "Their eyes go white, and then they . . ."

Cyril trailed off, studying the suds of the weeping tide that lingered on the sand.

"White," he repeated. "Of course. The weeping tide is the answer. When Beasts near it, they go into some sort of violent state. It explains Midsummer and Midwinter. It even explains all these attacks. With the weeping tide blooming more and more, any Beasts who come into contact with it become affected."

Cyril might've been rambling to himself, but his words made sense. And for the first time, Barclay felt a flare of respect for the Horn of Dawn. He still thought he was pompous, and he didn't forgive him for how he'd treated Viola. But Cyril had earned his reputation as much as Runa had.

Shazi's eyes widened. "Are the effects permanent?"

"I don't think so." Cyril placed protective hands on both

their shoulders. "Come on—we need to get you all back to the Guild House."

The next three hours passed in a blur. Thanks to Edwyn's healing Lore, Barclay slept for most of them, curled up on the floor with a blanket draped over his shoulders and large strips of silver Gunkwort crisscrossing his palms. Until a hand on his arm shook him awake.

"Barclay," Runa hissed. "Barclay, wake up."

Barclay blinked open bleary eyes. Despite the late hour, the Guild House boomed with the ruckus of Lore Keepers shouting at one another.

"What time is it?" he asked. "Are all the Brutopods gone?"

"It's two in the morning, and yes."

"What about Goath? Is he all right?"

"Goath is fine." Runa rolled up her right sleeve, where Goath's Mark wiggled over her skin. "I'm glad you're all safe, and you can sleep more tonight. But I thought you'd want to hear this—Orla is about to make an announcement."

Barclay straightened and looked up. Orla stood at the top of the spiral staircase. Her shawl was wrapped tightly around her bony shoulders. She looked exceptionally tired.

Beside him, Shazi snored loudly, and he elbowed her to wake up just as Orla called, "Quiet, all of you! I have a few words I'd like to say."

The commotion in the room died down as everyone stared up at the High Keeper.

"First, I want to thank you all for your show of strength and bravery tonight. It's thanks to you that there were no fatalities. A special thanks goes to Tadg Murdock and Yasha Robinovich, whose combined effort extinguished the fires that had spread across Herring Street."

A patter of applause swept through the Guild House. Barclay caught a glimpse of Tadg and Yasha, who grinned at each other near the foot of the stairs. Their clothes and faces were smeared with soot, but neither of them looked hurt.

"Next, I have some grave news," Orla continued. "As you can tell, there was a great deal of destruction tonight. Much of it was caused by the Brutopods, and some of it was from other sources. . . ."

Orla's gaze roamed over the countless heads in the room until it rested firmly on Barclay. Barclay sucked in a breath. He remembered the fence he'd broken, the shed that had collapsed. Did the High Keeper believe he'd made the destruction worse?

A moment later, she looked away. Maybe he'd only imagined it.

"But now, thanks to Cyril Harlow's clever deduction, we have reason to believe it was the weeping tide that was responsible for the violent state of the Brutopods and some of our own Beasts. And so this is my decree. Until we have determined why the weeping tide is flourishing, I'm afraid we cannot put our lives at risks. Beasts will only be permitted to leave their Marks when in your personal living quarters, except for a case of extreme circumstances." Orla cast a sad glance to Murph's usual spot by the fireplace, now empty. "We'll have to rely on ourselves to put a stop to all this madness."

THIRTEEN

Without the chirping, squawking, growling, chittering, and roaring of Beasts, the Guild House had been unusually somber in the two weeks since Orla's decree. The bread served for breakfast always tasted a little stale, and the milk seemed extra sour.

In the hall's corner, one Guardian sang a mournful shanty while another accompanied him on the fiddle.

When I came to the Sea, the land of storm,
I found a letter, and the message warned
That my bones would sleep in the ocean's bed
Unless I turned back to the old life I'd led.
But when I came to the Sea, the land of storm,
I left behind where I was born,

So I kissed the earth one final time.
Then I sailed in search of that grave of mine.

The only cheerful person in the hall was Cecily. She brandished a handful of champion cards with a mischievous glimmer in her eyes. "You strike a hard bargain. I respect that. But how about this? I'll trade you my Aoife Kearney for your Wei Meng."

"Not a chance," said Shazi. "My Meng card is special edition. See? Look at the stamp—"

"Can you two do that somewhere else?" Tadg snapped. The other five apprentices sat clustered together at the opposite end of the table, where Viola had spread out her notebook and sketches. "Now," Tadg said, turning back to Viola, "what were you saying?"

Viola cleared her throat. "We read every book we could find about Lochmordra in the library. Whatever items you need to make his snare, they're a mystery."

"Except the Polypop bells and Fire Coral," Tadg reminded her. "Dad was sure about those."

"Right, but even so, it's impossible to bond with Lochmordra without all six."

At that moment, Toadles leapt from the table onto Tadg's shoulder, his sticky, webby feet slapping down with a wet *splat*. But Tadg was so lost in thought he didn't seem to notice.

"What's wrong?" Hasu asked him. "This is good, isn't

it? This means that whatever is causing the weeping tide to bloom more often, it's not a Lore Keeper behind it."

"We can't know that for sure," Tadg said.

Viola gathered up all of her papers, sighing. "I know it would be easier to blame all this on someone, but I don't think there *is* someone this time. In the Woods, Soren—"

Tadg stood up with a jolt, making all the plates and glasses on the breakfast table rattle. "I don't want to talk about him," he grunted.

Then he stormed off.

Viola was probably right, but for once, Barclay agreed with Tadg. Ever since he and Root had spotted that monstrous Beast outside of Munsey, he'd had a dreadful feeling that he couldn't shake. But because of Orla's decree, Barclay hadn't gone running with Root in a long time. Maybe he was just anxious without his favorite way to clear his head.

"Good riddance," Viola muttered. "Why does Tadg have to be so grumpy all the time?"

"Because he's a bully," said Barclay.

"Maybe he misses Mar-Mar," Hasu said. "He can't exactly summon Mar-Mar inside, can he? I already miss Bitti. . . ." She sniffled and scratched the tip of her nose, where Bitti usually napped.

Suddenly Viola yelped. Orla stood behind her, patting Viola on the shoulder. Barclay shrunk down in his seat, as he did whenever Orla was around lately.

"Go easy on the Murdock boy," Orla told them. "It's hard for him, being home. Conley is still very missed."

The table fell silent, and Barclay felt a pinch of guilt for what he'd said about Tadg. Missing runs with Root was nothing in comparison to missing a father.

"How are your hands, Shazi? Barclay?" Orla asked.

Barclay stiffened beneath Orla's scrutiny. He'd told himself that he'd imagined the way she'd singled him out the night the Brutopods attacked, as though he was to blame for much of the destruction in Munsey. But there was still something especially piercing in her stare.

"They're better," Shazi said, holding up her palms. Thanks to a combination of Gunkwort and Edwyn's healing Lore, neither she nor Barclay had any scars.

Orla smiled, but not so wide as usual. "That's good to hear." And then, slowly, she made her way to her rocking chair. Even in a room crammed full of Guardians, she looked lonely without Murph beside her, warming himself in front of the fire.

"I'd like you to spar with one another," Runa announced at the start of their next lesson. "Now that you're all patched up from the incident with the Brutopods, it's time to identify your weaknesses and improve them. I have a feeling that will be far from the last time you'll see combat while at the Sea."

Barclay's mood lifted. He wasn't hopeless at sparring.

He'd done a lot of it during the apprenticeship Exhibition in the Woods, and even after all this time, he and Tadg had never had their proper match.

"Viola, you can spar with Cecily. I think you'll give each other a challenge," Runa said. "Shazi, you'll fight Tadg, since your metal will be vulnerable to his electricity. Please don't kill one another, though. And Yasha, you'll be with Hasu."

"What about me?" Barclay asked.

"You're going to keep working on the same assignment that I gave you after we left Knunx. It's important that you master it."

Feeling the burn of the others' eyes on him, Barclay flushed from his ears to his toes. "B-but . . ." He steadied his voice, not wanting to show that being singled out bothered him. "I can still spar fine. I fought the Brutopods, didn't I?"

"I know you can fight. But Orla feels that—"

"Orla?" Barclay's stomach twisted tighter than a fisherman's knot.

While the other apprentices exchanged nervous glances, Runa told them, "Off you all go. Barclay and I need a word together." Then the assigned pairs scattered across the beach and grass, and Runa led Barclay away. "Orla isn't important. What *is* important is—"

"She thinks I made a mess of things when the Brutopods attacked, doesn't she? Just like I did in Knunx."

Barclay *knew* it. He hadn't imagined it at all.

Runa sighed. "The Brutopods destroyed plenty without your help, and Cyril and I both told Orla that you did an impressive job helping to protect the other apprentices. A Brutopod makes a dangerous opponent for any Lore Keeper, and you students took on dozens of them. But Orla does have a point. Guardian Keepers need to be able to control their Lore. In the Woods, you were never asked to use your powers much in Sycomore itself. There was always space. But here, you need more precision. You don't want to accidentally hurt someone, do you?"

Barclay was so embarrassed and ashamed that he wanted to bury himself in the sand.

"Of course not," he said. "But—"

"That assignment might seem silly to you, but it really is a great place to start. I know you can handle it with a bit more practice—"

"I've been practicing nonstop ever since we left Knunx, and I still can't get it!" Barclay couldn't help it—his voice rose. And it kept rising, because he was tired of pushing himself and *still* falling behind the others. Tired of being the odd one out. "Everyone else already mastered their assignments ages ago. They're getting stronger, and I'm just . . . I'm just stuck! And I never *will* get stronger. Because I'm too much of an Elsie to ever be a Lore Keeper."

Runa's expression changed. Barclay had never seen

Runa scared before—he didn't think the Fang of Dusk *could* be scared—but that was how she looked now. Her face went ashen. Her brows knitted tightly together. And Barclay could think of no good reason why.

"What does your being an Elsie have to do with it?" Runa asked him slowly.

Barclay would've thought that was obvious. "Because everyone else can control their Lore, and I can't. It probably shouldn't even be a surprise—I grew up terrified of Beasts. And maybe I'll never be able to change that. Some part of me will always be an Elsie, just like everyone believes."

For several moments, Runa didn't speak. Barclay's heart hammered, and he braced himself for the words he'd been expecting to hear ever since Knunx. That Barclay didn't belong as one of her apprentices.

Finally, Runa said, "Barclay, I want you to listen to me carefully." She knelt in front of him so that they were closer to eye level. And Runa's eyes looked very, very sad. "You are going to become an incredible Guardian one day. Do you know why?"

Barclay was too shocked to respond, so he only shook his head.

"Because you have perspective that most of us don't, myself included. There is a lot of misunderstanding between the Elsewheres and the Wilderlands. But because of where you come from, you're able to see both sides. That might mean you have more to learn about the ways of Lore

Keepers than those of us who grew up with Beasts, but you already have knowledge that the other apprentices will probably never have. And that is a great strength."

Runa placed her hand on his shoulder and squeezed.

"I know that your home treated you unfairly—and Knunx wasn't much better. But I think it's important you keep in mind that not all the Elsewheres are the same, just like not all the Wilderlands are the same. The world isn't only split into one thing or the other. And you don't need to be either."

Barclay had never considered that being an Elsie would make him a stronger Lore Keeper, or that there was anything about the world that he could possibly know better than his friends or Runa.

"Maybe . . . ," Barclay said, still unsure. "But that doesn't explain why I can't control my Lore."

"No, it doesn't," Runa agreed. "But if it helps, one of the most powerful Lore Keepers I ever met was an Elsie."

"Really?" Barclay asked eagerly. "Who?"

"Oh, it was a long time ago." Runa scooped a shell off the sand and stood up. "Here. Let me see you try your assignment again."

Barclay broke out in a cold sweat as she dropped the shell into his palm. He stole a glance at the others sparring down the beach. Viola and Cecily looked equally matched, each girl's light or shadow devouring the other's. Yasha seemed nervous to aim any fire Lore at Hasu, even if she kept popping in and out of portals.

The only thing that made Barclay smile was spotting Tadg on the ground, the tip of Shazi's training sword pointed at his chest.

The world isn't only split into one thing or the other, Barclay repeated Runa's words to himself. *And you don't need to be either.*

Despite every kind thing Runa had told him, it still made him nervous to have her watching. He didn't want to let her down.

So he tried every trick he could think of. He took a deep breath. He focused. And, like Yasha had suggested, Barclay thought of something that would calm his nerves. But this time, instead of straining to remember the history from his textbook, he reached for something else.

Button, he thought. *Mourningtide Morel. Chaga. Bella.*

His mind ventured into pleasant memories, like the earthy smells of the mushroom caves and the thunderous sounds of Master Pilzmann's snores. Immediately he felt more at ease than he had in weeks. It didn't matter where he'd come from or why he'd left. Wherever he traveled, home was the place beneath his feet.

He took a deep breath, focused hard on the shell, and thought, *Wind!*

The shell lifted off his palm and soared into the air. For three seconds, then five seconds, then eight, it hovered in front of Barclay's eyes. Then the wind grew stronger, forcing the shell higher and higher—until it finally slipped away and plunked onto the sand.

It might not have been perfect, but it was far better than anything Barclay had managed yet.

"You nearly have it," Runa told him.

Barclay beamed. He nearly did.

But before Runa could leave to instruct the other apprentices, he said, "Wait! I wanted to ask you . . . That book you gave me to read . . . why did Tadg say it was all, um, make-believe?" He didn't want to accidentally insult Runa by calling the book a load of phooey.

"Book?" Runa repeated. "What book?"

"*The Nine Most Crucial Events of Lore Keeper History* by Grusha Dudnik."

Runa's expression changed to a *second* one Barclay had never seen on her before—embarrassment. Her ears flushed cherry pink, and she chuckled awkwardly.

"Well, isn't that a mix-up? Grusha is a distant—*very* distant—cousin of mine, who has a lot of silly ideas about Lore and Beasts. I bought a copy of her book because I was trying to be nice. I must've given it to you by mistake. You haven't read much of it, have you?"

Barclay had nearly memorized the entire thing. "Nope," he squeaked.

"Good. As if you need to waste time studying a plague that only affected geese."

"Should I study something else, then?" He still had a

long way to go to catch up to the other apprentices.

Runa smiled. "I think you've more than earned yourself a break, don't you?"

Barclay skipped dinner that evening. He wasn't hungry, and even after one of the best lessons he'd had in a long time, he was still too ashamed to face Orla, who clearly thought him more trouble than he was worth.

He rummaged through the bottom of his satchel and pulled out the conch shell he'd been given in Knunx. He hadn't looked at it in a long time, because Tadg or Yasha was normally in the room with him. And because looking at it embarrassed him. It reminded him of the useless charm *he'd* once carried.

But now all he felt was hope.

Barclay summoned Root from his Mark. Root stretched his back, no doubt bored of being cooped up for hours.

"I'm going to be a great Guardian one day," Barclay whispered to Root. The words were too bold to speak very loud. He didn't want to jinx them.

Root didn't seem worried about jinxes, though. He barked in agreement.

Barclay snuggled next to Root in bed and read, not a silly textbook, but an adventure story he'd borrowed from the library. It was exactly as a good book should be, an old, dusty tome with wrinkled pages and grains of sand stuck in its spine. In the opening chapter, a brave heroine named Maedigan—much like their cove—struck out on a quest to slay Lochmordra after he'd swallowed her father's ship.

Barclay happily tumbled into the adventure.

Until the smell of smoke wafted beneath the crack of the attic door.

"Ansley?" he called nervously. When no one responded, he set his book on the nightstand, and he and Root crept downstairs.

The Planty Shanty was eerily dark—all the shutters had been closed. The only light came from the red flames of the Fire Coral, which was out of its tank and burning in the center of the room. Ansley hunched over it, her back to him.

Now Barclay was twice as nervous.

"Ansley?" he said again. Beside him, Root's ears and tail were perked high on alert.

Ansley whipped around. She wore soot-stained goggles over her eyes and oven mitts on both hands. Coughing, she waved the smoke away from her face. "Barclay? I thought you were at the Guild House."

"I stayed behind. What are you doing?" By the look of it, burning her shop down.

"Oh, just some research. Orla asked me if I could find some sort of medicine to prevent Beasts from being affected by the weeping tide. I haven't found it yet, but I will. The weeping tide is a Trite class Beast, which is exactly the expertise of Apothecaries. And all Apothecaries know that if one sort of Lore does one thing, there's always another Lore to counteract it."

"But why would the Fire Coral make an antidote?" Barclay asked. "I thought the weeping tide liked the—"

Heat.

Of course. Why hadn't he pieced it together before?

"The vents have been making the Sea warmer." Barclay's words spilled out in a rush. "That's why the weeping tide keeps blooming. It likes the heat!"

Ansley did not look as surprised by this news as he'd expected. Instead she stroked an oven mitt over the Fire Coral's grooves. "Yes, yes. I've guessed as much about the weeping tide for a long time now. But as for the antidote, I think Fire Coral is worth the study. It's a rare, prized find after all. It's even one of the ingredients in Lochmordra's snare."

Barclay froze. "You know Lochmordra's bonding items?"

"Not all of them, but I have my suspicions. You get a feel for these things as an Apothecary. In fact, I wouldn't be surprised if you could purchase four or five of the items in this shop."

Barclay's gaze anxiously sped around the Planty Shanty. The seaweed looked far more frightening in the dark, colorless and fleshy, much of it in a dead man's float on the surface of its tanks. His eyes paused on the bells hanging on the front door. He had always thought they dangled on curly ribbons, but now that he examined them closer, he realized the ribbons were actually tentacles.

Polypop bells—the only other bonding item that Conley Murdock had been sure of.

The same dread that had kept Barclay company these past few weeks grew stronger all at once, like a rope about to snap.

"But wouldn't selling all those items make it easy for someone to bond with Lochmordra?" he choked.

Ansley slid her goggles back into place, so Barclay couldn't see her eyes. But her mouth slanted into a smile. "Bond with Lochmordra? No one has managed to bond with a Legendary Beast in hundreds of years."

Leaving Ansley to her research, Barclay and Root slinked upstairs and paced around the cramped attic. He'd gotten so nervous, he was sweating. He wrenched open the window. Outside, the sunset splashed the Sea a hundred marvelous shades of color. But when Barclay closed his eyes, he only saw weeping-tide white.

FOURTEEN

I don't get it," Hasu whispered to the other apprentices. "So the earthquakes are making the vents stronger, and the vents are making the Sea warmer, and that's making the weeping tide bloom? That sounds really complicated."

Across the deck, Edwyn shouted, "Barclay, let out those topsails, will you? No—no, the other rope! That one there!"

Barclay raced to the rope and yanked at its tangle of knots.

"And how is it looking, Navigator? That's the Isle of Trowe in the distance, so we must be getting close."

"We're not there yet!" Cecily called, crouched upon the skinny bowsprit like a seagull.

Because the weeks without their Beasts had left everyone cranky, Edwyn had gotten permission to borrow one of the Guild's vessels for today's lesson. Barclay wouldn't have thought Edwyn much of a sailor, as Ulick, the only sailor he knew, was so big and burly, and Edwyn always looked so tired and weary. But from the way he dished out orders, he clearly knew his way around a ship.

At last, the knots unraveled, and one of the square sails above Barclay rolled free. He ducked back to the bow, where the other apprentices huddled.

"That means whoever is trying to bond with Lochmordra *must* be causing the earthquakes," Tadg said firmly.

Viola groaned. "We've been over this. No one is trying to bond with Lochmordra."

"Besides," Shazi added, "there's no way any Lore Keeper is powerful enough to cause earthquakes all the way down on the ocean floor. Even if the Grand Keeper had stone Lore, I don't think he'd be that powerful."

"I agree," Yasha said tightly. "It's just not possible."

"I still don't think we should rule it out," Barclay said. "But it's all the more reason we need to find the Isle of Roane. So the Guardians can protect it—"

"I see it! I see it!" Cecily shouted, and the apprentices broke out of their huddle to peer over the starboard rail.

Ahead of them was a massive circle of clear water, crystal light in comparison to the murky depths of the Sea. Even from a distance, Barclay could spot bright colors below the surface: magentas, oranges, silvers, and greens. Excited, he helped Edwyn lower the rowboat while Yasha and Hasu furled the sails and dropped the anchor. Then everyone hauled their bags of spare clothes over their shoulders, and Shazi took off her prosthetic.

"This type of reef is called an atoll," Edwyn explained. "A long time ago, this was a small island, but it gradually sank back into the sea. What you're seeing here is the island's tip-top—probably the mouth of a volcano, from its round shape—and you can see it's made a sunken sort of pool. Now it's home to thousands of different animal and Beast species."

The apprentices nodded eagerly. This was far more interesting than Cyril's dull lessons or Runa's exhausting training sessions.

"Can anyone tell me what makes this reef special?" Edwyn asked.

"It has Beasts in it?" Hasu guessed.

Edwyn laughed. "Well, yes. There are reefs in other oceans, but this is the only one in a Wilderland. But what *else* is different about those versus this one?"

Viola's hand shot into the air.

"Yes, Viola—you know you don't have to raise your hand with me," Edwyn told her.

"Coral reefs prefer warm climates with lots of sun, and, well . . ." Viola looked up at the overcast sky. "The Sea has a colder climate and is usually cloudy."

"That's exactly right. The temperatures of this reef are the coldest of any reef in the world. It survives due to rich mineral deposits in the water from the Beasts. But enough of this boring Scholar stuff. Let's take a closer look, shall we?"

They hoisted their bags into the rowboat and—cramming together—paddled out to the atoll. Barclay gasped once they crossed over to the clear water. Beneath the boat darted hundreds of fish. Big fish with diamond-shimmery scales. Little fish with coiled tails. Round fish puffed out like balloons. Flat fish flipping through the water like golden coins. They all roamed amid the forest of coral and silver Gunkwort, a whole tiny world underneath the water.

Edwyn rummaged through all the bags he carried, each stuffed full of tools and gadgets. He had to yank out a bottle of Dungwasp repellent, a grappling hook, a jar of plumberry jam, a set of strange rocks that stuck together like magnets, a dagger shaped from a Jawbask tooth, and a pair of fuzzy socks—all before he *finally* found what he was looking for: Polypop masks. He handed one to each of them.

"Now," he said, "your assignment today is to find an Oystix, which is a type of mollusk Beast that lives within the reef. Be careful if you try to open them. Almost all Oystixes secrete a goo that explodes when it makes contact with air. My healing Lore is good, but it's not so good that I can reattach fingers."

"Ooh—do they have pearls?" Hasu asked.

"Indeed! Occasionally, instead of exploding goo, an Oystix will hold a pearl inside, which is valued at six hundred kritters!"

Cecily bounced with excitement beside Barclay, ready for the hunt. "Do we get to keep the Oystix pearl if we find one?"

"Of course," Edwyn told them. "And . . . three . . . two . . . begin!"

Cecily, Shazi, Viola, and Yasha all dove into the water, making the rowboat rock so much that Barclay's satchel went spilling overboard. He watched in dismay as his pouch of kritters, spare set of dry clothes, and his conch shell from Knunx went sinking amid the coral.

Tadg snorted and swam off. Edwyn and Hasu, however, stayed behind to help him collect his belongings.

Barclay tied on the Polypop mask and dove down. Thankfully, the atoll wasn't very deep, so none of the items sank far. Hasu dug up his kritter pouch from the sand, and Edwyn played tug of war with an anemone for Barclay's spare trousers. After a minute of searching, Barclay scooped up the conch. It was tangled in a bush of shimmery, silver Gunkwort, and worse—a snail-like Beast had burrowed into it. Barclay shrieked—air bubbles flying from his mouth—as the snail peered up at him with its single beady, black eye. Its whole body, from head to tail, began to glow scarlet like a hot coal.

Barclay shook it out, letting it sink back into the seaweed.

Then he heard a strange whirling noise. *Woooosh*. He looked around, unsure where it had come from. Apart from Edwyn and Hasu, the others had all swum off in search of an Oystix.

Then he realized it was coming from the conch. Curious, he lifted it up to his ear.

Woooooooooooooosh.

It sounded strongly of rushing water, but in all the weeks since he'd been given the conch, he'd never noticed the noise before. When Barclay broke the surface and dumped the excess water from the shell, he held it to his ear again. Only, this time, it was silent.

Hasu watched him quizzically.

"Isn't that one of those charms the Elsies carry in Knunx?" she asked.

"One of the villagers gave it to me," Barclay told her. "But listen to this! It only makes noise if it's in the water."

He thrust it into her hands, giving Hasu no choice but to test it out herself. She dunked her head beneath the surface and held the conch to her ear. When she reemerged, Barclay expected her to look impressed. Instead, she shrugged and passed it back to him.

"It's probably just the shape of it," she said. "Making the water rush through it or something."

"But it's so loud. Don't you think that's a bit strange?"

"But . . . it's just an Elsie charm." Then Hasu's eyes widened. "I mean, I know you were an Elsie too, but . . . it's just a pretty shell, isn't it?"

Barclay sighed. "I guess you're right."

While Hasu swam off to join the others, Barclay laid the rest of his wet clothes out to dry on the rowboat and slipped his conch and kritters back into the soaked satchel.

"Ah yes, I remember Runa mentioning you're from the Elsewheres, Barclay," Edwyn said.

Barclay grimaced. "Is it really that strange for a Lore Keeper to be from the Elsewheres? I'm tired of everyone acting like—"

"I'm an Elsie too," Edwyn told him.

Barclay's mouth fell open in surprise. "You are?"

"Yes. From a kingdom far from any of the Wilderlands—maybe about four or five weeks from the Sea, and at least ten or twelve from the Woods. Growing up, I barely knew what Lore Keepers were. They were just a story."

"Then how did you end up becoming one?"

"I decided I wanted to be one. I've always been the sort to chase after stories. I traveled to the Woods and bonded with the first Beast I could find."

"You have a Woods Beast?" Barclay asked.

"Oh, well . . ." He looked sheepish. "Not anymore. It was a long time ago. But can this just be between us, Barclay? I think Munsey has enough drama with Runa and Cyril trying to work together. I wouldn't want to start any gossip too."

Barclay nodded with understanding. "Yeah, that's fine."

He still had a few questions, though. Edwyn was the only other Lore Keeper he'd met from the Elsewheres, and while they clearly had come from very different places, Barclay wanted to learn more about him. How did his family reaction to him becoming a Lore Keeper? Did he ever go back to his home? What did his home think about Lore Keepers?

But then Cecily whined farther down the atoll. "How did you find one? I've looked everywhere!"

Tadg brandished his Oystix proudly. "I've dived for them with my dad before."

"Yasha found one too," Shazi said.

Yasha held out his empty hands and shrugged. "Mine was just a regular mussel."

"Well, are you going to open it, Tadg?" Hasu asked eagerly.

"Not if he wants to keep his fingers," Viola said.

"Actually," Tadg told them, "there's a way to make sure they don't explode. My dad would just . . ."

Tadg lifted the Oystix toward his face and kissed it right on its crevice. Hasu slapped her hands to her mouth, scandalized. Barclay and Shazi both let out roars of laughter.

A long, phlegmy tongue slipped out between the cracks of the Oystix shell—like it was licking its lips. Then it popped open, revealing . . .

"Muskrats," Cecily cursed. "It's empty."

Barclay swam over, hoping to also get a closer look at the slimy Beast. But then his Mark throbbed suddenly, and Barclay spotted something out of the corner of his eye. He turned. A long line of milky white stretched across the horizon, slowly drawing near.

Horror seeped through him. "H-hey, is that . . ."

Tadg frowned and looked to where Barclay was pointing. Then he paled. "The weeping tide."

Far, far in the distance, a low shriek rumbled through the water.

Lochmordra was coming.

FIFTEEN

Everyone, get back to the boat," Edwyn ordered. The apprentices swam frantically for the rowboat, groaning and oofing as they piled inside. No sooner did Barclay tumble on board than the weeping tide crept into the atoll, devouring whatever fish or Beasts floated on the water's surface.

Tadg looked out to the Isle of Trowe in the distance. "We need to go there and help them. They'll be the next island hit."

"Definitely not," Edwyn said. "What *you'll* all be doing is staying out of danger—"

"That roar was still far. If Lochmordra is only just waking up, we still have twenty, maybe thirty minutes before he arrives," Tadg said, making chills creep down Barclay's spine. The roar had been so *loud*, but Lochmordra was that far away? "At least let us help evacuate."

"I'm going to get Cyril," Hasu said fiercely. Then a golden hexagon glowed behind her.

"Wait!" Shazi told her. "That's too far. You'll get—"

Hasu disappeared.

"Doesn't she pass out if she travels long distances?" Viola asked with concern.

"Someone needs to warn Orla and the Guardians so that they can protect Trowe," Tadg said. He turned back to Edwyn, fuming. "And I don't care about the danger. You all can run away if you want, but I'll swim there with Mar-Mar if I have to."

After exploring the ruins of Glannock, the thought of encountering Lochmordra terrified Barclay. But if Tadg, who had faced the Legendary Beast before, who had lost his father to him, could sound so brave, then Barclay could muster up some courage as well. He wouldn't let what happened to his parents in Dullshire happen to anyone in Trowe.

"We're training to be Guardians," Barclay pointed out. "How can we ever become them if we don't learn how to help people?"

The others nodded in agreement.

"Fine," Edwyn relented. "We'll help evacuate, but none of you are to go off on your own. It's important we stick together."

They rowed back to their ship and sailed for the Isle of Trowe. Unlike Munsey, Trowe overlooked a steep cliff, and their uphill climb to the town was exhausting. By the time they arrived, the weeping tide was already lapping at the rocks below, but few in Trowe had noticed it from so high up.

"Knock on everyone's doors," Edwyn instructed. "Warn them that Lochmordra is coming."

"Got it!" the apprentices said in unison, and they split into three groups—Shazi with Cecily, Barclay with Viola and Tadg, and Edwyn with Yasha. Barclay and his friends raced to the cottages along the cliffside, banging on their brightly painted doors and hollering, "You need to leave! Lochmordra is coming!"

At Barclay's first door, a young man answered, looking ashen. "He's here? In Trowe?"

Barclay nodded. "The weeping tide has already surrounded the island."

The man fled back into the house to pack his belongings, and Barclay felt a flutter of pride. He might've been afraid, but he was helping people. And that was what mattered.

But the older woman at the second house wasn't as happy to evacuate. She scowled down at them. "I've lived in this house for thirty years. If it's going down, then so am I."

"It's not a ship," Tadg growled at her.

But she wouldn't change her mind, even after Tadg threatened to shove her in a barrel and let her roll down the hill to the beach. And so, frustrated, they moved on to the next house, where a woman needed help carrying her elderly father from his bedroom.

As they worked, a clock ticked in Barclay's mind, trying to keep track of how much time had passed since they first heard the roar. Had it been twenty minutes? Thirty?

While he helped hoist the woman's father into a cot, the daylight above them began to fade. Not from clouds in the sky—but a cloudlike mist around them. It swathed Trowe in fog so thick that droplets of water dribbled down Barclay's cheeks.

"What's going on?" he asked Viola, who was merely a silhouette beside him. His teeth chattered from the cold. "Is this— Is Lochmordra—?"

"This is Orla," Tadg told them. "I bet she and the other Guardians have arrived."

"Do you think they can stop Lochmordra?" Viola asked.

"The Guardians on the other Isles couldn't before," Tadg said. "But Orla had never made it in time, and those islands hadn't had the Horn of Dawn and the Fang of Dusk. If anyone can kill Lochmordra, they can."

"*Kill* Lochmordra?" Barclay repeated, aghast. But before he could question Tadg further, Orla and Murph emerged from the fog. Orla moved her arms in slow, steady waves, and the mist swirled around her and her Beast.

"You're all here, are you?" Orla asked sharply, her eyes trained on Barclay. "Hasu brought word to the Guardians just in time, and now they're gathering on the cliffside. You should evacuate with the rest of Trowe. There are ships waiting there prepared to sail everyone to Munsey."

"But we might be able to help," Tadg said.

"I know you put out the fires in Munsey, but don't overestimate yourself. This is Lochmordra. You'll only get in the Guardians' way."

Even though Orla hadn't singled Barclay out, it felt like she had. His control over his Lore still might've not been perfect, but it was far better than before. He'd never have a chance to redeem himself if Orla sent them away just as danger neared.

"We faced Gravaldor!" Barclay protested. "We could—"

"Yes, Runa told me. Just like she told me that you'd argue with me about this. But I'm the High Keeper here, and as Guild apprentices, you must respect my orders. You may finish evacuating the town, but you *will* evacuate with them."

Viola sighed and tugged on both of their sleeves. "She's right. Let's go."

Tadg ripped his arm away and stomped off to the next door, as though he was going to do what Orla instructed, but he wanted to make it clear that he wasn't happy about it.

Thankfully, since Orla's mist had draped over the town like an eerie shroud, everyone in Trowe knew that something was wrong, and word had spread quickly of the weeping tide's arrival. Nearly all the next houses the apprentices visited were already abandoned, and the streets had grown crowded as people ushered their families, Beasts, and livestock down the roads.

EEEEEEEEIIK!

A raspy, bloodcurdling shriek tore through the air, so loud and piercing that Barclay swore the mist around them rattled. Screams rang out in the distance. Barclay knew that the fog was meant to protect Trowe, but he wished he could see more than a few feet in front of him. It felt like anything could be out there, stalking them. His Mark twitched painfully.

"Let's go!" Viola called, and Tadg paused outside the door he was about to knock on.

"What if there are still people here?" he asked.

"Then they heard *that*! And we need to get out of here like Orla told us."

"Barclay, you can run faster than us," Tadg said, which was the first time that Tadg had admitted Barclay could do anything better than him. "Hurry and see if there's anyone who needs help up ahead. Then we'll turn back."

"Wait! That's still not—" Viola started, but Barclay had already taken off.

He sprinted so fast through the mist that droplets ran down his skin, and his feet slipped on the wet cobblestones.

With the weeping tide surrounding Trowe in all directions, Barclay knew it was dangerous to summon Root. But the algae bloom was hundreds of feet below him, and if Orla had Murph at her side, then surely Barclay could have his Beast too.

"Root! Come out, I need you," he said, and Root appeared next to him. His ears immediately perked up in alarm, sensing the danger that approached.

"We need to run fast," Barclay told him while he climbed onto Root's back. He grabbed a fistful of Root's shaggy black fur in each hand and braced himself as Root shot off down the street.

The edges of Barclay's skin and Root's fur blurred, and the bright blue and green doors of the houses around them smeared in the corners of Barclay's vision. What was up and what was down seemed to spin as they raced across the outskirts of Trowe. They were running faster than the wind, so fast that they had become part of the wind themselves.

Even though Barclay and Root had done this night after night, it felt different this time. His breaths sucked in more mist than air. And with no one on the streets but them, Trowe felt as haunted as a ghost town.

Within seconds they reached the edge of Trowe on the opposite cliffside, then skidded to a halt. The mist hung so thick that Barclay couldn't even glimpse the ocean, and chills prickled across his neck. It was dreadfully, dreadfully silent.

Until a low growl rumbled behind them.

Barclay and Root spun around. "Can you see anything?" Barclay rasped.

Root didn't respond, but he lifted his head into the air, sniffing. His claws were out, and his fangs bared.

Glowing red eyes appeared through the mist, staring straight at them.

Barclay opened his mouth. *Run. RUN!* he wanted to tell Root. But not a sound came out.

The eyes advanced toward them—slowly, each step so heavy that the ground quaked beneath Barclay's feet. The closer they neared, the more Barclay made out a tall—no, a *giant*—figure, with brown fur and large, pointed tusks.

It was the same Beast he'd seen before. Only, this time, it saw Barclay, too.

Crash!

A crimson tentacle—wide as an alleyway—slammed down to Barclay's right, crushing a nearby cottage. The tentacle was covered in suction cups, and each of them stretched open and closed, open and closed, as though they were breathing. Red, frothy water dripped from them—the weeping tide mixed with blood.

Lochmordra.

Barclay found his voice. "Go! Go!" he shouted at Root. Root turned, and they fled away from the monster and Lochmordra. As they raced back through the misty streets, several more crashes thundered behind them.

When he reunited with Tadg and Viola, all three of them were shaking.

"Here, get on Root," Barclay told them, sliding off Root's

back so they could switch places. "We need to run to the beach. Now!"

Neither of them argued, and they took off down the hill to the evacuees. Crowds of people thronged the beach, shoving and hollering at one another so they could board the ships as fast as possible. Several vessels had already set sail to Munsey.

"Viola! Barclay! Tadg!" a voice called, and they spotted Shazi and Cecily waiting in line for the *Bewlah*. Barclay returned Root to his Mark; then the three apprentices stumbled to the girls' sides.

"Are you hurt?" Cecily asked.

"We're fine," Viola answered, though that wasn't entirely true. Tadg had frozen so still, he was barely breathing, and Barclay couldn't stop his hands from trembling.

"I saw Lochmordra," Barclay choked. "I saw two of his tentacles. He's *huge*. And there was another Beast. It was tall, with red eyes, and—"

"What do you mean, another Beast?" asked Viola.

"There was a second Beast out there. I was sure it was going to attack me. It had tusks, I think."

"Maybe it was one of the Guardians' Beasts," Shazi said.

Maybe, but Barclay didn't think so. But the fear he felt facing the tusked Beast was nothing compared to the terror of Lochmordra. How could Runa and Cyril possibly battle a creature so gigantic and powerful?

They boarded the *Bewlah* amid such a tight crowd that

the kids were crammed against the port-side rail, shoulder to shoulder. Once Ulick set sail, Barclay held his breath as the last clouds of Trowe's mist dissipated.

Up on the cliffs, mere specks from this distance, Runa and Cyril readied themselves side by side, the other Guardians flanked around them. The last time the two of them had entered a battle together, they'd been fighting each other.

Runa and Cyril each had a Beast next to them. Though it was hard to make them out, Barclay could tell both creatures stood on all fours. Cyril's was wide and black, with curved horns on either side of its head. Runa's was smaller, with white fur and dark stripes—Klava, Tadg had once called her. A saber-toothed tiger, from whom Runa must've gotten her nickname, the Fang of Dusk.

Below them, Lochmordra raged at the foot of the cliffside, squeezing his tentacles around the island as though he hoped to drag all of Trowe into the ocean. Barclay could only see the back of his head from the *Bewlah*, and he felt a lurch of panic over what would happen if Lochmordra turned and spotted the vessels sneaking past behind him. He'd heard stories that Lochmordra's mouth was large enough to swallow ships whole.

But Lochmordra focused only on Trowe. He screeched again, making all the passengers cover their ears with their hands. He let go of the island, and his tentacles flailed in every direction. He was in some kind of frenzy.

Each time he reached for the Keepers, a wall of Runa's ice

shielded the town. And the wood of the trees along the cliffs twisted around the tentacles like shackles. That Lore, Barclay guessed, was Cyril's. But it was no use. Over and over again, Lochmordra managed to break free of his bindings and strike the wall. It shattered, raining shards into the Sea.

As the *Bewlah* sailed far from Lochmordra's sight, all that was left of Trowe was a cloud of smoke in the distance, billowing into the sky.

SIXTEEN

For ten days the people who'd lived on the Isle of Trowe crowded the streets of Munsey, and the apprentices' lessons were put on hold while they helped the struggling refugees whose homes had been ruined. Barclay and Tadg had been assigned the grueling chore of seaweed fishing, while the others had been tasked with building makeshift houses or weaving new bed linens and clothes.

"This would go a whole lot faster if you actually worked instead of reading," Tadg said gruffly. Groaning, he leaned on the top of the stake and hoisted a hulk of seaweed out of the ocean, dripping briny water all over the open book on the rowboat's floor.

"Careful," Barclay said worriedly. "This book is older than Orla."

"Nothing's older than Orla. Now help me with this. I don't know why you brought a book along, anyway."

Barclay absentmindedly swirled his wooden stake around the water. Today was his twelfth birthday, and back in Dullshire it had been a tradition of his to spend the day at the library. He didn't need to celebrate alone this year, but even so, he hadn't told anyone about it. Happy occasions felt wrong when the Sea was amid a crisis. It wouldn't be long before Lochmordra destroyed the few habitable islands they had left.

So Barclay was carrying on his tradition, at least in a little way.

"Listen to this, though," Barclay said, squinting down at the pages. He was nearing the end of the adventure book. "'Though the night sky was at its brightest, Maedigan did not sail to Lochmordra's home—for then she almost certainly would never have reached it. Instead, she swam below the surface. She brought with her the most beautiful gifts of the Sea, each of them shining silver.'"

"Let me look at that." Tadg set down his stake and snatched the book. "'When Maedigan lay the gifts out before Lochmordra, he stilled, and the two looked at each other as equals. She took aim. Though she had never missed her mark before, her trident grazed his stomach and sank into his limbs. She left and never returned.'" Tadg scowled. "I don't like this version. In the one my dad told, Maedigan cut off one of Lochmordra's tentacles and kept it as a trophy."

"But Lochmordra's home must mean the Isle of Roane, right?" Barclay asked. "Why wouldn't Maedigan have reached it if she'd sailed?"

"I don't know, but we should ask the others."

"They'll probably say that it's just a story."

Tadg glanced grimly back to Munsey, where the make-shift tents of refugees dotted the streets. "It's the only hope the Sea has left."

After they finished their fishing for the day, Barclay and Tadg sent messages to the other apprentices via a postal Fwisht to meet at Maedigan Cove. But even an hour after sunset, no one else but the two boys had arrived.

"What are they all doing?" Tadg asked, jabbing a stick into their puny fire. "If I'd known we'd be waiting all night, I would've made you take a bath."

"Made *me* take a bath?" Barclay said.

"You smell like fish."

"So do you."

"Well, your stench bothers me more."

It figured that Barclay would have to spend his entire birthday with Tadg. He'd rather be in the library.

"Croak!" Toadles bellowed, appearing uninvited on Tadg's shoulder. The sound of him echoed throughout the cave.

Croak! Croak! Croak!

"You again?" Tadg said flatly. He'd gotten so used to Toa-dles's sudden arrivals that he no longer screamed each time they happened. "You're not supposed to be out, you know. What do you want?"

"*Croak!*" Toadles responded, which was followed once again by *Croak! Croak! Croak!*

For some reason, the echoes struck Barclay as very funny. He snorted. And, surprisingly, Tadg snorted too.

"*Croak!*" Tadg repeated, mimicking the Beast's throaty voice.

Croak! Croak! Croak!

The two boys glanced at each other. Then suddenly both of them were laughing. Barclay laughed so hard he got a stitch in his side, and tears streaked down Tadg's cheeks.

"You know what's funny?" Tadg said. "Dad would've loved Toadles. He would've thought he was a great mystery, with his all his powerful, secret Lore."

Tadg wiggled his fingers in front of Toadles's face like a magician. Toadles stared back at him blankly.

"I think Toadles is worried that we're onto him," Barclay said.

"Oh, we're onto him, all right. We know all about his evil plans." Tadg poked the stone in the center of Toadles's forehead. "Do you have any power at all? Or do you just keep it all hidden on purpose?"

Toadles didn't so much as blink.

"Did your dad know how to coax the Lore out of a Beast?" Barclay asked. Tadg's father was usually a risky subject, but Tadg had already brought him up himself. "He must've, since he studied so many of them."

"He probably would've said you had to befriend them. Feed them a special treat. Or tickle them in the right spot."

Tadg tried to tickle Toadles underneath his armpit.

Toadles croaked once more, loudly.

Croak! Croak! Croak!

The boys laughed again, and Barclay forgot all wishes to spend the day alone in the library.

Until two people chorused, "Happy birthday!"

Viola and Yasha strolled through the mouth of the cave. Viola beamed and held out a present. It was wrapped neatly in parchment, with a piece of fishing twine tied into a bow.

"I-is that for me?" Barclay asked. The only birthday presents he'd ever received had been from Master Pilzmann, and they usually were tools for mushroom foraging. Last year he'd given Barclay a sensible pair of gardening gloves.

"Of course it's for you," Viola said. "It's not every day you turn twelve."

"Why didn't you tell me it was your birthday?" Tadg snapped. "I would've . . . I don't know . . ."

Barclay's cheeks flushed from all the attention. His hands were sweaty as he tore open the present, revealing a stationery kit.

"Thank you," he said, even though he was confused. Who was he going to write letters to?

"Postal dragons can be very sneaky, you know," Viola told him. "I thought maybe you'd like to write to your old teacher in Dullshire. The one you always used to talk about."

There was no teasing in Viola's voice, and yet Barclay instantly felt self-conscious. He might've missed Dullshire at times, but missing his old life and rekindling it were two very different things. If he was caught, Dullshire would probably send him back a parcel full of dung or rotten fruit.

Eager to change the subject, Barclay asked, "Does this mean you're finally writing to your father?"

Viola made a pinched face. "No. It doesn't."

Even Yasha had a brought a gift—a whole pack of Fillitot's Beast Treats. They might've been more for Root than Barclay, but Barclay felt so guilty about keeping Root cooped up in his Mark again that he was grateful for a chance to cheer him up.

Barclay barely got the chance to thank Yasha before Tadg impatiently cleared his throat. "It's about time you both got here. We want to show you something important. It's about the Isle of Roane."

Barclay retrieved the adventure book from his satchel and flipped to the story about Maedigan and her golden trident.

"She didn't sail to it?" Viola asked, furrowing her brow as she read. "She went beneath the Sea instead?"

"Maybe the Isle of Roane sank a long time ago, like the island that made the coral reef," Yasha suggested.

"Great," Tadg muttered. "Then we'll never find it."

The four of them fell into a grim silence. Barclay imagined that they, like him, were replaying the terrible scene in Trowe. The homes reduced to nothing more than rubble.

The shrieks that cut like scythes through the mist. The way Lochmordra had thrashed, destroying everything in sight . . .

Barclay's thoughts screeched to a halt. Lochmordra had been frenzied and out of control, just like the Sleábeaks, the Brutopods, and the other Beasts who'd been exposed too long to the weeping tide.

"What if it's not Lochmordra who causes the weeping tide?" Barclay asked. "What if it's the weeping tide that's affecting Lochmordra?"

"I don't know," Yasha said uncertainly. "The weeping tide is only a Trite Beast, and Lochmordra is a Legendary one."

"No, I think Barclay could be right," Viola said excitedly. "The weeping tide always shows first, doesn't it? Maybe it's not from Lochmordra's Lore as he wakes up. Maybe it's what is *waking* him up."

"We have to tell the Guardians," Tadg breathed.

"But what about Shazi, Hasu, and Cecily? Where are they?" Barclay asked.

"We'll wait for them," Viola said. "They deserve to know first. They've done as much research as we have."

Which meant that for the next two hours, the four of them had nothing to do except celebrate. Yasha used his Lore to turn Barclay and Tadg's pitiful flames into a roaring bonfire, whose light danced all across the cave. Feeling risky, they each summoned their Beasts, letting Root, Motya, and Mitzi join Toadles and stretch out their legs and wings. At some point, they even sang happy birthday.

Throughout the festivities, Barclay's thoughts kept wandering back to the present that Viola had given him. Briefly he let himself imagine how it would feel to write to his old teacher. To tell him that he'd become a new kind of apprentice. That he and Root were now best friends. That he was on an adventure at a far corner of the world.

"What's wrong?" Yasha asked him. "You shouldn't look so serious on your birthday." If Yasha thought he looked serious, Barclay's expression must've truly been grave.

Barclay hesitated, unsure how to explain his feelings—or even if he wanted to. Runa had said being an Elsie would be Barclay's strength, but Yasha might not see it that way.

Then again, Yasha had never poked fun at Barclay for being an Elsie before.

"I don't know if I should write to my old home again," Barclay confessed. "I doubt they want to hear from me." Nothing said *good riddance* like torches and pitchforks.

"I don't know . . . ," Yasha said. "If I had a home, I'd want to write to them."

"Oh," Barclay said awkwardly. He didn't mean to dig up painful memories for Yasha. And when he dwelled on it, he realized he didn't know that much about Yasha at all. Which was a shame, because he liked to think that they were friends. "I'm sorry. I didn't know."

Yasha stared into the bonfire. "It's fine. It was a long time ago."

"Is it all right if I ask you something?"

"Of course."

Barclay didn't want to admit that he'd *spied* on Yasha

once—that would be far too humiliating. And so he chose his words carefully. "I've always thought our types of Lore were alike. If you don't touch fire, it still burns. That makes it wild, like the wind is wild. And I was wondering how you learned to control it."

Yasha tilted his head curiously. "You know, there's something I've always wanted to ask *you*. If that's all right."

"It is," Barclay said slowly, worried he'd said the wrong thing again.

"If your home in the Elsewheres is so scared of Beasts, how did you manage to bond with a Lufthund?"

As though he'd heard his name, Root stood up from his resting spot near the fire and padded toward them. Barclay smiled and scratched him behind the ear.

"It was an accident," Barclay explained. "I'd gone into the Woods, and Root showed up. I thought he would eat me, but instead, he bonded with me."

Yasha clenched his jaw, like he was more than stern. Like he was *angry*. "If such a powerful Beast chose you, then how could you ever worry you won't be able to control your Lore? You were made for wind Lore. Doesn't matter if you're an Elsie or not."

Barclay had known this. He'd *felt* this, every time he rode with Root, every time dirt caked beneath his fingernails, every time he felt wild or free. And being chosen by a Beast was special, even among Lore Keepers. But at some point since arriving at the Sea, he'd forgotten how special it was.

What made Barclay a Lore Keeper wasn't that he was Runa's apprentice, or that he could always control his powers, or that he no longer thought like an Elsie. Barclay was a Lore Keeper because Root had chosen him, and he had chosen Root.

Swallowing down his nerves, Barclay grabbed the broken shell from his pocket. This time, he didn't even bother reciting anything to calm himself.

He locked eyes with Root. And he only told himself one thing.

I still choose Root.

Wind blew from his hand, and the shell lifted off his palm. And no matter how long the shell hovered there, the wind never once went out of control. Barclay had been terrified that his Lore had forgotten the sound of his voice, but now it listened to him like it had never stopped.

He let the Lore settle until the shell lowered gently back into his hand.

"I did it," Barclay breathed. Root licked his hand proudly.

"Of course you did," Yasha told him.

Barclay knew he still had more practice ahead of him, but he'd gladly stay up all night to do so, just so he could show Runa in the morning. He didn't feel one lick tired. He probably wouldn't ever feel tired again.

"You're a good teacher," Barclay told Yasha, hoping that the other boy would smile for once.

Yasha only shrugged. "You're not wrong. Our Lore has a lot in common."

"But still . . . thank you."

Finally, Yasha cracked a grin—though a small one. "If you ever wanted to practice together, we could—"

"There you are!" Viola called. Barclay looked up and spotted Shazi, Hasu, and Cecily standing at the cave's entrance. "What took you so long? It seems like you're never around lately."

"That's what we came here to talk about," Hasu said nervously. "We can't be friends anymore."

"What?" Barclay asked, unsure he'd heard right. "Why not?"

"Because Cyril told us everything about Runa," Shazi said. "The *truth*."

Tadg frowned. "I don't know what he told you, but this is more important. We figured out something about Lochmordra, and maybe even the Isle of Roane. That means we can finally tell—"

"*No,*" Cecily said. "I mean, we can tell the Guardians. But we can't tell Runa."

"What do you mean?" Tadg demanded. "Why wouldn't we tell Runa?"

Cyril's three apprentices exchanged a dark look.

When neither Hasu nor Cecily seemed willing to speak, Shazi blurted, "Because Runa is a murderer."

SEVENTEEN

Barclay had always known that Runa and Cyril hated each other, but he was still shocked that Cyril would make up such a horrid lie. Because of *course* it was a lie. Runa might've been intense at times, but Runa was, without question, *good*. And no matter what the girls said, Barclay had already decided not to believe a word of it.

Tadg seethed. "That's nonsense. And it wouldn't be the first time Cyril lied about Runa."

"Cyril isn't a liar," Shazi shot back.

"Shazi . . . ," Hasu squeaked. "We promised Cyril we wouldn't say—"

"But they *deserve* to know, don't they? I'd want to know, if she was my teacher. After all . . ." Shazi's voice went quiet and grave. "Any one of you three could be next."

"You think we're in danger?" Barclay asked. This was

growing more and more ridiculous. "How could any of you believe that?"

Even Root was getting caught up in the heat of the argument, and he barked twice in warning. Barclay returned him to his Mark, saving him from unneeded stress. His friends did the same for their Beasts.

"I've known Runa my whole life," Tadg snarled. Barclay had seen Tadg angry countless times, but none of them compared to how furious he looked right now. He clenched and unclenched his fists, and bright static crackled between his fingers. "She was my dad's best friend. You think I don't know her better than you do?"

"Think about it," Shazi said. "You know how much Cyril and Runa hate each other. What do you think caused that?"

"Maybe it's because Cyril is a slimy, stuck-up liar."

Shazi crossed her arms. "Well, we know the whole story now. After Lochmordra's attack, Cyril overheard me talking about . . . Well, I wanted Runa to sign my champion card of her." She cleared her throat. "Anyway, he said we ought to know the truth about her. Especially because we spend so much time with all of *you*."

"What did he say?" Viola asked uneasily.

Hasu sighed, seeming to realize their secret was doomed not to stay secret much longer. "Cyril and Runa were apprentices together."

"I already know that," said Viola. "They were my father's apprentices before he was the Grand Keeper."

"But there was a third apprentice," Cecily murmured.

Viola furrowed her brow. "Dad never mentioned a third."

But Barclay had already suspected this, from when they'd overheard Runa and Cyril argue the day the other apprentices arrived in Munsey. "Who was the third?" he asked.

"His name was Audrian Keyes," Cecily answered. "And near the end of their apprenticeship, there was some kind of disagreement—a fight. And Runa killed Audrian over it."

The cave went quiet except for the crackles of the fire and the sizzles of Tadg's static.

Barclay was still clutching the shell he'd practiced his Lore on, and he squeezed it so hard that its ridges dug into his palm. "*No*," he said, letting his voice carry across the stone walls. "Runa wouldn't do that."

"But that's what Cyril said." Hasu's voice wobbled slightly. "And I think he was telling the truth. He looked so angry."

"Well, what was the fight about?" Tadg demanded.

Hasu gasped. "Why would that matter? Nothing is worth killing someone over! And Cyril said . . . he said they were all *friends*."

"It's a lie," Tadg said, more firmly than ever.

"Then why doesn't the Grand Keeper speak to her either?" Shazi asked.

"If the Grand Keeper really thought Runa was a murderer, he would've sent her to prison," Barclay pointed out.

But Cecily shook her head. "Cyril said it was too complicated, that Runa claimed it was self-defense. And the Grand Keeper was worried about how it would look that his own apprentices fought one another."

Barclay had already gotten the impression from Viola that the Grand Keeper cared a lot about appearances. But *this* seemed a stretch, even for him.

Nonetheless, a look of uncertainty crossed Viola's face—but not Tadg's. He bit out, "I'm going back to the Guild House. Or you know what? I'll ask Runa myself. Maybe we should hear *her* side of the story—"

"No!" Hasu yelped. "If Cyril finds out we told you, he'll be furious!"

Barclay was feeling furious himself. It had taken weeks for the seven of them to put the past behind them and become friends. Now they felt more opposed than ever.

"Then why *did* you tell us?" Barclay asked.

"Because you deserve to know," Shazi said. "And because . . . what if it's Runa who's been trying to bond with Lochmordra?"

"That doesn't make any sense," Barclay snapped. "How could Runa be causing the earthquakes? She only has ice and bone Lore."

"Not to mention that Runa and the rest of us only got here the day before you did," Viola reminded them. "How could she be responsible for the Isle of Coad? For Kelligree or Slakey?"

"Barclay said that the scary Beast he saw had tusks," Cecily pointed out. "Maybe he saw Klava's fangs and just *thought* they were tusks."

"No way," Barclay said. "I know what I saw. They pointed up, not down, and Klava walks on four legs. So—"

"Runa was here last year," Shazi added. "She was here for Midsummer."

A bolt of Tadg's electricity shot down to the cave floor. The pebbles rattled and fizzled with sparks.

"You have *no idea what you're talking about!*" he shouted. "Last Summer, Runa wasn't even on the water when Lochmordra rose! I should know. I saw him when he did."

The apprentices quieted. Tadg was talking about the day his father died.

"Well, I still believe Cyril," Shazi said. "And I don't trust Runa."

Barclay groaned. "What if we can figure out who *really* is trying to bond with Lochmordra? Then will you stop suspecting Runa?"

"Maybe . . . ," Cecily answered. "But if it's not Runa, who is it?"

"It would have to be someone who's been here for every attack," Barclay said.

"But there's thousands of Lore Keepers who live in the Sea," Viola said. "What are we going to do—interrogate all of them?"

"Ansley knows a lot about the weeping tide," said Yasha.

Since the argument began, he had retreated into the cave's corner, so quiet that Barclay had nearly forgotten he was there.

"Ansley?" Viola repeated. "But why would she want to bond with Lochmordra?"

"There are dozens of reasons why someone would want to," said Tadg. "Soren was hardly the first person to try. He wasn't even the hundredth person, probably."

Viola hugged her arms to her chest. "I know that. I just . . . I guess I don't know Ansley very well. I don't know why she would do this."

Barclay didn't know why either, but he couldn't deny that there had been something suspicious about Ansley the night he'd stayed behind in the Planty Shanty.

"She talked to me about Lochmordra," Barclay said. "She mentioned his bonding items, and the way she was studying the Fire Coral . . . it definitely wasn't normal."

Shazi's eyes lit up. "And she keeps a tank of the weeping tide in her shop, doesn't she? She studies it. She probably knows more about how it works than anyone. She could've made up everything she told us about the vents."

"Then maybe it's time to talk to the Masters about it," Viola said. "Let them decide."

At that, Shazi's expression darkened again, and Hasu and Cecily kicked at the pebbles on the floor.

"I don't know if we should tell Runa . . . ," Hasu said.

Yasha stormed in between the two groups, forcing everyone else to stagger back out of his way. "As the only one *not* in the middle of this, this is what I think. If we don't tell the Guardians about this, and Ansley uses Lochmordra to destroy another island, then it would basically be our fault. Either we tell the Masters, or we let it happen."

All of them swallowed. That was a lot of responsibility to put on their shoulders.

"So what's more important to you—a feud from a bunch of years ago, or saving the Sea?" Yasha demanded. "Choose."

His voice was so loud that it echoed throughout the cave. *Choose. Choose. Choose.*

"Fine," Shazi said. "We'll tell all the Guardians about Ansley. We'll trust Runa until after this is over."

"After this is over," Tadg fumed, "we'll ask Runa *her* side of the story, no matter how mad Cyril gets."

The three girls exchanged wary glances, but finally, they nodded.

Barclay was relieved. The Guardians needed to know what the apprentices had found out. But after the Sea was saved, the apprentices deserved answers of their own.

Like what had really happened between Runa, Cyril, and Audrian all those years ago.

The seven of them raced back to the Guild House, where supper had ended hours ago. However, the lighthouse was as boisterous and jam-packed as ever. After Lochmordra destroyed Trowe, the Guardians rarely took a break to rest—they were always bickering, always strategizing their next move. Sometimes the musicians played their shanties long into the night.

The apprentices scrambled to where Orla, Cyril, Runa, and Edwyn spoke in hushed voices at the head table. It was hard for Barclay not to glare at Cyril, sitting so casually across from the woman he *claimed* had killed their friend. His rigid posture, his gleaming medals . . . Barclay took back every kind thought he'd had about him. Cyril really was a slimy, stuck-up liar.

"We need to talk to you," Viola said breathlessly. "In private."

Runa studied the dire expressions on their faces. "Is it important?"

Viola nodded. "Extremely."

"In that case," Orla said, "we can speak in my office."

They climbed the spiral staircase up several floors until they reached a cozy study, its walls covered in maritime maps and shelves displaying a collection of ships in glass bottles. Damp mist clung to the air, and Barclay couldn't guess why until he spotted Murph asleep beneath the desk, fog billowing out of his nostrils whenever he snored.

Once they'd all crowded inside, Runa asked, "So what is it?"

Viola fiddled with the glittery pins on her shirt. Barclay could tell keeping quiet about Cyril's story was bothering her as much as him.

"We believe that someone is summoning Lochmordra using the weeping tide," she said. "And we think that person is Ansley."

"Ansley MacGannon?" Orla said, aghast. "Why would Ansley do something like that?"

"I hope you realize that these are serious accusations," Runa told them carefully. "And that this would be a very poor way to show gratitude toward Ansley for letting several of you stay in her—"

"This is nonsense," Cyril cut in. "There's no way to summon Lochmordra, not one that's been discovered."

"But there might be," Barclay said. "Even without knowing the items to make his snare."

Barclay stiffened under the weight of the adults' heavy stares, especially Orla's.

"W-when Lochmordra attacked Trowe, he was in the same sort of frenzy as all the Beasts affected by the weeping tide," Barclay said. "I think—*we* think—that's because the weeping tide affects him, too."

"Really, Orla," Cyril said, sounding exasperated, "they're just children—"

"But they're Guardians in training," Edwyn reminded him. "Sometimes it takes a fresh perspective to see what we can't. I think they deserve to be heard out."

"W-we think it might be Ansley because . . ." Barclay cleared his throat. "Because Ansley keeps a tank of the weeping tide. She's been studying it. Feeding it."

"It's not just that," Yasha added. "Ansley could also have all the items you'd need to make a snare. We've seen the Fire Coral and Polypop bells in her shop."

Orla inspected them shrewdly. "I'm not sure how you lot found out about those two items—Conley's research on Lochmordra's snare was supposed to be between him and me—but all you're really saying is that Ansley has rare, valuable items in her shop. That's probably true of good Apothecaries in every Wilderland, and Ansley is one of the best."

"If what you said about the weeping tide is true—and I think it very well might be, Barclay," Edwyn said, "then it sounds like whoever controls the weeping tide controls Lochmordra."

"Do you think Ansley has some way to control it?" Cyril asked sharply.

"If she did, we would find evidence in her office," Edwyn said.

The adults each exchanged grave looks. Barclay could tell that Orla was still unconvinced, but Runa, Edwyn, and Cyril did seem unsure.

Orla sighed. "I hate to think it, but . . . I do believe it's worth some questions, at the very least."

Ten minutes later they entered the Planty Shanty. Ansley was seated at the desk, her knitting needles clutched in her hands. She glanced up in surprise as they all filed inside. "Well, I don't normally get this much business at this time of night. What can I help you with?"

"We understand you've been studying the weeping tide," Orla said. "Would you mind showing us your experiments? We have a few questions."

"Of course." Ansley set down her knitting and walked over to her array of new glass tanks along the windows. Whereas they had once brimmed with different colors of algae, now they were only filled with the weeping tide. "I've made some fascinating discoveries. Though it will eat meat of any sort, it clearly prefers Beast meat—maybe because of their Lore. Each time I've fed it that, it *grows* maybe three, four times in size! I believe it stimulates—"

"Have you been testing this on the Sea?" Orla asked. "Or just here?"

"Well, I've gone out to the Sea a few times. If I performed all the tests in my office, there are factors that could skew the results. But don't worry, I've been going out far into open water—wouldn't want to cause a fright to any dockworkers—"

"You've been growing the weeping tide out at Sea?" Cyril asked tightly.

"Why, yes, I think it's important we understand it. . . ." She frowned, examining their faces. "Am I in some kind of trouble?"

Runa lightly touched the Polypop bells above the door, making them jingle. "These are rather rare items to treat like a trinket. Did you know that these are believed to be one of the six bonding items in Lochmordra's snare?"

"I—I thought they made for a cute crafting project," she stammered. "Why? What exactly are you accusing me of?"

"I think you ought to come with us," Orla said.

Ansley's eyes went wide, magnified wider by her spectacles. "I—I haven't done anything. I only started these experiments a few weeks ago. How could I possibly be responsible for what is happening?"

"We just want to get this cleared up," Orla assured her.

"But my shop! My work! Who will look after it while I'm gone?"

"Ansley, please don't make me ask again," Orla said firmly.

Ansley's shoulders slumped in defeat. "All right, then," she murmured. She followed Orla and the other Guardians outside while the apprentices lingered in the Planty Shanty.

Shazi smiled smugly. "You were right. Imagine—feeding the weeping tide out in the open ocean!"

"Will the attacks stop now?" Hasu asked.

Barclay hoped so, but that familiar sense of dread in his stomach hadn't gone away. Though Ansley's actions certainly were suspicious, she had seemed so *shocked* by their accusations. And now that he thought about it, if the earthquakes were coincidence and the temperatures of the Sea weren't actually rising, then that didn't explain all the dead fish.

"What will happen to her if she's found guilty?" Barclay asked.

"She'll be banished from the Sea," Tadg answered.

Barclay shuddered, remembering all too well how it felt to be thrown out of his home. What if they were wrong? What if he had done that same thing to someone else?

"So that means . . ." His mouth felt awfully dry. "That means we can ask Runa now. We can find out the truth about Audrian Keyes."

Viola groaned. "We can't. They're all questioning Ansley."

"We could wait at the Guild House," Cecily suggested.

"No," Tadg snapped. "The three of us are *not* waiting with the three of you."

Hurt flickered across Shazi's face, but then her nostrils flared. "Fine. We're going home. It's not like we want to wait with you, either."

But Barclay didn't have it in him to fight anymore. Overwhelmed, he pushed past the others and fled outside. He didn't know where he was going. The library was closed at this hour. Maedigan Cove would only make him feel twice as guilty about what they'd accused Ansley of. And the streets of Munsey were so crammed with refugees that there was no solitude to be found, not even in the winding alleys.

So, with nowhere else to go, he found himself on the beach.

Except he wasn't alone. Ulick stood there, looking strangely lonesome without Bewlah perched on his shoulder. He stared out at the water.

Ulick turned as Barclay approached. "Ah, looking for a bit of thinking space?"

Barclay nodded.

"I was after that myself. Orla has suspended all but the absolutely necessary voyages between the Isles, and Bewlah and I miss our sea legs. Especially on a moon like tonight." He pointed at the full white moon that floated like a phantom over the Sea. "The tides will be strong."

"I'm sorry," Barclay told him.

"There's nothing to be sorry about. We spend our lives surrounded by Beasts and Lore, but Lore is still a mystery, isn't it? We like to pretend, but truth is, we don't have all the answers. A risk of the lifestyle, I suppose." He sighed, stroking his crimson beard. "I won't bother ya if ya want your space."

"No, it's fine. I'm just going to sit," Barclay told him. He peered up at the full moon, wondering if it was bright enough to read. It might've been, if he squinted hard. Then it would be almost like ending his birthday at the library. But even in Dullshire, he'd rarely felt this miserable. His friends weren't speaking. Half of them believed the worst of Runa, someone Barclay considered family. And worst of all, they might've gotten an innocent woman banished from her home.

While Barclay shrugged off his bag to grab his book, Ulick peered inside it curiously. "Ya got one of those river charms."

"What do you mean?" Barclay asked.

"The conch shell—it comes from a Ciansnail, a Beast that lives in underwater rivers. Their shells are mighty tricky to find. The rivers and currents deposit them out toward Knunx. They're real pretty, aren't they?"

Barclay's eyes widened. "Is that what the rushing sound is when I put it in the water? The underwater rivers?"

"Yep. They're like deep-sea compasses. Put them in the ocean, and they'll find ya a seafloor river. Put it in a river, and it'll lead ya to the source. At least, that's how the story goes."

"The source? The people of Knunx claim it warns you if you're approaching doom."

Ulick chuckled. "I bet they do. Maybe that's just the Elsie side to the story."

That might've been true, and Barclay wouldn't normally trust his Elsie instincts . . . but what if the reason that the people of Knunx thought the charms led toward doom was because they led to Lochmordra? The swirl symbol of the Isle of Roane even looked like the conch shell. And if the Lore Keepers found Lochmordra . . . maybe they could put a stop to this.

"I have to go," Barclay said, then took off running back to Munsey.

EIGHTEEN

Barclay raced back to the Guild House and dragged
Viola and Tadg out of earshot of the squabbling
Guardians.

"I figured it out," Barclay breathed. "I know how to get to
the Isle of Roane."

Viola nearly dropped the book she was reading. "You
did? How?"

Careful to be discreet, Barclay opened the flap of his
satchel and showed them the conch shell tucked inside.

Tadg scoffed. "That Elsie charm again? It doesn't—"

"It's not just an Elsie charm," Barclay said. "It's the shell
of a Ciansnail, and when you listen to it in an underwater
river, it leads you to the heart of the Sea. Don't you get it?
That's how Maedigan got to the Isle of Roane. *That's* why
she journeyed underneath the Sea."

Tadg's mouth slammed closed. For once he seemed unable to think of anything to argue.

"How do you know this?" Viola asked.

"Ulick and I were talking about it," Barclay replied.

"If the Isle of Roane *is* real, and we can find it," she said seriously, "then we should tell Runa."

"Great," Tadg grunted. "Let's just add that to our list. If we wait until they finish questioning Ansley, we could be waiting here all night."

"And what if . . . what if we're wrong about Ansley?" Barclay asked.

Tadg and Viola both gaped.

"But you're the one who told everyone she was studying the weeping tide," Tadg said. "You're the one who—"

"I know! I *know*." Barclay already felt terrible about what he said. He didn't need Tadg making him feel guilty too. "But something about it still feels wrong. And this time, if we tell the Guardian Keepers anything, I want to be sure."

"So what are you suggesting?" Viola asked.

"We'll leave now. We'll find the Isle of Roane and come back. Then Runa and Cyril can be the ones to face Lochmordra. They can save the Sea."

Barclay had expected it would take work to convince them—or worse, another argument. But to his shock, Tadg immediately said, "Barclay is right. We should go to the Isle of Roane so that we can be sure. And we can tell Runa about it when we come back."

Viola still looked uncertain, but she was outvoted two against one. So, fifteen minutes later, the three of them snuck into the Planty Shanty. Barclay felt bad about stealing Polypops from Ansley—the very crime he'd once scolded Cecily for committing. But he would make it up to Ansley by finding the Isle of Roane and proving her innocence.

Soon they tied the slimy Polypops around their faces, climbed onto Mar-Mar's even slimier back, and plunged beneath the ocean's surface. With the Firenekkies to light their way, they retraced the familiar route to the underwater river they'd once raced on. The temperature on the seafloor was the hottest Barclay had ever felt it, and it wasn't hard to guess the reason—the vents coughed up not just puffs of smoky water, but whole clouds. There hadn't been an earthquake in some time, but Barclay worried the vents were now overactive beyond repair.

Mar-Mar halted at the riverbank.

"Come on," Barclay told them. If they lingered here too long, they'd all be fried into fish sticks.

"How does the shell work?" Tadg asked.

"Ulick said I have to listen to it under the river." But that was easier said than done. The river's current roared past. Barclay would need to hold on to something so as not to be swept away.

"This better work," Viola muttered. "All this salt water has been a nightmare for my hair."

Barclay squeezed her hand as he lowered himself into the

river. At first the current was so strong that he thought he would be torn out of Viola's grasp. But then Viola gripped his arm with two hands—her nails digging painfully into his skin—and he submerged his head beneath the mucky water.

Whrrrrrrrl.

The whooshing was louder than when the shell was simply in the ocean. Barclay turned from side to side, trying to judge which direction the sound was coming from.

Then he hoisted himself out of the river and back onto Mar-Mar.

"It's toward the reef," he said. "But the river forks ahead, remember? If we want to follow the sound, then I need to stay in the water."

"We're not rescuing you if you fall down another trench," Tadg said flatly.

Viola sighed. "Then we'll *all* ride in the river."

"But we don't have any Sunboards this time," Barclay said.

"I have an idea." Viola swam a few yards away and yanked out a long rope of seaweed from the ocean floor. She knotted it around her waist and handed the boys more to do the same. "Here. We'll tie ourselves together so we don't get separated."

Barclay took it, grimacing at the seaweed's slippery texture. Once they'd fastened themselves together, they floated along the riverbank, and Tadg returned Mar-Mar to his Mark.

"I'll jump first," Tadg said.

"No," Viola told him. "We all need to jump at the same—"

Too late—Tadg leapt into the river, dragging Barclay and Viola with him. The current seized them and jetted them ahead. They clung to one another, all of them fighting and flailing to keep themselves upright and not spin out of control. Sand and pebbles peppered their skin, stinging like wasps.

"There!" Viola tried to raise her arm to point ahead, but she couldn't lift it from the water. "That's the first fork."

Barclay ducked his head below the surface, listening to the *whrrlllllll*, then he lurched back up.

"Right! Go right!" he shouted.

They continued this over several more bends. The underwater rivers were a labyrinth, and Barclay wouldn't be surprised if they stretched like a spiderweb across the entire seafloor.

The already fierce current grew fiercer. Barclay's head bobbed in and out of the river. Even though he could still breathe, thanks to the Polypop mask, the speed made him dizzy. He wished he hadn't drunk so much sour milk at supper.

"There's another bend up ahead," said Tadg.

Barclay fumbled trying to keep hold of the conch—the last thing he needed was to lose it to the rapids. But the current was so fast that before he had time to hear the whirl, they were already swept to one side of the fork.

"If this takes us to the Zapray territory or the poisonous

reefs, I still won't save you," Tadg said, but Barclay didn't care. He wouldn't want to be rescued by Tadg anyway.

"Maybe we should go back," Viola said nervously.

"No, I—" Barclay struggled to keep his head out of the water. "I—I hear it! It's getting louder. We're going the right way."

"Can you tell if we're *close*?" Tadg demanded. "My arms are cramping."

"I don't know." Barclay's own muscles were so tired that they trembled.

Then Barclay slammed into the side of a boulder, throwing him off balance. His arms gave out, and he was dragged beneath the surface. The seaweed rope around his stomach jerked Viola next, then Tadg, and soon all three of them were hurtling and spiraling down the river. They flailed, and Tadg—the strongest swimmer of the three of them—tried to pull them to the surface, but the weight of the others dragged him down. They spun and spun. It felt like falling downhill, except the hill never *stopped*.

"AHHHHHH!" Barclay shouted.

"Do something!" Viola screamed.

"I can't!" Tadg called. He tried to control the current with his Lore, but it was too powerful.

Barclay had no idea how long it lasted. It could've been minutes; it could've been hours. But eventually the rapids twisted around a bend and began to slow. The three of them were so exhausted that they could only drift there limply like pieces of kelp.

"Are we dead?" Viola asked, panting.

"If I could move right now," Tadg answered, "Barclay would be."

Barclay ignored him and peered around, squinting in the dim light of the Firenekkies. The river ended at the base of what looked like an underwater mountain, circling it like a moat.

"I think . . . I think we're here," Barclay breathed.

Apparently Tadg *could* move, because he jolted and turned to where Barclay was looking. "That's an island. It has to be," Tadg said. He untied the seaweed rope around their waists and hoisted himself out of the river. "But what are those?"

He pointed toward the surface, where twisty pillars of water hung down like stalactites. Barclay tried to count them but couldn't. There were too many.

"I think those are whirlpools," Viola answered. "A *lot* of whirlpools."

As Barclay heaved himself out of the river, a rock nestled in a bushel of seaweed caught his eye. A swirl was carved into it, just like the one he'd spotted on the trench. And a foot away was another, then another. Stone after stone of spiral carvings ran parallel to the riverbank.

"This is it," he said excitedly. "This *has* to be it. Tadg, didn't you say there's a region full of whirlpools? It was on your dad's map."

"Shipwreck Stretch." And it was just as Tadg spoke those

words that Barclay tore his gaze away from the whirlpools and the stones and actually took in the seafloor around them.

They were in a boat graveyard. Dozens—maybe hundreds—of shipwrecks surrounded them, each vessel in a different eerie stage of decay. Their decks were broken and crusted with grime. Fraying, shredded masts rippled in the ocean currents.

Shivers crept down Barclay's back. He had never seen anything so haunting.

"The Isle of Roane must've been at the center of Shipwreck Stretch this whole time," Tadg said. "That's why no sailor could ever reach it—the whirlpools sank all their ships before they could."

"And the whirlpools explain why a swirl is the island's symbol," Barclay said. "They look just like— Where are you going?"

Tadg took off swimming toward the surface.

"Tadg! Wait!" Viola called, climbing out of the river to follow after him. "Shouldn't we go back now? We can tell Runa—"

"But we're *here*," Tadg said. "Why shouldn't we find the way to Lochmordra ourselves?"

"I don't know . . . maybe because he's a giant kraken who could kill us? Is that what you want?"

Tadg didn't answer, and Barclay suspected Tadg was, in fact, eager for a fight. Lochmordra had killed his father.

He'd destroyed his home. It wasn't surprising that Tadg wanted revenge, but Lochmordra—like Gravaldor—wasn't just a Beast. He was a force of nature, the very essence of the Sea, and Tadg couldn't slay him any more than he could slay a monsoon. He would only end up hurting himself instead.

"Tadg!" Barclay called, swimming after him. He didn't like being slower in the water than on land.

Suddenly a shadow slinked to their right amid a shipwreck.

"What was that?" Viola asked sharply.

To their left, another dark shape shifted. It was massive, and a sharp fin jutted from the top of its head in the curve of a hook.

Barclay swallowed. "What does a Hookshark look like again?"

"Something like that," Viola squeaked, pointing to a third shadow behind them. This one hovered by the gaping hole in the belly of a ship, watching them with glowing yellow eyes.

Then it advanced toward them.

"Tadg!" Barclay screamed.

The Hookshark loomed into view. Its scales were brown like rotted wood, and it had tiny eyes and a blunt snout. It was also *huge*, easily large enough to swallow Barclay whole. When it opened its mouth, Barclay counted at least a dozen rows of razor-sharp teeth.

He screamed, bubbles bursting from his Polypop. The water around him suddenly felt a tiny bit warmer.

Then Mar-Mar slammed into the Hookshark's side, Tadg riding on Mar-Mar's back.

Viola grabbed Barclay by his shirt and twisted him around, where two other Hooksharks barreled closer.

"We're doomed," Barclay moaned. So deep in the water, both of their types of Lore were weaker. He wished he could run.

The first Hookshark thrashed back at Mar-Mar, snapping its jaw to try to take a bite of the Nathermara's tail. It missed—barely—and Mar-Mar swam back to Viola and Barclay. Barclay had never been so eager to hug Mar-Mar's slimy skin.

"We need to get back to Munsey!" Viola shouted.

"But the Isle of Roane is right here!" Tadg said.

"How do you plan to get past the whirlpools? If you don't take us back to Munsey right now, I will bury *you* in a bog!"

Tadg groaned loudly, then steered Mar-Mar around. The three Hooksharks raced toward them, knocking into one another to fight for who would get the first chomp.

"Let's go," Tadg told Mar-Mar.

Mar-Mar darted out of the Beasts' paths, so quick Barclay was almost thrown off his back. Then the water around Mar-Mar began to change, swirling fast, and they torpedoed forward as though shooting through a tunnel. The Isle of Roane disappeared behind them.

NINETEEN

Trembling, the three apprentices staggered onto the beach on the Isle of Munsey.

"We need to tell Runa," Barclay gasped, wringing the seawater out of his hair.

"But it's so late, and . . ." Viola swallowed. "Shouldn't we tell Orla first?"

Tadg glared at her. "Don't tell me—you believe what Cyril said about Runa, don't you?"

"N-no, of course not," she stammered.

"I don't get it. Ever since Midwinter you've been all Runa this and Runa that. You agree with everything she says. If Runa told you to eat dung, you'd run to grab a spoon. And now you suddenly believe Cyril over her?"

Viola clenched her hands. "You wouldn't understand."

"Can you both stop fighting?" Barclay cut in. "We have enough problems without—"

"It's not like I started it. It's always *you* who starts it." Viola jabbed her finger into Tadg's chest.

Tadg's nostrils flared. The water on the shoreline splashed up behind him, spraying all of them. Annoyed, Barclay wrung out his hair *again*.

"I could've gone to the Isle of Roane myself," Tadg snarled, "but instead, I went back to save you two. I didn't have to do that."

"Oh, you wish you'd just let us get eaten?" Viola asked.

"I wish that I'd gone alone."

"You never would've found the Isle of Roane without Barclay!"

"Stop!" Barclay shouted, shoving himself between them. Barclay didn't blame Viola for yelling at Tadg—Tadg definitely deserved it. And just because Tadg had acted nice to Barclay earlier that evening didn't change the fact that he was grumpy, arrogant, and rude the rest of the time. But fighting wouldn't solve anything. "You both are being—"

"You trust Runa, don't you, Barclay?" Tadg demanded.

"Of course I do," Barclay said. "But the Isle of Roane is more important. We have to—"

"No, you know what is important? Loyalty. And you both have none of it."

Tadg marched across the beach.

Barclay and Viola exchanged an alarmed look, and Barclay dashed after Tadg.

"Tadg—Tadg," Barclay huffed. "It's the middle of the

night. You can't just barge into Runa's room and ask if she *murdered somebody*."

"So you're on Viola's side too? You always are."

That might've been true, but Tadg made it hard for anyone to want to side with him. Barclay hadn't even realized Tadg wanted him to.

And Barclay *was* loyal, no matter what Tadg thought.

"You win," Barclay said. "We'll ask Runa. But *then* we're telling her about the Isle of Roane."

But when the three of them reached the Guild House, the ruckus inside had finally gone quiet. Barclay twisted the knob—locked. He grabbed Tadg's fist in midair before he could bang on the door.

"If you wake up all the Guardians, they're going to find out about Cyril's story," Barclay warned him. "That will only make things worse for Runa."

Tadg wrenched his hand away, seething. "*Fine.* We'll wait until morning."

Tadg stalked back toward the Planty Shanty. Once he was out of earshot, Barclay murmured to Viola, "We'll talk in the morning."

Barclay didn't feel they had any right to be in Ansley's store anymore. Yasha must've thought so too, because when the two boys stormed upstairs, the attic was empty. Amid all the drama, Yasha must've decided to stay with Edwyn.

Tadg threw himself onto his bed, not bothering to change into pajamas.

Tadg wasn't the only one who felt frustrated, but even so, Barclay took a deep breath and said, "I'm sorry for what Cyril said about Runa. I know that must've been hard to hear."

Barclay waited while holding his breath. Talking to Tadg when he was like this felt like jabbing a stick into the side of a sleeping Beast. But it also felt wrong not to say anything.

When Tadg didn't respond, only pressed his face into his pillow, Barclay continued. The silence was too awkward not to break it. "She's practically family to you. And, well, she's kind of like family to me, too. The closest I've got, anyway."

Tadg grunted something unintelligible into the pillow.

"What?" Barclay asked.

It took Tadg several seconds to speak again, and when he did, his voice cracked. "I *said* that they didn't even think about it."

"Think about what?"

"My dad died because he got in Soren's way when he tried to bond with Lochmordra, and Runa was my dad's best friend. So how could they think that she would be the one behind this?" Barclay could tell Tadg was crying, and that he was probably embarrassed about it, by how he scooted farther away from the window, more into the dark. "I—I don't want to tell her that part tomorrow. She'd only be upset."

"You're right. I don't think we should."

Barclay rifled through his belongings for his pajamas, making as much noise as he could while he did so. He didn't think there was anything wrong about Tadg crying—Barclay liked crying, and did so quite a lot. But he knew it would make Tadg feel better if he pretended that he couldn't hear.

When he finished and Tadg's side of the room went silent, Barclay slid into bed.

"Can I ask you something?"

"I guess," answered Tadg.

"A little while ago, the day we were at Trowe . . . you mentioned something about slaying Lochmordra. Why?"

"Because Lochmordra is a *monster*. Even if someone is controlling the weeping tide or causing the earthquakes or whatever, it's not the weeping tide destroying all the islands or killing anyone. It's him. And if he were gone for good, all of this would stop."

"But it's the Lore of the Legendary Beasts that maintain all the Wilderlands. Without them, the Beasts would invade everywhere. There'd be no order, or—"

"I don't care," Tadg snapped. "It's not like you get it, anyway. You're—"

"An Elsie?" Barclay finished for him. Now it was *his* turn to be angry. "Why do you think I didn't want to be a Lore Keeper, at first? Eight years ago, on Midsummer, Gravaldor killed my parents. So believe it or not, I know exactly how you feel."

"I didn't know that—"

"It isn't a secret. The only reason you don't know is

because you've never once tried to be my friend. You're too busy being mean and angry all the time."

Tadg didn't speak for a long while, so long that Barclay gave up, yanked his quilt up to his ears, and tried to go to sleep. He didn't realize until he closed his eyes how tired he was.

So by the time he heard Tadg mutter, "I'm sorry I didn't know. And I'm sorry about your birthday, too," Barclay was already drifting off to sleep.

The next day was a rare sunny one for the Sea. But you wouldn't know that from the somber mood in the Guild House. Ansley might've kept to her seaweed tanks and craft supplies, but clearly the people of Munsey considered her a friend. The news of her possible betrayal sat well with no one.

No one except Cyril. "Now that the perpetrator has been caught," he announced, "these attacks will cease, and I see no reason for me to remain in the Sea."

"The only true test of Ansley's guilt is whether this happens again," Runa said. "But if you want to run off before we're certain, by all means, leave."

Barclay, Tadg, and Viola squeezed their way past the onlooking Guardians. Cyril's three apprentices stood behind him, each staring glumly at their shoes. Yasha lurked in a far corner.

Cyril glowered, and Edwyn rested his hand on his shoulder. "Runa is right. I made the mistake of leaving only to have to return. Even if Ansley *is* guilty—and it certainly seems that she is—we should wait—"

He was cut off as Tadg stalked between them. "Runa, we'd like to talk to you in private. It's important."

"Again?" she asked. "If it's important, you can say it in front of all of us."

Tadg shot a furious glance at Cyril. "No. Just you. It has to be in private."

Runa studied the serious expressions all three of them wore. "Fine, then. We'll go upstairs."

They climbed up the spiral staircase past Orla's office and entered a small guest bedroom where Runa was staying. Her enormous saber-toothed tiger Beast lay on the bed, shedding white and black fur all over the quilt. As they entered, the Beast lifted her head and peered at them suspiciously. Then she bared her long fangs and hissed.

"This is Klava," Runa said. "She doesn't like people, but she won't attack you. Not while I'm here."

Runa's words hardly gave Barclay peace of mind. Klava's front teeth were so long that they could pierce him through.

"Now what is all this about?" Runa asked.

"We want to hear about Audrian Keyes," Tadg told her.

Runa blanched. "How do you know about Audrian?"

"Cyril told his apprentices, and they told us. He's saying the Grand Keeper had a third apprentice and *you* killed him. And we've told them that it's obviously not true, but they don't—"

"It is true," Runa said softly. "But there's more to the story than that."

Barclay sucked in his breath. Viola gasped.

"Wh-what?" Tadg stuttered. "What do you mean that it's true?"

"I should've known Cyril would say something," said Runa bitterly. "That's very like him. If one of us did something wrong, he was always the first to tell. But you all are kids. He had no right—"

"I think we have the right to know what happened," Tadg snapped.

She sighed. "Why don't you three sit down?" But when Barclay stepped toward the closest chair, Klava let out a low, threatening growl. "Give her space," Runa told Barclay sharply. And then, to Klava: "It's all right, girl. Go back to sleep."

Klava stopped growling, but she didn't go to sleep, either. She watched the three of them with narrowed eyes.

And so, cautiously, Viola took the rocking chair, and Barclay sat cross-legged on the floor. Tadg, who didn't seem to want to sit, stood in a corner, his arms crossed.

"The three of us became Leopold's apprentices when we were all your age," Runa said. "From the start, we were inseparable. Leopold wasn't the Grand Keeper yet—his mother was—but we were the top three students in our Exhibition that year, and we thought we were going to be the greatest Lore Keepers in the world together—or at least,

Audrian and I did. Cyril spent all his time chasing after us."

Runa smiled for a moment, as though remembering the times fondly. Then her expression darkened.

"We were all ambitious. We all had something to prove. But Audrian . . . he was the most ambitious of any of us. Audrian was an Elsie, and as we grew older, he began to change how he felt about the Elsewheres."

Now Barclay understood—when Runa had mentioned knowing another Lore Keeper who was an Elsie, she must've meant Audrian.

"Cyril and I were always able to go home, but Audrian wasn't. He grew bitter, and he started talking about how the Elsewheres needed to change. He felt that Lore Keepers were making a mistake keeping the Wilderlands and the Elsewheres so separate, and that there shouldn't be boundaries between the lands. He started acting strange. He became obsessed with the Legendary Beasts. He ended up leaving his apprenticeship the year before we finished, and Cyril and I completed our licensing exams without him.

"And then, a year after our exams, we ran into him again. Cyril and I were on an assignment investigating reports of unusual dragon patterns in the Mountains. Leopold was busy then—you weren't much older than a toddler, Viola, and he'd begun to take on your grandmother's duties as Grand Keeper when she'd fallen ill. When I told him that I suspected Audrian was responsible for disrupting the dragons, he didn't believe me.

"But then Cyril and I found evidence that proved Audrian was guilty. Audrian wanted to bond with Dimondaise to become so powerful that he could remove the Mountains' borders and consume the surrounding Elsewheres." Pain crossed Runa's face. "And even though bonding with a Legendary Beast is an incredible feat, I know he would've succeeded if I hadn't stopped him. We knew him better than anyone, and so I knew how brilliant he was. And what he was capable of. He would've destroyed the world on a quest to unite it. He was . . . lost.

"After I defeated Audrian, Cyril never forgave me," Runa said. "Despite Audrian trying to kill both of us, Cyril was convinced there could've been another way. He tried to duel me, but Leopold stopped us. Leopold wasn't there to see what happened with Dimondaise, but he took Cyril's side. I'd saved the Mountains—possibly more—and Leopold told me that was the only reason he didn't arrest me. That, and our history.

"And so I left. I joined the Dooling championships. I took assignments far from Cyril. We've passed each other on a few occasions since then, but this is the first time we've worked together since it happened eight years ago. Eight years might seem like a long time, but it certainly hasn't felt like it."

Now Barclay understood why Runa had looked so scared during their last lesson. Barclay had been angry and bitter because he thought being an Elsie made him weaker than everyone else. Runa must've grown worried that Barclay might start thinking like Audrian too.

But that would never happen. Barclay would always feel hurt that Dullshire had thrown him out, but he didn't want to make them fear Lore Keepers more than they already did. He wanted them to understand that Lore Keepers weren't as terrible as they thought they were. And if they never believed that, then Barclay would still protect them. He didn't belong in Dullshire anymore, but a part of him would always consider it his home, even if Root was his home too.

"So you see," Runa finished, "Cyril's story was true. But we don't see eye to eye about what happened. And I'm afraid we never will."

"But if you were both friends, isn't there a way you can—" Barclay started.

"It's better to be wronged by an enemy than betrayed by a friend, isn't it?" Runa said sadly.

Barclay did know a thing or two about betrayal. From Dullshire. From Ethel and Abel in the Woods.

"I've never told anyone about this, other than your father, Tadg," Runa said. "And up until now, I didn't realize that Cyril had either. He's hinted, certainly, but for him to tell his apprentices—I think he and I need to have a word."

Then she walked out the door.

"Wait!" Viola said, jumping to her feet. "We have something else we wanted to talk to you about!"

But Runa didn't turn back. She stormed down the staircase to where Cyril and Edwyn spoke by the fire.

"What happened to keeping your silence because you thought it would reflect badly on Leopold?" Runa hissed. The other Guardians in the hall might've been too far away to hear, but they sure did stare. One even hollered, as though hoping the Horn of Dawn and Fang of Dusk would duel again and make it a spectator sport. "How would the Grand Keeper react to know that High Keeper Mayani's and Chancellor Essam's daughters both know what happened? Not to mention his own daughter?"

Cyril, who'd been leaning against the fireplace mantel, lost his balance. He swiftly collected himself, straightening his medals and puffing out his chest. "They're my students. I can't protect them all the time, but I wanted them to be careful. Viola, too, even if she's not my student anymore."

At all the attention, Edwyn turned to several Guardians ogling at a nearby table. One had a fiddle resting on her lap. "Well?" he barked. "Don't just sit there gawking. Play us some music."

At his orders, they scrambled to their feet. The noise of them drowned out any of Runa's and Cyril's conversation.

When I came to the Sea, the land of storm,
I found a letter, and the message warned . . .

"What do you take me for?" Runa asked Cyril. Her voice was so icy that frost shimmered out at her breath. "You can't 'protect them all the time'? They're a bunch of kids."

"We were barely older than kids," he said darkly.

In all the weeks Runa and Cyril had spent together at the Sea, never once could Barclay picture them as anything other than enemies. But something weighed in that moment, something heavy. It made Barclay wonder whether it had been Cyril or Audrian who'd given Runa that scar.

Finally, Runa slumped her shoulders. "You win, then. My apprentices and I will leave in the morning."

Surprise flicked across Cyril's face; then he molded it into his usual pompous frown. "I think that's for the best."

So I kissed the earth one final time.
Then I sailed in search of that grave of mine.

Then, without warning, Viola marched between both of her teachers.

"No one can leave yet," she declared. "Because what happened in the Mountains wasn't the only reason we wanted to talk to you. The three of us found the Isle of Roane. Which means we can find Lochmordra."

Four hours later the seven apprentices waited on the beach for their mentors to return.

Barclay, Tadg, and Viola had told the teachers everything. The Ciansnail shell. The underwater rivers. The whirlpools. The Hooksharks. The book about Maedigan.

And so Runa, Cyril, and Edwyn had left immediately to investigate.

"Maybe this all really will be over now," Hasu said hopefully.

Tadg grumbled something unintelligible.

"What?" Hasu asked.

"I *said* that I doubt it. Even if they find Lochmordra's home, if it's not Ansley who's causing this, then they still have no idea how to stop him. Unless they slay . . ." Tadg trailed off and shot a glance at Barclay that Barclay couldn't read.

"Funny that that's how *you* would solve the problem," Shazi sneered.

"What is that supposed to mean?"

"You're Runa's apprentices. You know what I mean."

"You're wrong about what happened between Runa and Cyril," Barclay told her. "Runa was only protecting herself. Audrian gave her no choice."

"Which makes Cyril a liar," Tadg finished.

While the others bickered, Cecily nudged Barclay in the side. "I believe you," she whispered, as though it were a secret she didn't want her friends to overhear. "I like Runa. She's so scary. I want to be scary like that when I get my license."

Barclay stared at Cecily's shadow wiggling like fish bait along the sand. He had no doubt that she'd grow up to be just as creepy as she hoped.

"Won't Cyril be angry you feel that way?" Barclay asked her.

Cecily shrugged. "I know you probably don't like Cyril,

but I owe him a lot. If it wasn't for him, I'd never have thought someone like me could've been in the Guild."

"What do you mean? You have a Mythic class Beast."

"Yeah, but testing for a Guild license is expensive, and you don't get paid much as an apprentice, do you? I have a lot of little brothers and sisters at home to help feed."

"How did he become your teacher, then?" Barclay asked.

"I was on my usual corner in Halois, which is right outside the Guild Capitol. It's really busy there, especially in the morning, when everyone is rushing to work. And I saw Cyril walking by, with all his fancy gold medals, and so Oudie and I pickpocketed him."

Barclay gawked. "You *stole* from the Horn of Dawn?"

"I didn't know who he was. I just thought he'd have some kritters on him," Cecily said. "He didn't catch me, not until later that day, when he realized his coin purse was missing. He tracked me down, and he was really angry, at first. He'd just come back from the Woods, and he was in a bad mood. He threatened to have me thrown in jail. But he made me tell him how I'd done it, because he thought he was too powerful for a little kid to steal from him. After I showed him, he was really impressed. He told me that he had a slot open for a new student, and that he'd personally make sure that kritters were sent to my family every few weeks. And it was way more than I was earning as a thief."

Barclay didn't know what to make of the story. Before Cecily, Cyril had only taught the children of important people, because—so Barclay guessed—it made *him* look really important. Maybe after Viola had told him she'd rather be Runa's student, he'd tried a little bit to change.

"He still lied," Barclay said firmly. "There was a lot more to the story about Audrian than he made it seem."

"I know," Cecily said sadly. "But he's not *all* bad. I just thought you might like to know that."

"Look!" Yasha said, standing and pointing out to the ocean, where the Guardians emerged.

Runa ripped her Polypop mask off and stomped onto the sand. Without a word, she threw it aside and stormed back to Munsey. Even Edwyn, who was always in a good mood, shook his head in frustration.

"What happened?" Barclay asked. "Did you find the Isle of Roane?"

"Next time," Cyril fumed, thrusting the Ciansnail shell back into Barclay's hands, "you would do better not to believe in stories. Whatever underwater river you claim led you to the Isle of Roane doesn't exist. The *island* doesn't exist."

TWENTY

I still don't get it," Barclay groaned. "How could one of the rivers just be *gone*?"

He and the other apprentices toiled in the Guild House, books from the library open and scattered across their tabletop. In his frustration, Cyril had assigned each of them an essay on the life stages of a Lepinfish—of which there were forty-two. Barclay had written a page already, but it was hard to focus. His thoughts kept veering back to the Isle of Roane.

"You probably just got mixed up," Hasu told him gently.

"But the whirlpools haven't disappeared," said Barclay. "They could've sailed for them. Or sent a flying Beast."

"Then they'd just get their ships shredded on Shipwreck Stretch," Shazi said. "And Orla won't risk any Beasts right now to the weeping tide."

Barclay saw her point—all their options were dangerous. And he, Viola, and Tadg hadn't brought back any proof that they'd found an island at all. But Barclay *knew* they were right. They'd seen those stones with the swirl carvings. And the whirlpools were the only explanation for why the Isle of Roane was so hard to find.

He flipped through his library book about Maedigan. He kept reading and rereading the same few lines about her traveling beneath the Sea. When Barclay had shown the book to the Guardians, they'd seemed impressed—Edwyn even said he'd stayed up all night reading it cover to cover, even despite failing to find the island. But now it might as well have been worthless.

"The myth of the Isle of Roane had to come from *somewhere*," Barclay said.

"Maybe someone dreamed it," Shazi said. "Or someone just made it up."

"No, that doesn't make sense."

"But the legend doesn't make sense. Lochmordra has to live in the water, not on some island. So how can the island lead you to his home?"

"Can you both just shut up?" Viola snapped. "Some of us are trying to work."

Barclay and Shazi quieted. Seeming satisfied, Viola lowered her head back to her notebook, where Barclay saw she'd already finished three whole pages. Behind her, Cecily lurked over her shoulder, copying what Viola wrote.

Barclay gaped. "But even you agreed it was the Isle of Roane."

"Even if it was," Viola said, "Yasha got to go with the Guardians on their work today because he's the only one who hasn't been spilling secrets and breaking rules."

"We had a good reason," Barclay argued.

"But we still got in trouble, didn't we?"

Barclay didn't bother bickering with her. He knew the real reason Viola was upset wasn't because they broke the rules, but because it had been Cyril who'd punished them for it.

Suddenly a bell tolled—the same bell as when the Brutopods had attacked. They dropped their quills, splattering ink over their parchment.

"That's the emergency bell," Tadg said. "Something must be wrong."

Abandoning their papers, the six apprentices scrambled to their feet and raced across Munsey. The town had fallen into chaos. People were fleeing from their homes, carrying what precious few items they could manage in their arms. Those who'd already left a devastated island had nothing else to bring.

And as for *why*, the answer was obvious. Even from the edges of town, they could see the white of the weeping tide looming on the horizon.

"Maybe it's just a leftover bloom," Barclay said anxiously. "Like when the Brutopods attacked."

There was only one way to be sure.

They returned to the Guild House and raced up the spiral staircase. Up, up, up. Barclay, being the fastest, reached the top first, and he panted as he looked out over the tower ledge to the dark, open water.

A menacing white inked across the horizon from every direction. North, west, south, east—no matter where Barclay turned, the weeping tide was there, as though it was going to swallow Munsey and Dunsey whole.

This was no leftover bloom.

Cecily reached the tower next, shortly followed by Hasu, Shazi, and Viola.

"If Lochmordra attacks Munsey and Dunsey," Viola said, panting heavily, "there'll be almost none of the Sea left."

"Would everyone have to leave?" Hasu asked. "Where would they go?"

"If the Lore Keepers left the Sea, then the Elsewheres nearby would also be in trouble," Barclay pointed out.

"But Lochmordra might not give the Lore Keepers a choice," Shazi said. She winced and held her hands to her ears—the bell was awfully loud.

"What do we do?" Cecily asked. "We don't even know what direction Lochmordra will come from."

"But we can't just sit here and wait," Hasu squeaked.

"Don't panic," Viola said, ever the leader in a crisis. "We still have time before Lochmordra rises. If we can evacuate to a nearby island . . ."

"Trowe is the next closest, but that's already been attacked," Barclay said.

"Then somewhere else. Anywhere else. Hasu, can you get the Guardian Keepers?"

"They said they were going to investigate where Ansley was studying, and I don't know where that is! I can only use my Lore for places I've been—"

"Ansley," Barclay breathed, his eyes widening. The others turned to stare at him. "Ansley is still locked in the cellar! We need to free her before Lochmordra comes."

"But what if she's the one . . . ," Hasu started, then stopped. "But she has to be innocent. She hasn't fed the weeping tide in days. This can't be her fault!"

They raced down the steps to the lighthouse's lowest level. It was dreadfully dark, and the walls were a cool, damp stone, like in a grotto.

Viola shined a beacon from her palms, illuminating Ansley in her cell. Her hair looked greasy and her glasses dusty, but otherwise she seemed all right—Orla had allowed her to bring her knitting to the cell to keep her occupied. She stood up, spotting them.

"I heard the alarm bell," she croaked. "Is Lochmordra coming?"

Barclay nodded. "The weeping tide—it's *everywhere*. And we know this can't be your fault. We're sorry that we thought it was your fault in the first place."

"It's all right, dear," Ansley said. "I should've told Orla

about my experiments ahead of time instead of doing things by myself like I always do. Maybe we could've figured out the cause of this before it all got so bad." She peered around at their group. "Where are Yasha and Tadg?"

"Yasha went out with—" Viola started, then stopped, whipping around. The apprentices gawked at one another, realizing that they were only five in number. "Where's Tadg? Wasn't he with us a few minutes ago?"

Tadg must've slipped away when they were distracted climbing to the tower. And Barclay could only think of one place that he would go. His mouth tasted salty with dread.

"I know where Tadg went," he rasped. "He's gone to Shipwreck Stretch. He's gone to try to kill Lochmordra."

TWENTY-ONE

We have to go after him," Barclay said. If Tadg fought Lochmordra, then there was little chance of Tadg escaping the battle alive.

"But what about Munsey?" Hasu asked. Outside the Guild House, the bell tolled as loudly as ever, but even that didn't drown out the noises of havoc. Carts rumbled across the cobblestones. People shouted. Fwishts squawked overhead, and hooves and boots stampeded past. Munsey was already the largest city of the Sea, but now it was crowded to bursting with refugees, and every one of those people needed to evacuate.

"They've sounded the alarm," Viola said. "There's nothing a bunch of apprentices can do that will help now. But we can still save Tadg."

"But how does he know where to find Lochmordra?" asked Shazi.

"Because we *did* find the Isle of Roane," Barclay said fiercely. "And even if the underwater river that we took there is gone, there's still another way to get there."

"No, no way," Shazi said. "If we sail through Shipwreck Stretch, we'll all drown! Or be eaten by Hooksharks!"

But Barclay had made up his mind. "Fine. Evacuate with the rest of Munsey if you want. But I'm going after Tadg."

"Me too," Viola said.

"You'll need me," Cecily said. "I can help steal a ship!"

"I'd like to help, if I can," Hasu said.

That left Shazi, who scowled. "All right. I'm coming too."

"Then let's go," Barclay said.

They bolted down the streets, where passersby jostled one another in their panicked race to the harbor. Barclay only made it two steps out the Guild House's door before someone collided hard with his shoulder.

"How are we going to steal a ship if they're all taken?" Viola asked. "The people need them to escape Munsey."

She was right. They needed to find another way to reach the Isle of Roane. But sailing was their only option, and all the ships were docked at the harbor . . .

All the ships except one.

"Ulick! I bet he'll take us," Barclay said. "But what if he's already left?"

"You run ahead first," Viola said. "Make sure he's still there. We'll be right behind you."

Barclay nodded—then he summoned Root. Having

Beasts out of their Marks was still against the rules, but certainly Orla would count this as an exception.

Root crouched in a defensive stance, wary from all the chaos around them.

Barclay pressed his forehead against Root's. "It's all right, boy. But we need to run."

Root bent lower so Barclay could swing his leg over Root's back. He grabbed fistfuls of Root's shaggy black fur and squeezed tight.

A moment later they took off.

They wove through the buildings, dodging the pedestrians who barreled past. As soon as they reached the edge of town, Root broke out into a sprint. The cattle that roamed the field blurred as they rushed past. The blades of grass whistled. The air around them went so still that all Barclay could feel was the pounding of his heart. Even if slaying Lochmordra would put a stop to the attacks, Barclay knew the real reason Tadg wanted to kill the Legendary Beast: to avenge his father.

Thankfully, when Barclay reached Ulick's shack on the Isle of Munsey's northern shore, he spotted Ulick hauling supplies onto the *Bewlah*.

"Ulick!" Barclay called, and Ulick nearly dropped the crate he was holding.

"Barclay? What are ya doing here?" Ulick asked. "Haven't ya heard the bell?"

Root skidded to a stop at the water's edge, and Barclay slid off his back.

"We need your help," Barclay told him. "Tadg's gone. He left on his own to try to kill Lochmordra."

Ulick's jaw dropped. "Where'd the boy get an idea like that?"

"We *need* to go after him. He's gone to the Isle of Roane, but I know how to get there. If we leave right away, we might be able to stop him before it's too late."

"You found the Isle of Roane, did you?" Ulick looked impressed.

"We did, but . . ." He hesitated. "It's in the center of Shipwreck Stretch, and it's surrounded by Hooksharks. It'll be dangerous."

Ulick grinned, his mother-of-pearl tooth glinting in the daylight. "It's been mine and Bewlah's lifelong dream to sail through there! But are we going alone?"

As though on cue, the four girls appeared at the edge of the beach, each panting.

"Well, then," Ulick said. "Let's weigh anchor! There's no time to waste!"

They hurried aboard the *Bewlah*. Barclay and Hasu helped Ulick let down the sails while Cecily wheeled up the anchor. Salty wind tore across the open water, and Barclay realized with dread that the winds were coming from the north—exactly the direction they needed to go.

Ulick must've been thinking the same thing, because he shot Barclay a nervous look. "We're gonna need all the wind ya can give, or we have a long, slow voyage ahead of us. Can ya manage it?"

Barclay nodded. He hadn't had time to practice his power since Yasha had helped him yesterday, but he wouldn't let his Lore be the reason they didn't reach Tadg in time.

But if they *did* make it to the Isle of Roane, how would Barclay stop Tadg? Tadg had been talking about slaying Lochmordra for ages. Words might not be enough to convince him otherwise.

Barclay took a deep breath that did nothing to calm his nerves. Last night, it was Tadg who'd made fun of Barclay for being an Elsie. But it wasn't Tadg Barclay needed to prove anything to—it was himself. And so Barclay lifted his hands to the ship's sails, and he summoned all the wind he could muster.

They set off. After the Isle of Munsey and its surrounding ring of weeping tide vanished behind them, Ulick summoned Bewlah, so she could join them for the all-time dangerous voyage of their dreams. As soon as she appeared, she started wailing atop Ulick's shoulder.

The monster is coming by Sea,
And what a hideous killer is he.
Us heroes sail brave
To our watery grave,
But wise men know better to flee.

"When we reach the whirlpools," Ulick told them, "we'll need to be ready. If the ship gets sucked into one, we'll all be shark food. So I need someone up on the mast to keep watch."

"I can do that!" Cecily said. Then she scampered up the wooden beams to the highest point of the ship. With incredible balance, she stood at the top, Ulick's spyglass in her hand.

"And you three," Ulick told Viola, Shazi, and Hasu. "There will be lots of the weeping tide near the Isle of Roane, so I wouldn't be surprised if we meet more than Hooksharks out there. Can ya be ready?"

"We will be," Shazi said, then stalked to the ship's stern and unsheathed both her swords. She pointed one out to the horizon, as though daring a Hookshark to challenge her.

With the full force of Barclay's wind, the ship blasted across the choppy waves at a stomach-lurching speed. Twenty minutes later, the whirlpools of Shipwreck Stretch roared in the distance. The white of the weeping tide frothed and foamed in patches across the water, and Barclay tried to ignore the fearful knot twisting in his gut. He'd heard stories of Lochmordra devouring ships whole. The *Bewlah* probably wasn't even enough for a meal.

"I see the whirlpools!" Cecily called from atop the mast. "Go right! Go right!"

Ulick spun the helm, and the *Bewlah* lurched to the side.

"There's something in the water!" Hasu called from where she manned Ulick's speargun. The contraption looked comically large compared to her, clearly built for Ulick's size. She clutched the trigger with her whole hand.

Barclay sprinted to the side of the ship. Sure enough, a large shadow lurked in the water, swimming warning laps around the *Bewlah*. It was shaped like a diamond, with a long, skinny tail.

"That's a Zapray," Viola said. "It has electric Lore, like a Nathermara."

"Should I use the harpoon?" Hasu asked nervously.

"Save it," Shazi answered. "Look over there."

Up ahead, a dozen fins emerged from the waves, each one curled like a sickle.

"Hooksharks," Barclay said hoarsely.

"Hold on tight!" Ulick called, and the *Bewlah* veered around its first whirlpool. The entire ship shuddered as the currents tried to drag it into their depths. "Barclay! Give us some more push!"

With one hand still braced on the port-side rail, Barclay raised the other toward the sails. *Wind!* he thought, and gusts sprang from his palm. The *Bewlah* heaved forward, tearing itself away from the grasp of the currents.

"There's another one up ahead!" Cecily called. "No! There's two!"

Ulick grunted and spun the wheel. The *Bewlah* lurched so strongly that Barclay nearly toppled to the deck.

Suddenly something knocked against the ship.

"What—?" Barclay gasped out. Then he *did* fall. He landed painfully on his side. Above, Cecily shrieked and clung to the mast with both arms and legs.

"What was that?" Viola shouted.

They had their answer when a Hookshark vaulted from the water. It reached so high that its white eyes were level with the *Bewlah*'s rail, and it opened its mouth, exposing hundreds of sharp teeth. Hasu screamed and fired the harpoon, but it missed. The Hookshark splashed back into the water.

"Barclay!" Ulick bellowed.

Barclay scrambled to his feet and aimed more wind at the sails. The *Bewlah* narrowly dodged the second whirlpool.

"Cecily!" Ulick yelled. "Is the island ahead?"

Still hugging the mast, Cecily peered ahead through the spyglass. "Not yet!"

A terrible doubt wheedled itself into Barclay's mind. What if they hadn't found the Isle of Roane at all? What if he was leading them all to their doom?

Another Hookshark surfaced. It leapt so high that when it fell, it tore off a chunk of the *Bewlah*'s starboard rail. Wooden beams and crates plunked into the ocean, and the shock of impact sent the ship quaking from side to side.

Barclay held on to the boat for dear life and gave all his power to the sails. That was the only way they would make it to the island. He blew gust after gust. Faster. Faster. The *Bewlah* danced around the dozens of whirlpools, until at last, Cecily shouted, "I see it! I see an island to the northwest!"

Before Barclay could cheer or sigh with relief, another Hookshark sprang out of the water. It landed *on* the *Bewlah*, and the boat groaned as it tilted downward from the weight of the Hookshark's massive body. Even Ulick shrieked this time—surprisingly high-pitched for a man his size—as the ship nearly tipped over. The Hookshark flailed, trying to squirm its way farther up the deck. It opened its jaw wide, *wide*.

Viola screamed. The ropes she held slipped from her grasp, and she skidded down the deck—right toward the Hookshark's mouth.

"Help!" she wailed.

"Wind!" Barclay shouted desperately. The gust sent Viola rolling out of the Beast's path. She grabbed ahold of what remained of the rail and squeezed tight.

The Hookshark thrashed, and the *Bewlah* groaned louder beneath it. Any moment now the Beast would snap the ship in two.

Then Shazi took off running down the sloping deck. After nearly losing her balance twice, she whacked the Hookshark hard on its snout with both her swords. It jerked away and sank into the water.

The *Bewlah* whipped back to an upright position and continued onward. The Isle of Roane came into view in the distance. It was smaller than Barclay had expected, and he scanned its shores for Tadg. But from this far, he couldn't see anything.

"We need more wind!" Ulick told him, and Barclay snapped his focus back to his job. Tadg had to be there—alive. He *had* to be.

"There's something else out there!" Cecily shouted.

"More Hooksharks?" Viola called fearfully.

"No, but it has a very long nose!"

"A nose?" Barclay repeated, confused.

Beside him, Ulick gasped. "That's no nose. That's a Daggerfish."

Something shiny burst from the water, and a massive blade struck the starboard side and came out the port. Everyone—even Ulick—fell. Barclay tumbled painfully down the steps of the quarterdeck. Shazi stabbed a sword into the floor to keep from plunging overboard. And above, Cecily grabbed ahold of a rope and swung through the air like bait dangling on a fishing line. The shadow of a gigantic Beast writhed in the milky water. It had pierced the *Bewlah* clean through.

The wood of the ship groaned; then the deck began to collapse. Whole planks of wood caved inward and toppled into the waves below, and the *Bewlah* folded like a massive jaw snapping closed.

No, Barclay thought frantically. The Isle of Roane wasn't even a mile ahead. They were so close. They could still make it.

But then the *Bewlah* spun. It had been sucked into a nearby whirlpool, and it circled around and around, sinking deeper with each rotation. The last thing Barclay saw was white swirling in all directions, and then it swallowed them whole.

TWENTY-TWO

Barclay retched salt water onto the sand. His chest *hurt* from how much Sea he'd breathed in, and his arms trembled just from holding himself upright.

What had happened after the *Bewlah* sank was a blur. Barclay remembered the weeping tide—patches of his skin now stung red and blistered where it had eaten him. He remembered the Daggerfish and Hooksharks, fleeing as a great, low groan echoed from deep within the ocean. And he remembered the pain of his Mark burning, urging Barclay to do whatever it took to swim to shore.

"Barclay!" shouted a voice.

Barclay didn't look up right away—he was still too busy hacking up seawater. When he finished, he rolled onto his back and stared up at Viola, who'd staggered over to him. Like Barclay, she was drenched and shaky.

"Are you all right?" she rasped.

"Barely. Are you?"

"I don't know."

Wincing, she bunched up what remained of her tattered sleeve. The skin of her arm burned an angry scarlet and was swollen and speckled with blood. Gingerly she smeared away the mess, and Barclay realized the weeping tide had hurt her on her Beast Mark. The golden tattoo was so inflamed that Barclay could barely make out Mitzi's shape.

"I can't summon Mitzi," she choked. "And I can't use my Lore, either."

"Is Mitzi all right?" he asked, alarmed.

"I think so—I can sense her. But . . ." She wrung out her hands, clearly trying not to panic. "It can't be good."

Barclay sat up and looked out to Sea, scanning the water for any sign of his other friends or the *Bewlah*. The whirlpools churned with a steady roar.

"Where is everyone else?" he asked.

"I'm not sure. It all happened so fast. But Hasu could've used her Lore to transport them out of there. They must be all right."

Barclay hoped so. He didn't want to think about the alternative.

Barclay turned around and examined the island. It was smaller than any of the other isles he'd visited, little more than a knobby hill. Way up at the peak, Barclay glimpsed a number of stone pillars, too clean cut to be a natural rock formation.

"Do you think this is it?" he asked. "The Isle of Roane?"

"It has to be. And if Tadg's here, he would've climbed to the top."

Barclay took Viola's offered hand and clambered to his feet. The two of them set off to climb the slope. A path of pebbles had been laid up it to avoid the steepest parts of the incline, and as they walked, Barclay realized it was in the shape of a spiral.

At the summit, the stone pillars formed a circle. They were so ancient and swathed in moss that the carvings on them were barely visible. But the ones he could make out, Barclay recognized as spirals—the Isle of Roane's symbol.

In the center of the pillars was a large pool of water, the currents twisting in a whirlpool that sank deep into the island's core.

And at the edge of the pool, staring into the vortex, was Tadg. He seemed to be debating whether or not to jump.

"You can't do this," Barclay said, making Tadg's head jerk up in surprise.

Tadg scowled. "How did you two follow me here?"

"We all did—us, Shazi, Cecily, and Hasu. Ulick sailed with us. But . . ." Barclay swallowed.

"The *Bewlah* sank," Viola finished for him. "We got separated."

Tadg's eyes widened. "You did? How long has it been?"

"A while," Barclay answered. From this height, he could

look far out over the water, but he saw nothing except marbled white waves.

"Hasu would've taken them back," Tadg said, echoing what Viola said earlier. "The best we can do now is stop Lochmordra for good."

"And how do you plan on doing that?" Viola demanded. "All the Guardian Keepers couldn't stop him."

"The Guardians were forced to hold back. They didn't want to kill him." Tadg stepped closer to the edge, making Barclay lurch forward. He'd wrestle Tadg to the ground if he had to. Beside him, Viola shot Barclay a worried glance. She must've been thinking the same thing he was.

"I remember when Root calmed Gravaldor," Tadg said. "If Mar-Mar can do that, I can summon my electric Lore to kill Lochmordra. I'm strong enough now. It will only take one shot."

"Lochmordra is a *Legendary Beast*," Viola said. "He's as old as the Sea itself. To him, you're no more significant than a Firenekkie."

"And the Woods doesn't have anything like the weeping tide," Barclay added. "Gravaldor only rose in the Woods because of Midwinter. This isn't the same—"

"Then I don't care," Tadg spat. "Even if he's at full strength, I don't care."

"But the Sea *needs* Lochmordra," Barclay said desperately. "Without his Lore, the Beasts won't remain in the Wilderland."

"If he's allowed to live, there won't *be* a Wilderland much longer."

"I understand why you're angry. You *know* that I under-stand. But the two of us aren't going to stand by and watch you get yourself hurt."

At first it looked like Barclay's words had gotten through to Tadg. He sagged his shoulders, and his gaze drifted out to the murky white ocean as though his thoughts had taken him somewhere else.

But then when he looked back at them, he glared. "You have two choices. You can either let me go, or you can come with me."

"Or . . ." Barclay stepped closer to him. "We'll stop you."

"Barclay—" Viola said in warning, but was interrupted when Tadg snorted.

"You couldn't beat me even if you tried," Tadg sneered.

Maybe so, but they had no way of knowing that. During their Exhibition, Barclay and Tadg had never gotten to have their final match. And since Mar-Mar couldn't fight on land, Barclay had the advantage. There was enough dis-tance between them and the weeping tide for Barclay to summon Root.

Tadg stiffened when Root appeared at Barclay's side. Tadg might've been powerful, but even he couldn't win two against one.

And so Barclay raised his hand, palm facing out, and thought, *Wind!*

A funnel blasted toward Tadg, sweeping him back until he slammed against one of the stone pillars. He groaned and crumpled to the dirt, then stood up, his expression furious.

He pointed toward Barclay, and sparks began to crackle at his fingertips. A bolt of lightning erupted from his hand, and Barclay dove out of its path. It landed on the ground just where he'd been standing. The grass sizzled, its blades scorched black.

Viola ducked for cover behind one of the pillars. "Stop this! Both of you! You're going to hurt each other!"

But no sooner had Barclay dodged than Tadg fired another bolt. Barclay darted away. Even so, the lightning grazed some of his hair, making it smoke at the ends.

From Tadg's other side, Root pounced, knocking Tadg into the grass. Tadg thrashed as Root placed a paw on each of his shoulders and pinned him down.

Panting, Barclay straightened and walked closer.

"You don't want to slay Lochmordra to save the Sea," Barclay said. "You want to kill him because he killed your father."

"Shut *up*!" Tadg seethed.

"No, you need to hear this. Killing Lochmordra won't bring your dad back. Your dad wouldn't have wanted—"

Barclay was cut off when a wave of water crashed over him, smacking him to the ground. He sputtered—the water was cold, and the salt stung his eyes. By the time he pushed himself to all fours, he saw that Root had also been caught beneath the wave. Tadg had drawn the water out of the pool, and now a rope of it twisted around him.

Tadg hurled the water at him like a whip. When Barclay dove out of its path, Tadg seized the opening and sprinted to the pool.

"Tadg!" Viola called. "You're making a mistake!"

Wind! Barclay thought, and a funnel of air shot up from beneath Tadg. It caught him the moment after he dove but before he could reach the water's surface. He hovered in the air, kicking and flailing wildly, a human-sized version of the shell and bottle cap that Barclay had practiced on.

Finally, Barclay threw him back against the ground. Then he lunged in front of him, blocking any other runaway attempts to the pool.

Tadg pounded his fist into the dirt. "Why can't you just let me go?"

"Because we're your friends," Barclay answered coolly.

EEEEEEIIIIIIIIIKKKKKKKKKKKK!

The Isle of Roane rumbled below them, the sound so loud that it drummed against Barclay's bones. Soon Lochmordra would rise and destroy Munsey and Dunsey, and Barclay, Viola, and Tadg would be stranded—and with no way to help.

Seeming to realize this, Tadg stood up, chest heaving. He pointed his finger at Barclay, and Barclay braced himself for another bolt of lightning.

"If you won't stop, then I'll take you down with me."

Then, instead of summoning Lore, he charged at Barclay. Barclay was so surprised that he didn't have time to react. Tadg's shoulder collided with Barclay's stomach, and the two hurtled off the edge. They splashed into the pool—then the vortex sucked them down, down, into the heart of the Sea below.

TWENTY-THREE

Barclay and Tadg clung to each other as the whirlpool spit them out in deep, warm water. Blue Firenekkies were scattered about, illuminating a massive cavern. At its bottom, a pool of green, briny currents swirled like a cloud of mist—an underwater lake.

Already Barclay's chest felt tight from holding his breath. But with the whirlpool above ever churning, they couldn't escape the way they'd come.

Tadg pried himself out of Barclay's grip and pointed below.

Two red tentacles thrashed amid the lake as white seeped over its surface. Lochmordra rose up, up, the force of his movement sending currents pushing Barclay and Tadg back against the prickly cave wall, crusted with barnacles and coral. Had it not wasted breath, Barclay would've screamed when Lochmordra came into full view. His eyes glowed white, and the beaklike mouth—beneath his head—opened wide as he let out a vicious scream.

EEEEEEEIIIIIIIIKKKKKKKK!

Lochmordra whipped his tentacles all at once, propelling him into the darkness of what Barclay realized was a tunnel. He was leaving for the surface.

The *surface*.

Tadg must've had the same thought, because he immediately summoned Mar-Mar. He and Barclay grasped onto the Nathermara's back and hurtled after the Legendary Beast. Barclay knew that open water meant Hooksharks, Daggerfish, and who knew what else, but he didn't care. His chest hurt so badly, he thought his lungs might burst.

They emerged from the tunnel into the ocean, where it seemed the other Beasts of Shipwreck Stretch had fled— possibly out of terror of Lochmordra. The Legendary Beast continued to rise higher, to the milky film atop the water. The boys followed.

The more they swam, the more Mar-Mar began to tremble. Lights like bolts of electricity shone beneath his translucent skin, and his body jerked from side to side. Barclay's grip came loose, and he somersaulted through the water. But he didn't look back. All that mattered was swimming as fast as possible toward the surface.

He broke through and gasped for air. Though not even two minutes had passed since they'd fallen into the pool, he felt as though he hadn't breathed in lifetimes.

To his right, Lochmordra had yet to rear his head from beneath the waves but was instead flailing below the surface. Thankfully, he hadn't noticed Barclay. In his frenzied state, he probably couldn't notice *anything*.

The seconds ticked by, and Tadg had yet to surface. Worry settled like an anchor in Barclay's gut. Could Tadg, who used water Lore, have accidentally drowned? Or what if the Hooksharks weren't gone like Barclay had thought?

Barclay took a great gulp of air and dove.

He spotted Tadg instantly, still clinging to Mar-Mar's back as the Beast sped in wonky patterns through the water.

Then Tadg let go. Or rather, he couldn't hold on anymore. He drifted limply, then sank down toward the ocean floor.

"Tadg!" Barclay screamed, which was a useless waste of air, since Tadg was too far away to hear. Barclay frantically swam after him. Mar-Mar dove deeper, not seeming to notice his Keeper's state. But once Barclay hooked his arms around Tadg's shoulders—Tadg's eyes were closed—Barclay saw that Mar-Mar wasn't swimming without a purpose. He was covering himself in the glowing blue Firenekkies.

Barclay kicked back to the surface. He was slower without the use of his arms and from Tadg's extra weight, and so, like in the race across the underwater rivers, he summoned a wind to propel him faster. They hurtled up—up—

At *last* they reached the air. Barclay's arm burned, and he caught sight of a frothy puddle of the weeping tide drifting beside him. He splashed it away, then—cringing from the pain—turned his attention to Tadg. But Tadg's eyes didn't open, and he didn't breathe. Instead, his head lolled back. He was very pale.

"No. *No*," Barclay rasped. He slapped Tadg's cheeks, but Tadg didn't stir. Barclay needed to get Tadg to the beach, but it was a long swim. The weeping tide was everywhere. Barclay was growing tired. And he didn't even know if Tadg would last that long. If he wasn't already . . .

"Grab on!" shouted a voice behind him, and Barclay was so surprised he nearly leapt out of his skin.

A life buoy plopped onto the water beside him, splashing droplets into Barclay's eyes. Barclay grasped it, thankful to rest. The rope reeling them in connected to a ship, which floated out of reach of the whirlpools in the distance. It was large, larger even than the *Bewlah*. And it had *not* been there when the *Bewlah* sank.

Yasha waved from the deck, then began reeling the boys in.

At first Barclay was relieved. This must've been the Guardian Keepers' ship. Maybe when they saw the weeping tide, they'd heeded Barclay's information and sailed for Shipwreck Stretch. But Barclay didn't spot Runa, Cyril, or Orla on the deck. Instead he only saw Edwyn, steering the ship with his attention fixed on the Legendary Beast.

But Edwyn was still a welcome sight. Not only could he get Barclay, Tadg, and Viola home, but they all desperately needed his healing Lore right now.

"Hurry up!" Yasha told them. When the life buoy reached the ship's side, Barclay hoisted Tadg over his shoulder and climbed aboard. Yasha grasped Tadg by his arm, and his body spilled limply onto the deck.

Yasha's face darkened as he studied Tadg. "It's too late. He's—"

"No. No, he can't be," Barclay croaked. He pressed with two hands on Tadg's chest, over and over. He didn't know what he was doing, not really. He'd only read about it in an adventure book. "Come on. Come on."

Nothing happened.

Then Edwyn knelt beside Tadg. He traced two fingers from Tadg's chest to his mouth, and Tadg's eyes flew open. He rolled onto his side and coughed up phlegmy seawater. Every one of Barclay's muscles relaxed in relief. He might've hugged Tadg if he thought Tadg would let him.

"You gave us a scare," Edwyn said.

While Tadg continued to spew up the Sea, Barclay looked around the ship and knitted his brow. "Where are the other Guardians?"

"We were separated near the Isle of Veir. With the weeping tide blooming, we found ourselves in the face of six angry Silberwals. Lucky for Yasha and me that we had this ship tucked away for safekeeping."

"Safekeeping?" Barclay said.

"For this moment, of course. I have to hand it to you, Barclay. The conch shell's clue was brilliant. I doubt any Lore Keeper other than an Elsie would've paid it any mind."

Barclay should've felt a flutter of pride in his chest, but instead, he felt uneasy. Edwyn's voice had a sharp edge that he didn't recognize.

Edwyn returned to the wheel. "We should be ready. Lochmordra will rise any moment now. Yasha, lower the anchor."

"Lower the anchor?" Barclay repeated, aghast. "But we need to get Viola and run! If Lochmordra attacks us, we'll be done for!" Barclay and Tadg were in no state to protect themselves, and though Yasha's fire Lore was powerful, Edwyn's healing Lore was useless in battle.

"Oh, I hardly think we're in that much danger," said Edwyn calmly. "I have everything we need. And after we're finished, Lochmordra won't be terrorizing the Sea any-more."

For a delirious moment, Barclay thought that Edwyn, too, meant to slay the Legendary Beast. But then Edwyn grabbed one of his many leather knapsacks and tossed it over his shoulder. Two jars inside it spilled out and rolled across the deck. Inside one was a knob of Fire Coral. And in the other, a rare Oystix pearl.

"You don't want to stop Lochmordra," Tadg choked out, pushing himself to a sitting position. "You want to bond with him. That's what your lessons have really been about all this time—you've been looking for the items for his snare."

"Are you truly surprised?" Edwyn asked. "Great Lore Keepers have been bonding with the Legendary Beasts for thousands of years."

"It was *you*? You're the one trying to bond with Lochmordra?" Barclay asked, stunned. "But you were gone! You weren't here when Lochmordra attacked Kelligree."

"I only left to throw Orla off my trail. And it's convenient that the effects of my stone Lore last for some time. I knew it would take weeks for the vents to return to normal."

"Th-the earthquakes," Barclay stammered. "That was you?"

"Yes. Lira is hardly my only Beast, but I've had to keep my Tarmacedon secret. It stirs up too many old memories. This entire mission has already threatened to expose me at every turn. I couldn't run the risk of anyone seeing my Tarmacedon and remembering who I am."

Barclay had no idea what he meant. He was still grappling to understand how everyone's favorite teacher had been behind all of this from the start.

Another growl erupted from the Sea.

EEEEEEEIIIIIIKKKKKK!

The water trembled, making the ship sway back and forth.

"If it wasn't for you," Edwyn told Barclay, "I don't think any of this would've been possible. I realized the truth about the weeping tide last Winter, and each time Lochmordra has awoken, I've tried to bond with him. But he was too destructive. And I never had the right ingredients for his snare. It was that book you gave me about Maedigan that finally showed me the truth—silver! Imagine my surprise to learn the bonding item I'd been getting wrong all this time was the common Gunkwort I already carried on me."

Barclay's heart seemed to stutter. He'd been so focused on how Maedigan had gotten to the Isle of Roane that he'd paid no attention to the legend's clues about the bonding items. And he'd lent Edwyn the book that had led him right to the answer.

"With the proper snare *and* the Isle of Roane," Edwyn continued, "I will catch Lochmordra the moment he rises. This is our chance to change the whole world. The Wilderlands *and* the Elsewheres."

He held out his hand to Barclay.

"What do you say, Barclay? Will you help me, one Elsie to another?"

Barclay hesitated. If Edwyn bonded with Lochmordra, then these attacks would end. The Sea would be saved.

But it was *Edwyn*, not Lochmordra, that the Sea needed saving from in the first place.

"Don't listen to him," Tadg growled. "He isn't who he says he is."

"What do you mean?" Barclay asked.

"Don't you remember the scars on his stomach when

we first met? Like two fangs. Klava's fangs. His name isn't Edwyn. His name is Audrian Keyes."

Edwyn's face twisted in displeasure. "Can you blame me for concealing my identity after my closest friends tried to kill me? When one of them almost *did*?"

Barclay gaped. Edwyn was actually Audrian Keyes, the young man Runa had killed?

"B-but that doesn't make sense," Barclay sputtered. "How can you be Keyes? Why wouldn't Runa and Cyril recognize you?"

"After I used my healing Lore to save myself, I went into hiding," Edwyn—Keyes—explained. "I had to use some rather . . . extraordinary means to change my face, and I spent years in the Elsewheres, planning for when I would try again. After Murdock died, leaving behind the knowledge of Lochmordra's snare, I came to the Sea to find his research. To finally claim a Legendary Beast as my own. I never expected Orla to send for Cyril and Runa. Imagine my position, hearing them fight over *my* death, all those years ago? As though they weren't the ones responsible."

"Runa was only protecting the Mountains from *you*," Tadg growled. "You're the one who attacked them."

"And none of it would've happened if my friends had only been able to understand my desires, to *see* the future I saw. A world where Lore has no boundaries or limits. We would all have more power than we could possibly imagine."

"That would destroy the Elsewheres," Barclay said, horrified.

"Destroy them? No, the Elsewheres would be part of it—a world that is one great Wilderland. Even if they *are* consumed, it is a worthwhile price. From then on, Lore would be everywhere. And no one would be needlessly afraid."

Barclay backed away from Keyes. "No. No. I won't help you."

Keyes's face fell. "That's a shame. We could make a great team, the four of us." He turned to Yasha. "Bind them here."

Barclay looked to Yasha, expecting his friend to be as shocked and horrified by this news as he was. But Yasha wore a steely grimace.

After what had happened with Abel and Ethel, Barclay should've understood betrayal well. Yet the truth about Yasha was an unexpected blow. Because Yasha had always known his teacher's true identity and motives. Every night spent in the Planty Shanty, every lesson, Yasha had been lying.

Yasha reached in his pocket and pulled out a handful of stones, ones Barclay had once spotted among Edwyn's tools. He tossed them on the deck, and they moved on their own, darting like magnets. They formed a circle around Barclay and Tadg, and an iridescent dome stretched over them.

A cage.

Barclay pounded his fist on it, but the dome didn't budge. "No! You can't just leave us—"

"Don't worry," Keyes said. "Lochmordra will be in his Mark before he's able to attack you."

While Keyes left to climb into the rowboat, Barclay slammed on the dome once more. "Yasha! Yasha, wait! I don't understand. Why would you—"

"I have my reasons," Yasha said flatly.

Then he followed Keyes into the rowboat.

"No!" Tadg called after them, but they ignored him. Tadg seethed and kicked the barrier. "There has to be a way out of this."

Barclay reached down to try to grab one of the stones, but it was as though they'd been cemented to the deck. They wouldn't budge.

EEEEIIIIKKKKK!

Red tentacles sprang out of the water, and Lochmordra rose from the Sea. Up close and in broad daylight, he was larger and more monstrous than Barclay had ever realized. His head was long and narrow like a squid's, and ruby-like scales glimmered across his trunk. Strange markings swirled around his eyes—spirals. Etched deep into his flesh, they made him look as mysterious and ancient as the stone pillars on the island. As the Sea itself.

On one of his tentacles, something gold glinted in the sunlight. A magnificent trident, buried into Lochmordra's gut. There was no wound, but the trident remained there all the same, as though it was now a piece of him. A memento from the fable of Maedigan.

In the distance, Keyes and Yasha had reached the shore of the Isle of Roane. While Lochmordra shrieked, Yasha went to work setting down each of the jars in a line. After he finished, the sand beneath them rumbled and shook, then Keyes's stone Lore broke through and lifted them higher, creating a mountain so tall they stood eye-level with the Beast.

Barclay frantically scanned the island for any sign of Viola, but she was nowhere.

Tadg growled and shot a bolt of lightning at the barrier. Rather than split it apart, the bolt ricocheted off it, nearly striking Barclay in the leg. Barclay dodged out of the way just in time, and it burned a sizzling, thumb-sized hole in the deck.

"Are you trying to kill us?" Barclay shouted.

"I'm *trying* to get us out of here!"

"Croak!"

By accident, the Stonetoad appeared on Tadg's shoulder. "What the—? Toadles? I knew I should've fed you to Mar-Mar. Get back—"

Toadles leapt off Tadg's shoulder to the deck. He hopped to a nearby stone. Then his stomach convulsed, and his eyes bulged. He vomited a thick, purple sludge onto the rock, which melted with a *hiss*.

The barrier flickered out.

Rather than seeming pleased, Tadg looked possibly

angrier. "You could do *that* this whole time? Where have you been hiding that?"

Toadles only croaked in response.

Overhead, Lochmordra shrieked. His tentacles lashed out against the mountain of stone where Keyes and Yasha stood. At its base, a light began to glow, engulfing the six items of Lochmordra's snare. The light swelled, sweeping up the mountain, across the island. A brilliant, terrible net.

It collapsed over Lochmordra, and the Legendary Beast froze. He couldn't break free. He couldn't move at all.

Except for his eyes. His white pupils darted around wildly as Keyes grasped the trident on his tentacle with two hands. With a wrench, he pulled it free. Lochmordra let out a shriek so loud, so anguished, that all of the Sea seemed to tremor. A wave crashed into the side of Keyes's boat, sending Tadg and Barclay clambering for anything to hold on to. Barclay reached for a dangling rope and missed. He landed in a heap on the deck, while Tadg skidded back and collided with the port-side rail.

Then all at once, the net of light vanished. Barclay jumped to his feet and stared out at the snare on the beach. Viola stood among the jars. She'd stolen one and slammed it against the stone tower, smashing it.

Lochmordra roared. His tentacles flared back to life, writhing and battering in every direction. While Keyes tried to calm him, Yasha sprinted down the stony mountain back to the beach. To Viola.

But Yasha wasn't the only one Viola hadn't noticed. Behind her, a monster loomed. It was the same Beast Barclay had encountered three times now, though in the daylight, he was finally able to see it clearly. It reminded Barclay of a bull, except instead of horns, huge tusks curved upward from its jaws, each made of solid stone. Matching armored plates wrapped around its head like a skull. It stood on its hind legs, and slowly, its head turned to Viola. Part of its armor chipped away, as though brittle rock.

The Tarmacedon.

"Viola! Behind you!" Barclay called, but she was too far away to hear. He spun back around to Tadg. "We have to help her! She doesn't have her Lore!"

On the beach, Viola was rummaging around on the sand. She didn't notice the Beast until its shadow swallowed her, blocking out the sun.

Slowly she looked up, straight into the Beast's red eyes.

"Why isn't she moving?" Barclay moaned to Tadg. "She needs to run. She can't just . . ."

The Beast raised its front hooves in the air, ready to pummel Viola where she stood.

Viola turned her back to it and pressed something small to her face. Just as the legs lowered to crush her, there was a flash of light, and Viola vanished and reappeared at Barclay's side, making him yelp in shock. She held a cracked silver shard of Starglass in front of her eye like a monocle.

"How did you do that?" he asked.

"Starglass lets you use sunlight to leap from one place to—"

Before she could finish, Tadg sprinted to the bow of the ship, pointed his hand, and shot a massive bolt of lightning straight at Lochmordra.

"No!" Barclay shouted, then tackled Tadg to the deck. They landed with a painful thud. "You can't kill him! It's Keyes we need to stop—"

"I wasn't trying to *kill* him. I was only trying to get him to—"

With another shriek, Lochmordra turned. His eerie white eyes locked onto their ship, and he started to swim away from Keyes.

Toward *them*.

The apprentices scrambled to their feet.

"I'll get the wheel!" Viola shouted.

"I'll man the sails!" Barclay called.

"I'll reel in the anchor!" Tadg finished.

Barclay yanked the ropes, undoing their knots and freeing the sails. As Lochmordra loomed closer, his tentacles reaching for them, Barclay summoned all of his strength.

Wind!

The ship was hurled ahead. It leapt over the jagged waves, and the breeze whipped Barclay's hair across his face. Viola spun the helm, steering the ship to draw Lochmordra as far from Keyes and Yasha as possible.

"We can't outrun him!" Barclay shouted. Even if they tried, the whirlpools of Shipwreck Stretch loomed closer by the second. They would capsize all over again.

"And we can't fight him either," Tadg said.

Then something else cannoned out of the water, and Barclay stopped his Lore and braced himself, expecting a tentacle to seize the ship and drag them below the surface. Instead, it was Mar-Mar, his skin coated in blue Firenekkies.

Barclay's stomach dropped. Now they had to face not one frenzied Beast, but two.

But as Mar-Mar swam closer, Barclay realized he wasn't thrashing the way he had before. In fact, the white puddles of the weeping tide in the water dispersed around him, as though repelled.

"Look! Look!" Barclay shouted at Tadg.

Tadg leaned out over the rail. "I don't get it. What's happening?"

"It must be the Firenekkies! Ansley told me that whenever one kind of Lore does one thing, there's always something else that counteracts it. The Firenekkies must counteract the weeping tide! That's why the weeping tide never clustered around the hot sea vents."

"Which means the Firenekkies can fix Lochmordra," Viola said. "But they're all underwater. Should we dive?"

"No," Tadg said. "I'll do it."

Tadg reached both of his arms out over the water. Then he made a lifting motion, his body shaking from the strain.

Below them, the ocean began to rumble.

Waves quaked, then rose. Higher, higher. They knocked

the ship in every direction, and Barclay clung to a mast to keep from falling.

Then geysers of water erupted across the surface. Firenekkies sprayed everywhere, and the white froth on the Sea began to recede.

But it was no use. Lochmordra's tentacle reached forward, and Barclay lunged out of its path as it snaked around the deck once, then twice.

Lochmordra pulled, and the vessel lurched back. Behind them, the Beast's mouth opened wide. His throat was a pitch-black tunnel of endless teeth.

"It's no use!" Tadg called. "We need to jump!"

"And swim *where*?" Viola demanded.

She was right. They had nowhere to go. In the water was Lochmordra. On the island was Keyes.

"Do it again!" Barclay shouted to Tadg. "With the Firenekkies!"

"But I just—"

"Do it *again*!"

Muttering to himself, Tadg turned back to the water. He made the same lifting motion, and streams of water spouted from the ocean hundreds of feet into the air. Salt water and Firenekkies rained around them, just as Lochmordra's tentacle began to squeeze tighter. The wood of the floorboards cracked. The masts teetered and crashed.

Lochmordra's mouth was close. So close that Barclay could make out his sharp, serrated tongue.

This was their last chance to escape without being eaten.

Instead, Barclay raised his hands to the sky. He thought about conch shells, whirlpools, and spirals. He thought about his weeks of practice, so certain that he was too much of an Elsie to become a great Lore Keeper, when instead being an Elsie was what helped him solve this mystery when no one else could. He thought about the day Root had bonded with him. And he thought of Dullshire and the people he had sworn to protect. The reason he had become a Guardian apprentice in the first place.

Hundreds of small vortexes began to blow around them, each one catching a shimmering cluster of Firenekkies and suspending them in the air. They surrounded the ship as though it was cradled in blue starlight.

Lochmordra stretched his mouth open even wider, ready for his feast. Barclay braced his feet against the crumpled deck to keep from falling. Just before they passed through Lochmordra's lips, Barclay seized all of the wind he could and threw it at the Legendary Beast, coating him in the Firenekkies.

The Beast jerked his head back, and the tentacles grasping the ship receded. Glittering blue water sloshed up the ruined deck. The vessel was sinking. Tadg grabbed the life buoy and tossed it into the waves.

"Come on!" he yelled, motioning for Barclay and Viola to follow.

The three of them dove and swam for the life buoy.

Above, Lochmordra was blanketed in the glowing blue Firenekkies, and he stopped thrashing and lowered his tentacles. He still heaved—as though panting—but as the minutes passed, that also slowed. And then finally, the Legendary Beast went still.

The three apprentices climbed back onto the shoreline. On the stony mountain above, Keyes and Yasha were gone.

"We let them escape," Tadg choked.

"They can't have gotten far," Viola said.

"You don't know that! What other types of Lore could they be hiding?"

Lochmordra's gaze swept over them. As though *he*, a magnificent, monstrous Beast, as old as the first drop of water in the Sea, was assessing *them*, three exhausted and drenched apprentices, too scared to even breathe. Barclay had the urge to flee, to escape what was sure to be one final, deadly attack. But he couldn't look away. Lochmordra's eyes now churned a cloudy gray and flashed with light. Looking at him felt like staring straight into a storm.

Then, satisfied—or, perhaps, grateful—Lochmordra sank back beneath the waves.

And he was gone.

Next to him, Barclay realized that Tadg was crying.

Tadg wiped his eyes on his arm. "Don't. Say. Anything."

"I wasn't going to," Barclay told him. "Well, I was going to say that I'm sorry. About your dad, and about your home. It's okay to be angry about what happened."

Tadg sighed. "I just remember what it was like. The white water. The whirlpool that opened up, with Lochmordra's mouth at the bottom. If I'd rowed faster, I would've reached him."

"Or you would've been swallowed too."

Tadg sat on the sand and rested his head between his knees. "I know," he said softly, and Viola gave his shoulder a tight, supportive squeeze.

After another minute, the crest of Lochmordra's fin disappeared into the Sea, and the water—blue once more—became still at last.

TWENTY-FOUR

The next morning, Barclay and the apprentices gathered around Ulick's sickbed as he showed off the gruesome scar along his arm where a Hookshark had bitten him.

"He thought he had me, he did," Ulick said. "But *I'm* the one who took a bit of him! Reached in there and yanked it out!"

He brandished a jagged shark tooth and let out a bellowing laugh.

While the apprentices oohed and aahed, Orla ripped the tooth from Ulick's hand. "Nearly getting yourself killed is nothing to brag about."

"I think it is," Cecily said giddily.

"Ha!" Ulick barked. "We saved the Sea! Bewlah and I are heroes!"

On the bedpost behind him, Bewlah squawked happily—then shrieked when Oudie swooped in and tackled her, hoping to claim the best perch. Though they might've been scuffling, the pair of them and the other Beasts were a welcome sight. The weeping tide wouldn't bloom again until Midsummer, and so the Beasts of the Sea were free to roam as they pleased.

"If anyone is a hero, Ulick, it's these four." Orla nodded at Barclay, Tadg, Viola, and Hasu.

They beamed at one another, and Mitzi, now safe and sound on Viola's shoulder, chirped proudly.

"What are *you* proud of?" Viola asked her whelp. Strips of Gunkwort crisscrossed Viola's arms, courtesy of Ansley. "You missed all the action."

Mitzi fluffed out her tail feathers, ignoring her.

"In fact," Orla continued, "I believe I owe Barclay in particular an apology." She placed her wrinkled hand on Barclay's shoulder. "You'd think someone as old as me would be wise by now, but I still make mistakes. And I was too harsh on you. I'm sorry. The Sea was lucky to have a Lore Keeper as fine as you in our midst."

"Th-thank you," Barclay said, embarrassed to be singled out—but a good deal grateful.

Orla cast Ulick a stern look. "And *you*. You and I need to have a conversation about sailing five apprentices to what easily could've been their doom."

"But it wasn't, was it?" Ulick winked.

After the *Bewlah* had sunk, Hasu had used her spatial Lore to portal each of them to the closest inhabited island, the Isle of Veir. It had been the most power she'd ever used, and even after a full night's sleep, her eyes still drooped as she sat in the chair beside Ulick, and Bitti was fast asleep on her nose. Without the pair of them, their friends would certainly have been eaten by Hooksharks.

"I'm sorry about the *Bewlah*," Barclay said to Ulick.

"Don't be! That was the *Bewlah VII*. Seems about time for the *Bewlah VIII*."

"What do you mean?"

"My ships sink all the time! But Bewlah and I always find a way back out on the water."

Considering Ulick's excitement to sail during all manner of storms and Beastly frenzies, this made a lot of sense.

"Still, if we'd figured out why the underwater rivers changed," Barclay told him, "this never would've happened."

"Ah! I think I might have an answer for ya," Ulick said. "Ol' Maedigan traveled underwater 'when the night sky was brightest.' Well, that's obvious! The brightest night is the night of a full moon."

"It's like the riddle!" Viola said, so excited she practically squealed. "'Not even the sun knows where it lies, and the stars won't spill the secret.' The underwater rivers only travel to Roane on the full moon."

"There was a full moon the night we found it," Tadg said, nodding.

Ulick beamed. "See? Don't need a Scholar to tell ya stuff! Us sailors know the ways of the Sea just fine."

"All right, all right, that's enough from you. Go back to resting," Orla said. Then she took Shazi and Tadg by the shoulders and ushered everyone to the Guild House's spiral staircase.

The other Guardians awaited them on the ground floor. Now that Lochmordra's attacks had finally come to an end, the Guild House boomed with the ruckus of celebration. Musicians played. Drinking mugs clattered on tabletops. Beasts chittered, cawed, honked, and hissed.

Runa and Cyril were the only ones who didn't join the merriment. Last night, when Tadg, Viola, and Barclay had ridden Mar-Mar back to Munsey, they told the two Lore Masters and the High Keeper everything. About how Edwyn Lusk had really been Audrian Keyes. How he'd kept his stone Lore secret and used it to shift the sea vents and warm the water and make the weeping tide bloom. How he'd lured Lochmordra out each time hoping to bond with him.

For two people who'd spent so much time arguing with each other, Runa and Cyril had been shocked into silence. Runa hadn't even punished Tadg for sneaking out on his own or Barclay and the others for running after him without telling anyone. But now they each wore dour expressions, and Barclay braced himself for the worst.

Instead, Cyril declared, "Shazi, Hasu, Cecily—the four of us are leaving."

"What?" Cecily asked, helping herself to the bowl of sweets on a nearby table. "Already? But it's the middle of a party!"

"And the Sea still needs so much help," Hasu said. "Couldn't we—"

"I've written to the Grand Keeper about what happened, and he is concerned that, even if Audrian Keyes was thwarted from bonding with Lochmordra, this is a pattern, and he is dangerous. We have every reason to believe he will strike again somewhere else. While he and I investigate that, you'll be continuing your training in the Mountains."

The apprentices all exchanged sorry looks. Even after competitions, rivalries, and disagreements, the six of them had become good friends over the course of this adventure.

"Really, Cyril—" Orla started.

"We'll be leaving immediately," Cyril said tightly, "so say your goodbyes."

After narrowly escaping danger the day before, Barclay didn't see why they couldn't stay and rest one more night. He suspected it had to do with the way that Cyril looked nervously at Runa when she wasn't paying attention.

At this, the three girls turned to the other apprentices. But before they could say anything, Cyril strode between them and cleared his throat.

"Viola?" he said. "I was wondering if I could speak with you for a moment in private."

Viola stiffened. "Me?" She glanced at Runa anxiously.

"It'll only be a moment," Cyril said.

Runa placed a protective hand on Viola's shoulder. "Fine," she told Cyril. "But you better choose your words perfectly—you've had half a year to dwell on them."

While the two of them left to speak in a quieter corner, Hasu threw her arms around Barclay and Tadg. "I'm going to miss all of you."

Shazi, who wasn't the sort for hugs, held out her hand to shake. She squeezed Tadg's so hard that his skin whitened. "Next time we Dool, I won't take it easy on you."

Tadg snorted. "I was taking it easy on *you*."

Saif and Root also said their goodbyes, which included a very hesitant butt sniff. Oudie's shadow tickled Barclay underneath his arm.

"Bitti will be sad she slept through it all," Hasu said. The tiny Beast's wings fluttered on Hasu's nose, as though she was having pleasant dreams.

"Oh! This reminds me!" Cecily said brightly. "I should probably give all these things back to you." She shrugged her bag off her shoulders and began pulling out various items, so many Barclay wondered how she'd fit them all in a small sack. She crammed them into Barclay's and Tadg's arms. A loose sock. Several of Viola's gold pins. Tadg's leather bracelet. A lost button from one of Barclay's shirts. Many snacks. Even Conley Murdock's massive sack of fan mail, which fell to the floor with a heavy *thump*.

Annoyed, Barclay sifted through his missing belongings.

He'd been looking for that sock. "You've been stealing from us for weeks?"

She smiled mischieviously. "I like the practice, though you're all easy marks."

"Do you think we'll see each other again?" Hasu asked.

"I'm sure we will at the licensing exam," Shazi said glumly. That reunion would be years and years away. Then she grinned. "But you three better be ready, because *I* won't be staying an apprentice any longer than I have to."

"We'll be ready even sooner than you," Tadg said, which Barclay thought might've been wishful thinking. Other than Cecily, Cyril's apprentices all had been training a year longer than they had.

But for weeks, Barclay had been convinced that he would never catch up to his friends who'd grown up in the Lore Keeper world. Yet he'd saved Lochmordra. He'd faced Gravaldor. No matter what exams or adventures awaited him in his future, he needed to start believing in himself. He *would* be ready.

Viola returned in time to give Cyril's apprentices a last goodbye. She wore a colorful seaweed garland around her neck, which Barclay saw was one of many being handed out by a happy Lore Keeper across the hall. Even Murph was wearing one, and his mustache had been dyed a cheery pink.

"It was good to see one another again," Viola told the other girls. "And I wish you didn't have to go."

"Me too," Hasu said. "But I'm glad you're happier now.

And Runa makes a really great teacher for you."

"She does," Shazi agreed. "So you better train really hard, because I won't take it easy on you, either."

Reluctantly they gathered the rest of their belongings and trudged to the door.

Cyril shook Orla's hand. "Leopold sends his regards. According to the letter I received via dragon post this morning, he's very pleased that the situation was resolved."

"I bet he is," Orla said dryly. "So he wouldn't have to pay for any of it. But safe travels. Don't let the girls bully you too much."

He smirked. "Oh, there's no way around that." Then he asked Runa, "This entire time with Edwyn . . . did you ever suspect who he was?"

"Maybe once—I considered the resemblance, but I thought Audrian was gone," Runa answered. "Did you?"

"No, I didn't," Cyril said softly. Then without an apology, a handshake, or even a smile, he added, "Leopold will soon be in touch."

"I'm sure he will," Runa said flatly.

Barclay leaned over and whispered in Viola's ear. "If Runa never killed Keyes, shouldn't they be able to forgive each other? What they're fighting about never happened!"

"I don't think it'll be that simple," she said.

While Cyril and his apprentices waved a final goodbye, Barclay also asked her, "What did Cyril say to you?"

"He apologized for giving up on me as a student. He said

that if he'd been a better teacher, he would've realized why I was struggling instead of punishing me for it. And he said that he's glad that I've found my footing now."

"How uncharacteristically thoughtful of him," Runa spoke. When Viola looked embarrassed, Runa said, "Sorry, was I not supposed to eavesdrop?"

"No, it's fine. And I think . . . I think I'm going to write to my father. I understand why he was worried now, because of everything that happened with Keyes. But I want to tell him that I'm doing fine. That I'm doing really well, actually."

Runa nodded. "That is definitely what Leopold cares about most."

"But if they're returning to the Mountains, where are we going?" Barclay asked.

"We'll be staying here for the time being. Hasu was quite right—after all the damage to the islands, the Sea needs help rebuilding. And staying in one Wilderland will give you three the time you need to train."

"We're staying here?" Viola said, sounding disappointed. "I'm not sure I can drink any more milk."

Barclay grinned, peering around the happy mayhem of the party. He didn't think staying at the Sea sounded so bad.

"It's already decided, I'm afraid. But before we begin discussing training or rebuilding, you should know that you're all being punished until Midsummer. You left in the middle of a crisis, telling *no one*, with one very irresponsible adult, and nearly got yourselves killed for it. And Tadg," Runa seethed, "slaying Lochmordra? What would I have done if something happened to you? Next time you have the urge to spar someone who will knock you flat on your face, Klava and I will happily do it for you."

Tadg perked up. "Really?"

"No, obviously not. I promised Conley I'd watch out for you, not break all your bones." Then Runa's face softened. "But I'm proud of you. Especially you, Barclay. You figured out what no one else could have. It goes to show that there is just as much to learn from the Elsewheres as there is in the Wilderlands."

Barclay beamed.

"Also, you'll each be working part-time fishing seaweed until you pay Ulick back for his boat."

The three of them groaned.

"But that'll take the whole Summer!" Tadg said.

Runa shrugged. "Longer, probably. So you better get to work, then, if you intend to still have any time to train in the next year. You wouldn't want to fall behind Cyril's students, would you?"

After such a taunt, the three apprentices barely lingered to enjoy the party. They grabbed as many sweet cakes as they could carry, then took off running toward the docks.

Truthfully, punishment or not, Barclay was glad to help rebuild the Sea. He did love to be on the road, but they needed the time to train and grow stronger. Because despite all the celebration, this aftermath was different from the time the three of them had saved the Woods. The man who was responsible for so much destruction was still out there. And maybe it would be weeks from now. Maybe it would be years. But without a doubt, Audrian Keyes would strike again.

And Barclay would be ready.

The three apprentices boarded one of the boats and sailed out onto open water. As usual, Viola had brought along a book to study, and they each took turns quizzing one another while gathering seaweed.

"'How many species of dragons are there?'" Barclay read.

"Ninety-three," Viola answered, then shouted, "Mitzi! No! Don't eat that! That's supposed to be people food!"

Mitzi obediently spat out a mouthful of stringy seaweed, but she didn't look happy about it.

"'What is the capital city of the Tundra?'" Barclay asked.

"Permafrosk," Tadg said. Viola shot him a competitive glare. They were tied.

Barclay grinned at the next question. They all knew the answer to this one. "'What are the nine isles of the Sea?'"

"The *ten* isles," Viola blurted, so fast the words spilled out of her mouth, "are Munsey, Dunsey, Coad—"

"Glannock," Tadg cut in. "Slakey—"

"Orn! Kelli—"

"Veir!"

"Growe—I mean Trowe—"

"Croak!"

"AHHHH!" Tadg jolted and flailed out his arms, mak-

ing the small rowboat teeter until it tipped over. All three apprentices shrieked as they went plunging into the ocean. When they each resurfaced, all of them netted with seaweed, Toadles sat at the top of Tadg's head. His warty face curved into a smile, as though proud of the mess he'd made.

"And Roane!" Viola gasped out, not letting a little capsizing hold her back from finishing the contest. "Ha! I win!"

"I want to play against Barclay next," Tadg said quickly. "Because then I'll . . ." He hesitated.

"You'll have the advantage, because I'm an Elsie?" Barclay finished for him and smirked. "Is it that hard for you to win otherwise? That's just sad."

"Hey! I was going to offer to let you have double points. I was going to be *nice*."

While the three of them swam, bickering and laughing, a shimmering light began to dance across the water. They looked up. A parade of Polypops soared overheard, their tentacles waving like streamers. There must've been hundreds of them, all swimming across the sky.

Faintly, no louder than a whisper, bells tinkled. A message from the wilds.

The sound brought good luck, so the legends claimed. But it also brought a warning. Whatever path their futures took, that luck would be needed.

Because it wouldn't be long before adventure came calling again.

AN EXCERPT FROM

A TRAVELER'S LOG OF DANGEROUS BEASTS,
VOL. 2

BY CONLEY MURDOCK

BRUTOPODS

Wilderland: the Sea
Class: Prime
These crustaceans are known for their powerful claws and violent attitudes. What many don't know about them is that they continue growing their entire lives, even in adulthood. I once met one twice my own height, and sixteen years later, I'm still shell-shocked!

CALADRIUS

Wilderland: the Mountains, the Woods, the Jungle
Class: Mythic
Considered among the most powerful of healing Beasts; for years Scholars believed they held the secret to everlasting life. This may be a myth, but they remain a prized companion for any Lore Keeper who often faces danger. Make sure to plan accordingly, though—their Lore will knock you straight to sleep!

DRAGON

Wilderland: the Mountains
Class: varies
A collective term for Beasts of a mixture of reptilian and avian natures, who vary in size, power, and type of Lore.

FIRENEKKIE

Wilderland: the Sea
Class: Trite
These phytoplankton cover the seafloor, providing light to all the Wilderland's underwater plants and creatures. In the late Summer, they become so numerous that some of the Sea's waves glow a vibrant blue.

FWISHT

Wilderland: the Sea
Class: Familiar

Capable of carrying objects twice their size, these pelican-like Beasts make excellent postal birds. And their healing Lore might not work on humans, but it does just the trick for a Beast's minor scrapes or bruises.

GLUPPYFISH

Wilderland: The Sea, the Jungle, the Mountains
Class: Trite

These tiny colorful fish make beautiful additions to home aquariums. They develop their rainbow scales from the foods they eat, and so Gluppyfish from various Wilderlands often look different from one another, as their diets vary with each environment.

GRAVALDOR

Wilderland: the Woods
Class: Legendary

Resembling a massive bear, the Legendary Beast of the Woods slumbers for most of the year, and some Keepers credit hearing a low rumbling in the forest that could be his snores. When awakened, he has been known to destroy entire towns, especially when feeling threatened.

GRUIGNAD

Wilderland: the Sea, the Mountains, the Desert
Class: Trite

These sea lice live within tangles of algae, but their favorite home is human hair. To rid yourself of them, Siggykelp water makes for a useful shampoo, but a mayonnaise mask will substitute in a pinch!

HADDISSS

Wilderland: the Desert, the Mountains, the Jungle
Class: Mythic
Being only skeleton, these serpentine Beasts have no brain, no stomach, and no insides at all. They don't seem to eat or age, and much about their lives remains a mystery. Though I'm positive I heard one burp once.

HOOKSHARK

Wilderland: the Sea
Class: Prime
The heads of these sharks resemble large hooks, which they use with their sand Lore to dig bottom-dwelling fish out from the seafloor. Beware—they are known to indulge in humans as well.

JAWBASK

Wilderland: the Sea
Class: Prime
These sharks suck up small Beasts and animals from the ocean floor like vacuums.

KARKADANN

Wilderland: the Desert, the Jungle
Class: Prime
A large, hairless horse with an ivory horn and the attitude of a wolverine. I desperately wished for one as a child only to later learn they are nothing like ponies.

LEPINFISH

Wilderland: the Sea
Class: Familiar
The bane of all sailors, these "flying fish" jump so high that they can leap onto even the mightiest of ships.

LOCHMORDRA

Wilderland: the Sea
Class: Legendary

Lochmordra dwells in an unknown place deep within the Sea, rising to terrorize sailors or devastate coastal villages. His mouth is so large, he can swallow ships whole.

LUFTHUND

Wilderland: the Woods
Class: Mythic

Tricky to find and trickier to tame, as they are fiercely independent. Resembling large black wolves, they can grow up to six feet long and four feet tall. They can turn entirely into wind, like a rush of smoke billowing past, and their Lore can conjure storms and wind gusts. Absolutely magnificent! Also highly dangerous.

MADHUCHABEE

Wilderland: the Jungle
Class: Mythic

Unlike the more common, Trite-class Stingurs, Madhuchabees are exceptionally hard to find, as they can portal long distances with their spatial Lore. I would personally be honored to be stung by one.

MUIRMARÚ

Wilderland: the Sea, the Tundra
Class: Prime

These clever Beasts use sound Lore to send their cries hundreds of miles through the ocean. I've spent countless hours trying to decode their noises, but their language has proven too complex for human ears.

NATHERMARA

Wilderland: the Sea
Class: Mythic
A giant lamprey, capable of both water and electric Lore, that can only be found in the Sea's darkest depths. One also happens to be my most cherished friend.

OYSTIX

Wilderland: the Sea
Class: Trite
Producers of beautiful pearls or perilous explosives? One may never know until opening its shell to discover what lies inside.

POLYPOP

Wilderland: the Sea
Class: Familiar
These jellyfish secrete a slimy film in the Winter for warmth, which they shed in the warmer seasons. The gummy skins that they leave behind make useful masks for breathing underwater. On rare occasion, a Polypop will be born with bells within its tentacles, which you may hear chime if ever a smack of Polypops passes overhead, using their wind Lore to swim through the sky.

REPTILLY

Wilderland: the Sea, the Tundra
Class: Trite
These tiny saltwater snakes shed their skin every day, which makes for an excellent, savory snack. I've also heard their exfoliating properties do wonders for pimples!

SCORMODDIN

Wilderland: the Desert
Class: Mythic
With over three hundred individual steel plates covering
their bodies, these scorpion Beasts are almost impossible
to wound. Their long sharp tails make excellent blades. One
even won the gold medal in Menneset's swordsmen competition for six years in a row.

SILBERWAL

Wilderland: the Sea
Class: Mythic
Though nicknamed a "whale dragon," these Beasts are not
dragons, as they do not have wings and cannot fly. But
similar to dragons, they love anything shiny, and their
underwater caves are often full of sunken treasure.

SLANNTRAMÓR

Wilderland: the Sea
Class: Mythic
The beautiful armor of these whales has led them to be
hunted to near extinction. Anyone who wishes to bond with
one must receive special permission from the High Keeper
of the Sea.

SLEÁBEAK

Wilderland: the Sea, the Tundra
Class: Prime
This seagull Beast skewers fish out of the water with its
long, spearlike beak. But when it comes to vexing the Sea's
beaches, it's unclear which is worse: its front end or its back
end!

SMYNX

Wilderland: the Tundra
Class: Mythic
These lynxlike Beasts can survive in the coldest parts of the Tundra due to their powerful fire Lore. Wandering travelers have often mistaken them for demons, as they can turn their entire body into flame.

TARMACEDON

Wilderland: the Mountains, the Woods
Class: Mythic
These massive creatures can stand comfortably on either four legs or two, a talent which I believe evolved from their ability to slam their front legs on the ground and generate earthquakes. They hibernate in the Winters by turning their entire bodies to stone. Warning: do not approach wearing the color red.

TENEPIE

Wilderland: the Mountains, the Desert
Class: Mythic
These cunning crowlike Beasts can control their bodies and shadows separately, though each always remains attached to the other. Their shadows are especially ticklish.

TORTAR

Wilderland: the Sea, the Desert, the Jungle, the Mountains
Class: Mythic
With a lifespan of almost five hundred years, these tortoise Beasts could probably tell us much about forgotten Lore Keeper history. Unfortunately, they are exceptionally hard to find, as their mist Lore often hides them within a mirage.

WATERMOOSE

Wilderland: The Tundra, the Woods
Class: Prime

These water-breathing mooselike Beasts can be tricky to find. The best way to spot them is their antlers, which rise from lakes and rivers and look like bramble.

ZAPRAY

Wilderland: the Sea
Class: Mythic

These large stingray Beasts dwell in the deep waters of the Sea, especially off the coast of the Isle of Veir. Their powerful electric Lore makes them among the deadliest Beasts of the Sea. Avoid their territory unless you'd like to find yourself deep-fried!

STONETOAD (ENTRY BY TADG MURDOCK)

WILDERLAND: THE SEA
CLASS: ???

AN UGLY, WARTY TOAD WITH A GEMSTONE IN ITS FOREHEAD. ~~PEES~~ SECRETES POISON. DOES NOT RESPECT AUTHORITY.

ACKNOWLEDGMENTS

A sequel is a difficult task for any writer, but it is thanks to the support of so many people that *The Weeping Tide* faced nothing but smooth sailing.

To my editor, Kate Prosswimmer: without your feedback, Barclay would never have found his sea legs. Thank you for the amount of effort you put into what you do—it always shows, and it is always tremendously appreciated.

To my agent, Whitney Ross: thank you for your insight, your patience, and your dedication. I am so lucky to have you as a first mate.

To the entire McElderry team, including Nicole Fiorica, Justin Chanda, Karen Wojtyla, Bridget Madsen, Caitlin Sweeny, Nicole Russo, Cassie Malmo, Jenny Lu, Alissa Nigro, Anna Jarzab, Kate Bouchard, and Nadia Almahadi: I couldn't have asked for a better crew!

Thank you to Petur Antonsson for illustrating another stunning cover, and to Sonia Chaghatzbanian and Karyn Lee for the book's incredible design, inside and out.

To Christine Lynn Herman: I've run out of creative ways to thank you in these acknowledgments, but you will always retain a dedicated paragraph in every book I write.

Thank you to my early readers, Axie Oh and Amanda Haas—after an extremely messy first draft, both of your advice helped me to correct my course. Thank you to Claribel Ortega and Lauren Magaziner, whose enthusiasm and guidance have meant so much to me, a newcomer to the delightful world of middle grade. Thank you to fellow critique group members Janella Angeles, Katy Rose Pool, Kat Cho, Mara Fitzgerald, Alex Castellanos, Meg Kohlmann, Erin Bay, Ashley Burdin, Maddy Colis, Akshaya Raman, Melody Simpson, and Tara Sim. Thank you to Zoe Sivak, the cleverest of best friends.

Thank you to Mairead Fitzgerald-Mumford. Without your Irish language expertise, the names of the Beasts of the Sea would have fallen abysmally short of their inspiration.

Thank you to my fiancé, who will be my husband by the time this book is published.

Thank you to Jelly Bean, my spunky orange tabby, who has always been my inspiration for Mitzi.

To my readers: I cannot tell you how many times your kind messages have brought a smile to my face. From the beginning, writing this series meant venturing into uncharted waters, but it is thanks to you that it has been the most wonderful of adventures, and I'm so excited for everything we still have in store.

Turn the page to for a sneak peak of
Barclay's next adventure in

THE EVER STORMS

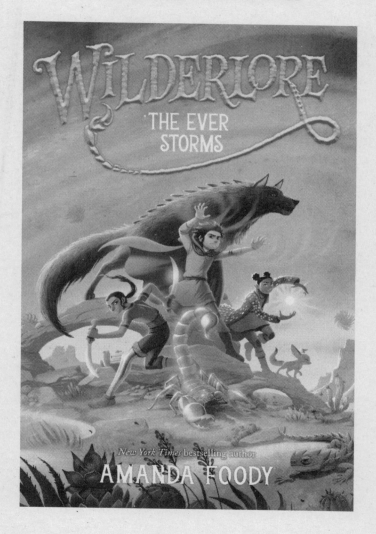

WILDERLORE

THE EVER
STORMS

New York Times bestselling author
AMANDA FOODY

B arclay Thorne groaned and covered his ears, trying to muffle the ferocious rumbles of the dragon's stomach—the dragon he was now riding.

This was Barclay's first time traveling by carrier dragon, and for the most part, he liked it. The passenger caravan strapped to the Beast's back was comfy and spacious, with wide windows perfect for admiring the breathtaking views. And the speedy flight had shortened an otherwise thirty-week journey on foot to a mere four days.

What he didn't like was all the *noise*. The wind whizzed shrilly in his ears. The pilot hollered directions from his saddle, no matter the time of day or night. And the carrier dragon, named Justine, was clearly suffering from a bad case of indigestion.

"Are we there yet?" Barclay grumbled.

"For the fifth time, no," answered his closest friend, Viola

Dumont, who sat cross-legged on the window bench beside him. "We'll land at sundown."

As she spoke, Mitzi—Viola's own dragon—reached a silver wing over Viola's shoulder and clawed at one of the hundreds of gold pins on her tunic. Viola yelped and shot Mitzi a dirty look.

Mitzi used to be sneakier—and a *lot* smaller. Only a baby whelp when Barclay had first met her, Mitzi had since grown to the size of a sheepdog. Two nubby horns had sprouted between her ears, and the feathers on her tail now climbed up her back and wings. But despite how much she'd changed, Mitzi still loved nothing more than all things shiny.

"Mitzi, we talked about this," Viola scolded her. "You need to be better behaved."

Mitzi paid her no mind. She jabbed a talon at a glimmering button on Viola's sleeve.

Both Justine and Mitzi were Beasts, which were animals with magical powers called Lore. Beasts came in many shapes and sizes, from tiny, harmless creatures to gigantic, terrifying monsters, and they dwelled in six regions of the world known as the Wilderlands. The people who lived there with them, like Barclay and Viola, were called Lore Keepers, and they bonded with Beasts in order to share their magic.

"You should try to relax," Viola told Barclay, ignoring Mitzi's pokes and prods. "Haven't you read that book twice already?"

Barclay peeled his attention away from *Beastly Biographies of Brilliant Keepers*, which Viola had gifted him for his thirteenth birthday earlier that Summer. "But what if I missed something? There are going to be apprentices from all across the Wilderlands at the Symposium, but I didn't grow up in the Wilderlands like everyone else. I don't want to fall behind."

The Symposium was a set of courses that all apprentices of the Lore Keeper Guild were required to pass before they could sit for their licensing exam. It took place every year at the University of Al Faradh, the most famous school in all the Wilderlands.

Being an apprentice himself, Barclay had always known that he'd have to attend the Symposium, but he'd assumed that would be years and years away. Until four days ago, when their teacher, Runa Rasgar, had abruptly announced their travels to the Desert for the Symposium. And four days was *definitely* not enough time to prepare.

Viola shook her head. "You've been a Lore Keeper for a year and a half now, and you know as much about Beasts as Tadg and I do. You have nothing to worry about."

Tadg Murdock was their fellow apprentice, a hotheaded boy who always found something to be grumpy about. After complaining all afternoon about how boring and long their flight was, he'd fallen asleep on the cushions in the caravan's corner. His wavy light brown hair was matted from his pillow, and one of his Beasts, Toadles, had nestled himself into the crook of his arm.

Barclay hoped that Viola was right. Even if he ended up being the only student from the Elsewheres, which were the regions of the world without magical Beasts, he no longer felt like the scared mushroom farmer who'd accidentally wandered into the Woods. He'd faced not one but two Legendary Beasts. And after more than a year spent training at the Sea, he was smarter, stronger, and faster than he'd ever been.

Gurrrrrrrrrg. The floor tremored with Justine's latest stomach cramp.

The sound made Root wake with a start. Root was Barclay's Lufthund, a wolflike Beast with powerful wind Lore. Side by side, the pair of them looked similarly wild. Root had shaggy fur, hooked claws, and sharp teeth. He was all black except for the white bones that jutted out from the base of his spine. Meanwhile, Barclay had long, tangled dark hair to match, pale skin, and fingernails far too often caked with dirt.

Unlike Barclay, who was still as short as ever, Root had grown far bigger this past year. When he padded up to Barclay, he had to bend down to nudge his Keeper's head.

"I know," Barclay told him, scratching him beneath the chin. "I'm tired of being cooped up too. But we'll land soon."

Root huffed impatiently. Then he sat down and rested his head on Barclay's knees.

Barclay turned back to Viola. "Maybe you're right and I've been studying too much. But how come you're not?" That wasn't like Viola, who didn't deem a book finished until she'd read it three times over.

Viola shrugged. "Oh, I've been studying for the Symposium since I was seven, so I've spent the trip doing more important things. Like mapping out my to-do list for when I get home."

Mitzi and Root weren't the only ones to have grown this past year. When Viola stood to fetch her satchel, she towered over Barclay. She might've always been tall, but lately she seemed to stretch another inch every season, and her two hair buns of tight brown curls only added to her height. She was even taller than Runa now.

Viola sat down and flipped through the pages of her leather-bound notebook.

"Your mom lives in the Desert, right?" Barclay asked. "How long has it been since you last saw her?"

"Almost two years, since I first became an apprentice." Barclay was no expert on families, as his parents had died when he was small, but two years seemed like a long time to be apart. "Which is why the first thing I'm going to do when I get home is eat as much of my mom's cooking as possible."

Barclay agreed this task was very important. The food at the Sea left a lot to be desired.

"Second," Viola continued, "I'm going to meet Gamila Asfour. She's the new High Keeper of the Desert, now that Idir Ziani retired. I've heard she's very impressive, and I need her to like me if I'm going to be Grand Keeper one day."

Whereas High Keepers governed each Wilderland, the Grand Keeper was the leader of the Guild and the entire Lore Keeper world. Though the job was elected, not inherited, the Dumonts had been the Grand Keepers for three generations. And Viola was determined to follow in her family's footsteps. Barclay had no doubt she'd succeed. She'd already traveled to four of the six Wilderlands. She was an expert on languages. And she spent all her free time studying and preparing for a job that was years away.

"Last, I'm going to bond with a second Beast," Viola finished.

Barclay smirked. "Will Mitzi like that?"

Mitzi now creeped across the floor toward Toadles, her best friend—or, as Tadg referred to him, her partner in crime.

"Mitzi and I have had a lot of long talks," Viola replied. "And we agree that I'm more than ready for a second Beast."

Meanwhile, Mitzi tapped Toadles on the gemstone in the center of his forehead. The tiny Beast's bulging eyes flew open with surprise, and purple goo squirted out of his webbed hands. Tadg jolted awake, seething. Toadles's poison Lore had made his fair skin swell violet with an itchy rash.

"You're supposed to stay in your Mark!" Tadg snapped at Toadles, who only stared at him blankly.

Suddenly, the caravan lurched as Justine swooped to the right. Root howled. Viola collided with Barclay. And Mitzi frantically stretched out her long wings to take flight, smacking Tadg in the face.

"Whoa, girl! Steady!" the pilot hollered, tugging on Justine's reins.

In the span of a blink, Runa rose from her sleeping roll in the corner and darted toward the pilot's side. "What's going on?" she asked, her voice calm even as Justine plunged into a steep dive.

Runa Rasgar was never afraid of anything, because no matter where she was, *she* was always the scariest thing in the room. Her chain mail clothes looked fit for a warrior, and a jagged scar cleaved down the pale skin on the right side of her face. Her famous reputation as a Guardian and a Dooling champion had earned her the nickname the Fang of Dusk.

"I . . . Look! Over there!" The pilot pointed southward, and Barclay and Viola twisted around to peer out the windows.

In the distance, a dark, menacing pillar stretched up from ground to sky. It was as wide as a city or even a mountain, as though a vast hole had been torn through the world. It took Barclay several seconds to realize that the pillar was *moving*. Its surface swirled and billowed like plumes of smoke.

"What is that?" Barclay rasped. Beside him, Root sprang up to take in the sight as well, and he let out a low, threatening growl.

"It's a sandstorm," Runa answered gravely.

"But it's so small," said Viola, which made Barclay gape. The storm might've taken up only a sliver of the otherwise blue and sunny sky, but it still felt ridiculous to describe something so frightening as small. "If it was a sandstorm, it would be—"

"I don't think it's a normal one. Can you take us closer?" Runa asked the pilot.

"C-closer?" the pilot sputtered. "That's much too dangerous. You see how Justine reacts."

"We don't need to fly close enough to put us in harm's way. I just want to get a better look."

The pilot muttered something under his breath, then tapped his foot against Justine's long neck, steering her to the right. The caravan tilted, forcing Barclay and Viola to grasp onto the window frames to keep from falling, and Root's claws raked across the seat cushions. Along the back wall, a rack of pamphlets advertising *SKYBACK CARRIER DRAGONS, the #1 Keeper-recommended draconic flight service* toppled down with a crash.

Tadg pried Mitzi off him—she'd been clinging to his face—and stumbled toward Runa. "You told us that you didn't have any work to do in the Desert. You said that while we were studying, you'd be taking a vacation."

"Did I?" Runa said innocently, with a not-so-innocent twinkle in her icy blue gaze.

Runa was a Guardian, which was one of the four types of Lore Keepers licensed by the Guild, so it was her job to protect the Wilderlands from dangerous Beasts. Last year, Runa had been summoned to the Sea to investigate a carnivorous algae bloom called the weeping tide, which had been making Lochmordra, the Sea's Legendary Beast, attack islands and ships. But as it turned out, the seaweed wasn't to blame. The real culprits were a Lore Keeper named Audrian Keyes and his apprentice, Yasha Robinovich, who were trying to destroy the borders between the Wilderlands and the Elsewheres to let Lore consume the entire world. Even though Barclay and his friends had saved the Sea, Keyes and Yasha had escaped, and no one had seen them since.

"I *knew* there was a reason you were sticking us in the Symposium," Tadg said smugly. "You've been sent to investigate something in the Desert, haven't you?"

"High Keeper Asfour might've requested my presence," Runa admitted. "But the three of you don't need to concern yourselves with it. You should be focusing on your studies."

"No way! We'd rather help you than be stuck in some class." When Runa didn't respond, Tadg whipped his head toward Barclay and Viola. "Well? Don't you two agree with me?"

Barclay was only half paying attention. As they neared the sandstorm, he could make out huge, whirling currents of dust within it, twisting around one another like snakes. It looked as though the Desert was writhing. The sand that soared in the air was so thick that no light could break through from above, creating a deep, deep darkness.

"Is that what sandstorms usually look like?" Barclay asked Viola.

"No," she answered tightly.

Justine let out a fearful cry and lurched a second time, so strongly that Viola shrieked and Tadg was thrown to the floor.

"I'm sorry," the pilot told Runa. "She won't take us any closer."

Runa stared at the sandstorm through shrewd, narrowed eyes.

"Ma'am?" the pilot asked nervously.

"That's fine. Get us back on course to Menneset."

Justine swerved around, and Barclay breathed a sigh of relief. Just looking at the sandstorm had made goose bumps prickle across his skin. He wrapped his arm around Root's back, and after a few moments, Root relaxed and withdrew his claws from the shredded cushions.

As they soared away, something dark moved in the corner of Barclay's vision. He turned back to the window, and his heart stuttered to a stop.

One of the columns of sand had bent away from the storm and stretched out toward them, like a massive hand reaching for a candle flame.

No sooner did Barclay scream than the hand closed over them.

And the world snuffed out.

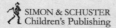

WHEN ADVENTURE CALLS, THE WILDS ANSWER.

A NEW YORK TIMES BESTSELLER

★"Wholesome, delightful, and jam-packed with adventure."
—*Kirkus Reviews*, starred review for
The Accidental Apprentice